THE
BODY MARKET

Also by Donna Freitas

Unplugged

THE
BODY MARKET

Donna Freitas

HARPER TEEN
An Imprint of HarperCollins*Publishers*

HarperTeen is an imprint of HarperCollins Publishers.

The Body Market

Copyright © 2017 by Donna Freitas

All rights reserved. Printed in the United States of America.

No part of this book may be used or reproduced in any manner whatsoever without written permission except in the case of brief quotations embodied in critical articles and reviews. For information address HarperCollins Children's Books, a division of HarperCollins Publishers, 195 Broadway, New York, NY 10007.

www.epicreads.com

Library of Congress Control Number: 2016958059

ISBN 978-0-06-211863-9

17 18 19 20 21   PC/LSCH   10 9 8 7 6 5 4 3 2 1

First Edition

Nature teaches me that my own body is surrounded by many other bodies, some of which I have to seek after, and others to shun. And indeed, as I perceive different sorts of colors, sounds, odors, tastes, heat, hardness, etc., I safely conclude that . . . some are agreeable, and others disagreeable, [and] there can be no doubt that my body, or rather my entire self, in as far as I am composed of body and mind, may be variously affected, both beneficially and hurtfully, by surrounding bodies.

—René Descartes,
"Of the Existence of Material Things and of the Real Distinction Between the Mind and Body of Man,"
Meditations on First Philosophy (1641)

PART ONE

1

Skylar

sleeping beauties

I ADJUSTED THE scarf around my head.

Only my eyes were visible.

I stepped into the crush of tourists heading inside. A great canopy stretched over us, blocking out the cold winter sun. The floor was polished marble, and it shined so clean and new it was slick as ice. To my right, people emerged from the lobby of the tall, glittering hotel, with its carefully trimmed topiaries lining the entrance.

All around me were voices.

They were speaking in languages I didn't understand. I wished for an App to translate what they were saying and then almost laughed. It seemed like a lifetime ago that Apps were a part of everyday life. An entire world away from the one I was in now. Literally.

I concentrated on the man next to me as we inched forward under the canopy. He held the hand of a woman, maybe his wife. They were nearly the same height, both shorter than me, their hair black as ink, their eyes almond-shaped. I listened to the sounds coming from their mouths, their accents, the tonal cadence of their words. Even with all my gaming and paying attention in Real World History, I couldn't translate the meaning, but with a little effort I could recognize the language.

They were speaking Japanese.

I listened to the others milling around me now, all of us trying to get closer to the main attraction, the reason we'd come. In the span of five minutes I heard a total of seven different languages. First there were the young men speaking in French, and then a large group of people shuffling along whispering to one another in Chinese. There was the tall blond couple talking intimately in Dutch, and another nearly shouting in Spanish. I heard snatches of Italian but I couldn't tell from which direction they'd come, and the same went for the female voice speaking in German. Even more languages swirled in the air around me that I couldn't quite place.

People had dressed for the occasion.

Many of the women had chosen smart skirted suits, spindly heels on their feet and lavish thick coats to protect them from the cold, jewels dropping from their ears. But there were also a few in colorful saris and even more with veils that revealed only their eyes. The men seemed to have coordinated with one another, all of them donning formal black suits and boxy wool coats. The world's wealthiest had spared no expense, traveling from far and wide for this momentous occasion. My flight from the ball and the fire on the opening night of the Body Market had certainly made a dent in my sister's plans, but in the end it had only delayed the inevitable.

Moving forward was all that mattered.

That's why I was here.

Rain didn't think it should be me, fought me on it. He thought it was too dangerous given my relationship to this place and its founder. But it was because of that relationship that it needed to be me. And then, Rain wasn't high on my list of trusted advisors at the moment. He'd hidden from me the truth about my sister, and he'd openly lied about Lacy.

He didn't get to tell me what to do anymore.

The full extent of the exhibits was a winding labyrinth that covered entire city blocks and extended down, down, down under the earth. The tourists were anxious to get started, excited for the preview they'd been promised. The priciest merchandise had been trotted out to entice and seduce, the rest of it stored away in the underground caverns, waiting and ready. An entire city's worth of goods. We shuffled along together, slowly moving forward in the line. Some people had their heads buried in a map, trying to pinpoint where we were in relation to the various displays.

Finally, we rounded the corner.

At the end of the aisle, someone had constructed a dais made of gleaming white marble. A set of stairs covered in lush red carpet led up to the star attraction. People stood within the space marked out by velvet ropes to get a closer look. I got in the back, and soon dozens more tourists took their places behind me. At least thirty minutes passed as we snaked our way through the maze. By now I could see the ends of the long glass box. It was illuminated from the inside, to highlight the preciousness of its contents.

The two tourists ahead of me—a man and a woman speaking Chinese—talked excitedly as they strode forward. I watched as they circled the box, whispering, pointing things out to each other. They glanced back at me and nodded, just before funneling through the velvet ropes toward the exit.

Then it was my turn.

I stepped up to the box and forced myself to look at what lay before me.

At *who.*

Jude was trying to punish me for my escape.

And she'd done an excellent job.

I pressed my hands against the glass, even though the sign warned me not to. I took in the delicate limbs, the elegant fingers painted a pale pink for the occasion. The way the chest gently rose and fell, shifting the covering that lay across the lower and upper halves of the body. Lips painted red and eyes closed peacefully. Long blond hair that fell across the forehead and down along the shoulders and arms, curled and impeccably styled to show off its lustrous shine. The skin was smooth and unblemished, or nearly so.

A tiny scar curved underneath the elbow.

You had to know it was there to see it.

You had to know it was there to even look.

I stared at the body of Inara, my best friend, on display for all the world to see.

To admire. To envy.

To covet and to buy.

Trader had failed in his attempt to help her escape, and soon Inara would be sold to the highest bidder.

The Body Market was open for business.

2

Skylar

the will to live

I WAS TAKING too long.

The crowd in line behind me began to whisper, impatient hisses erupting among the people waiting—Body Tourists, they were called. New Port City was the Real World's newest and therefore most popular site for Body Tourism, following on the heels of Beijing, Moscow, Paris, Buenos Aires, and a few other smaller, less cosmopolitan cities. They could sanitize the words for what was happening all they wanted, but deep down everyone knew what was really going on at this market.

Human trafficking.

They'd even tiered the sales. Starting today they'd offer only the least desirable bodies, those that had been deemed the lowest tier in value, and little by little, they would work their way up to the most valuable bodies, the prettiest ones, the most handsome, the ones that would fetch the most capital. The Body Tourists had to wait for those. It was a method for building demand, I'd heard one man say.

"Move along," the guard said to me. He sounded bored, immune to the display, barely aware of the precious merchandise to his left.

But I didn't move. I didn't want to leave Inara.

Her presence here was all my fault.

It's supposed to be me, my mind taunted. In two weeks' time, the Body Market would begin to hold the special auctions for its priciest wares and Inara would be gone, and quickly.

The guard turned.

I felt his eyes.

"Move along," he said again, this time a little less bored, this time with more force.

I pulled the scarf tighter around my head.

I retracted my hand from the glass and gave Inara one last look. Then I descended the dais, the carpet thick and soft under my feet. I wound my way through the market toward the exit and I was nearly there, I could see the way out through the crowd, I could see the signs of the city streets that lay beyond the market's walls, when something else stopped me cold.

Someone else.

In the back-right corner of the market was a cluster of bodies, also in glass boxes, displayed under a long red banner that matched the color of the carpet on the floor. The sign read:

HEALTHY HEARTS, Good for Parts!

A man was standing underneath it, the smile on his face more of a sneer. His eyes were laughing, but in a way that made my skin crawl, that showed how proud he was of the sick rhyme he'd come up with to advertise his merchandise.

He saw me watching. "Would you like to get a closer look, my dear? I can sense your interest all the way over here."

I swallowed. He was right.

I was interested.

And I did want a closer look.

One body in particular had caught my attention, and I went to it. I studied the face, the hair, the mouth.

I wasn't mistaken.

It was her.

My stomach churned.

"She's a strong one," the man said, his voice oozing with the anticipation of a sale. "One of the first to be taken off the plugs without incident. She's not going to go cheap, but I'll make you a good deal."

I could feel him next to me, smell the sweat coming off him despite the cold, nearly hear the way his heart pounded because of my interest. Maybe I was the first to show any. I hoped I was. I felt so helpless. I wanted to be sick. I knew I should leave, that I should get out of here as quickly as my legs could carry me, but I couldn't seem to budge.

Finally, I managed a few words. "If you hang on to this one until my return, I promise I'll give you more for her than you could possibly dream of getting."

"You like the look of her that much? She seems kind of plain to me," he added under his breath.

Never once in our conversation had I taken my eyes from the girl before me.

Sylvia.

It was her. I was certain. After all this time wondering what had happened to Sylvia, her body taken before she could unplug on her own, there she was. I stared at her body, lying there, and my heart sank as I thought of how Zeera would feel when I told her this news. Would it be all horror, or would there be a sliver of relief, to at least know where to find her?

At least Sylvia was still alive.

At least Sylvia was . . . still, technically, Sylvia.

"You want her or not?" the vendor asked, his voice growing impatient.

I dug around in the pockets of my coat and pulled out nearly all the capital Rain had given me. *Just in case you need it*, he'd said. We both knew what he'd meant. Just in case I needed to buy a body or two. "I'd like to put a deposit on her," I told the man. The capital was piled high in my outstretched hands. There was a lot of it.

He stared like he couldn't believe what he was seeing, like his dreams were finally coming true. But then he recovered and managed to tear his eyes away to look at me again. "A deposit?"

"Yes," I said. "I'm not in a position to take her today. I need to make arrangements."

He was already shaking his head. "I don't know. . . ."

I dug around in my pockets and pulled out the rest of the capital, adding it to the pile. "Is this enough to convince you?" I shoved it toward him and he took it. "There's a lot more where that came from if you keep your word."

The man stuffed the capital into the pockets of his coat. "All righty, miss, if that's what you'd really like to do," he said, then turned to a couple that were waiting for him to finish with me, that sneer of a smile on his face again. "How can I help ye today? In need of a new set of lungs? Perhaps a liver?"

"I'll be back for her soon," I said, but the man was already engrossed in conversation with his new customers.

A shiver passed over me. My body shuddered with it.

My right hand reached up and curled around the back of my neck.

I was being watched. I could feel it. Without looking back, I raced away, my heart hammering in my chest, desperate for the fresh wintry air of the city. I neared the market's exit, where guests were streaming in and out of the nearby hotel, bundled up against the cold, chattering excitedly about the day of window-shopping ahead, so many glass boxes to see, to peer into, bodies to inspect and evaluate for their worth. It wasn't until I stepped beyond the market's walls and until I could no longer sense the hotel rising up behind me that I could breathe.

There was talk that my sister had installed herself in the penthouse.

What if she was at her windows at this very moment, surveying her city? Would she look down right onto the spot where I stood? Would she set her guards upon me again?

I straightened up. Shook off this eerie feeling.

No one was watching me.

Not my sister. Not anyone else.

I was imagining things.

I started to make my way toward the edge of the city where Rain's car sat hidden, parked where I left it. My thoughts turned to the task of coming up with a plan to get Inara and Sylvia out of there, not to mention everyone else. My mind was whirring with ideas, when suddenly there was a little stirring in my brain, like a tiny warning light flashing red.

I stopped and looked up.

Slowly, I turned my head to the left, then to the right. The feeling that someone was watching me was there again, but then it slipped away.

The red light disappeared and everything grew quiet.

I carried on, hurrying, until my breaths grew even. I paused once, trying to gain my bearings, locating the familiar Water Tower in the sky, the way it loomed above New Port City and reflected its oceans all around. Today, it glowed a deep, dark blue, to match the gloom and mood of the sea in winter. When I picked up my pace, I felt something cold and wet smack my cheek. I reached up a hand to touch my skin, and my fingers came away icy. I studied the sky.

Snow.

My jaw fell open.

It was snowing.

I'd walked through snow before, run through it, played in it, built a snowman and a snow woman. An entire snow family in the park across from Singles Hall. But that was in the App World.

This snow was real.

I had a single memory of it from when I was a child, of my mother calling me to the windows to see the winter wonderland that had appeared outside overnight while we slept. Of how she took my hand and led me out into a world of white, how we'd gathered the snow into our arms and laughed.

My mother.

Where was she now? I took a deep breath and let it out. Then I held up my hand and watched as each individual flake drifted onto my palm and melted away to water.

For a second, for one glorious instant, I felt a sense of beauty and magic that has only ever seemed possible in the Real World. Ironic, since the App World is spun out of so much technological fantasy, designed to make sure we are never bored and never without something new and exciting to watch, to play, to enjoy. But the fragility of the Real World always trumped the manufactured, the coded, the virtual. This I'd learned quickly. The fragility itself, the randomness of each thing's existence, no matter how small, was what spun this world's beauty. Memories of downloading the Blizzard App with Inara when we were little, sipping hot chocolate by a warm fire, watching the snow blur the City, rushed through me, pushing away all other thoughts.

My shoulders slumped.

Inara wouldn't marvel at the real snow today. Neither would Sylvia.

The snow came down harder.

A thin blanket of white already covered the ground.

I started forward again, the icy flakes swirling around

me. The others would be worried I wasn't back yet, Adam, the Keeper, and Rain—Rain especially. But ever since I'd learned about his lies, ever since I'd learned the truth about my sister, lived that awful night at the ball, I couldn't seem to root myself anywhere, couldn't seem to get my bearings. Now, I focused on the snow. It pushed away my dark mood as it fell down heavier, muffling the city of its typical bustle. I felt protected by it, hidden.

Then a sound, a loud guttural roar, broke through the silence and the beauty.

Was that . . . a motorcycle?

Yes. A motorcycle was coming up the street, fast. It stopped at the corner, the sound cutting out. In a city where cars were nearly nonexistent, where Rain's was a precious and wild luxury, to see it there was strange. I couldn't stop staring at it—and the boy riding it. Anger rolled off his body in waves, his mouth twisted and scowling. He was dressed in a thick black leather jacket and black gloves, snowflakes skittering off the sleeves and down along black pants and thick black boots. His eyes were hidden behind dark sunglasses even though the sun had not shown itself in days. A black-and-white checked scarf encircled his neck, rising to cover the bottom of his chin. The boy didn't seem cold, despite the weather and the fact that he was traveling in the open, wintry air unprotected.

"Hello," he said.

Even though there was no one else around, I turned to look behind me, to see if his hello was meant for another person.

But we were alone.

"Yes, you," he said. His voice was as steady and blank as his face.

"Hello," I said back, uncertainly.

He got off his bike, pressed the kickstand down with his boot, and walked toward me. He didn't stop until he was right there, maybe a foot away. That warning light in my brain flashed maniacally, a frantic red, telling me to go, go, go *now*, but I didn't move. I didn't even look away.

What was wrong with me?

What had happened to my instinct for self-preservation? Had it been dulled or even deadened? It had seemed sluggish the last couple of months, too weak to do me much good. Or was there something else going on—something to do with this boy that refused to let me leave?

He took off his sunglasses and for the first time I saw his eyes. They were dark and strange, vigilant but empty, and framed by long lashes. He narrowed them. "I know who you are," he said.

"So?" I said, trying to sound as impassive as he did. "Who am I then?"

He put out his hand, as though we'd just been introduced at a party and he was trying to be polite. "You're the most wanted girl in all of New Port City." The right side of his mouth curled into a menacing half smile. "And I, a lucky bounty hunter."

There was a moment, a pause between those words and what happened next, long enough for the fear to sear my insides like a firebomb, but not long enough that my gaming instincts could save me. They eventually kicked in and I was about to run, my brain automatically calculating the distance between me and the dark alley nearby, but I was too late.

I felt his hands on me.

They were strong. He was strong—stronger than he looked for his size.

"Don't worry, Skylar," he whispered. "I'm not going to hurt you. I promise," he added, then he gripped my middle and pulled me onto his bike like I weighed nothing. Before I could even shout, he'd cuffed my wrists so that my arms were around his waist, my body pressed into his back. There came a great roar, and suddenly we were moving.

No, we were flying.

My scarf was ripped away from my head and floated up into the air, taken along on the wind. The cold was so fierce it burned, the snow like tiny sharp blades against my skin. I found myself gripping the boy tighter, pressing my bare cheek against the cold leather of his jacket.

If I didn't, I'd fall, and in truth, I didn't want to die.

I don't want to die.

I don't *want to die.*

These words repeated themselves again and again inside me as we sped through the city, my eyes tearing from the storm and the harsh wind beating at us on all sides.

As we headed across a bridge and the snow subsided for a moment, I took advantage of the reprieve and peered over the boy's shoulder. I studied his face, reflected in the mirrors on the bike. His eyes were hidden behind dark glasses again, his mouth a straight, inexpressive line, as though he was carrying innocuous cargo, having just stopped at the store. Yet in taking me, threatening me, this boy had jolted me back from the dead. I'd been sleep-walking through existence for the last several months. Aside from wanting to see Inara, to save her, out of love, and out of guilt, I'd been adrift. Floating from one day to the next, without much purpose or will.

Not anymore.

I wanted to *live.*

I was going to *live.*

For the first time in months I *felt* things.

The boy moved right then, only slightly, his chin shifting a bit. His mouth was still a tight, thin line, but I could tell he was watching me, too, through the mirror, that he was doing so with interest.

With a curiosity not unlike mine.

For a second, I felt sad.

I'm not sure how or why, if it was my gaming instincts alerting me that something was happening, but I knew this boy was going to become important to whatever came next in this world and my part in it.

And the sadness, well, it was on his behalf.

I'd killed before and I'd do it again.

If my survival was at stake, I would do it without a second thought.

"Hang on," he shouted over the roar of the engine and the wind.

So I did. I buried my face once more in the smooth cold leather of his jacket and let my thoughts turn to nothing. It was easier that way. For now.

3

Rain

helpless

I LOST HER.

Skylar was gone.

Maybe for good this time.

The railing was cold and hard in my hand, as cold as the air and the snow coming down outside the mansion. My palm wanted to bend it. If I was still in the App World I could find a way to mold it to my wishes, but here, in the real body, I was powerless to do such things.

"Rain?"

It was early morning, and the training floor was empty below the balcony where I stood. I'd come to be alone for a while. To think. To wallow, perhaps. To wonder where Skylar was and how I could get her back. I sighed. "Lacy,"

I said, turning around. "How did you sleep?"

She twirled a lock of long red hair around her fingers. It stood out against the blue of the concrete wall behind her. "You'd already know the answer if you'd joined me last night." Now she was the one to sigh. "Or any night."

Her soft green eyes were tired. I preferred the muted colors of Lacy's real self to the bright, harsh ones so highlighted and drawn out in the virtual version I'd grown used to over the years. Lacy felt differently, believed her real self was too literally pale and unremarkable in comparison to the virtual her, but I wondered if someday she would come around and see things the way I did.

"I know and I'm sorry," I said. The Lacy Mills of the App World I never could take seriously. Or fall for in any true way. But the Lacy Mills of the Real World was another story. I found myself thinking that maybe I could be hers. Maybe I could finally give her what she'd always wanted from me. I put out my hand and watched as her eyes came alive at the gesture.

Slowly, she wove her fingers through mine. "I could be yours," she whispered. "Again."

"Lacy."

Her eyelashes fluttered. "Yes?" She sounded so hopeful.

It nearly broke my heart. Lacy had a reputation of being cold and hard and conniving, but I knew better. Deep down, she was as vulnerable as the next person, full of longing and plenty of loss. She was just good at hiding it.

I couldn't lie to her now. "I'm grateful you're willing to help with my plans, both the ones from before . . . ," I said, unable to articulate further which *before* I was referring to, pained by the mistakes I'd made, mistakes that came with a cost I could never pay out, no matter how much I offered Skylar. I squeezed Lacy's hand. "And the new ones. I know how much you've given up for me and . . . how you feel about me. I never meant to lead you on, or give you false hope. I never wanted to hurt your feelings."

Lacy's green eyes dimmed. She slipped her hand from mine and hid it behind her back as though she couldn't trust it. "Apparently, hurt feelings are your specialty."

"Don't say that."

"I wasn't referring to myself, Rain."

I breathed deeply. "I know."

"She's never going to forgive you," Lacy said. "Not really. It's been months and she still doesn't trust you. That sort of damage is difficult to repair. It's like . . . she lost her way completely after that night."

"Wouldn't you?" I asked, unable to keep the frustration from my tone.

Lacy's eyes flashed. "What? If I suddenly found out the sister I gave up everything to see was willing to sacrifice me like I meant nothing? That everyone around me knew the entire time and didn't say a word to me about it?" She laughed bitterly. "I'd say so, yes. I almost feel . . . sorry for her."

I closed my eyes.

Lacy was right. This was my fault. All of it. The before and the now, which seemed to involve Skylar going missing again. Or worse, running away from us. In the middle of a storm.

And I let her go.

Like an idiot.

Skylar's bright-blue eyes had lost their light that terrible night, and her only interest became finding Inara and getting her back. She'd been like a ghost walking these halls. Even the sea, which she loved, couldn't wake her. The Skylar I knew during her first months in this world had vanished.

I wanted her back.

I'd thought that if she went to the Body Market to case the place, it might breathe life into her again. I'd even lent her my car when she asked for it.

"What are you thinking?" Lacy asked.

I opened my eyes. I'd nearly forgotten Lacy was standing there. She watched me strangely. "Why?" I asked.

Lacy hesitated. "You just . . ."

"Finish your thought," I said when she trailed off. "Please."

"You look . . . lost," she said.

I raked a hand through my hair. I tried to wipe away

whatever it was that showed on my face, trading it for something more benign. I used to be so controlled, and now it seemed that I revealed everything to whoever happened to be nearby. "Oh?"

Lacy nodded. "It's not a look I'm used to on you," she said. Her face grew pained. "It's her, isn't it? Skylar, Skylar, everything is always about Skylar. You can't let things go, even when all signs tell you that you should!"

"You're wrong," I lied. "Skylar is merely important to our interests here, on many fronts, including my father's. You know that already. I'm only worried about what her absence means for our plans. You're letting your jealousy get the best of you."

Lacy nodded her head. "Right."

"I made a mistake, that's all," I went on. "I shouldn't have let Skylar go yesterday, never mind alone, and when a storm was brewing."

"But you *did* let her go," Lacy observed, her exact meaning unclear.

I looked away. She was right.

And regret was making me pay dearly for my mistakes.

4

Skylar

blizzard

"PEOPLE WILL COME looking for me," I said.

The boy turned away from the closet where he'd hung up his jacket, though he hadn't yet shed his scarf. He laughed, but the laughter was dark and edged with something sharp. "You've got that right. People have been looking for you for months. Your sister made sure of that. She put quite a price on your head." He sounded so pleased.

I shifted in the chair where he'd sat me down. It was hard and wooden and uncomfortable, and pressed up against a small table. We were in a tiny kitchen, open to an equally tiny living room with a battered gray couch, a thick blanket thrown over the arm of it, and shelves on the walls that were full of books. There was a rug on the floor, old and worn and faded. At the center of everything was a short, black iron stove, a thick round pipe reaching up and through the low ceiling. The boy threw wood into its belly and soon a fire roared red and orange inside of it.

"I meant *other* people," I said.

He regarded me. "Even better."

I shivered, my coat heavy and wet, trying not to let my teeth chatter. I hadn't felt cold like this maybe ever, and certainly never in the App World. Even when I downloaded the Snow App, my virtual self was bundled in puffy jackets, a hat, a scarf, and mittens, and the temperature stayed at a balmy and comfortable seventy degrees. I longed to be warm, longed for a download that would flow through my code and burn my insides like the sun.

The boy took a step toward me, then another, the old wooden floorboards creaking under his feet. Thick round knots dotted it. "You're freezing," he said.

Sympathy crept into his voice, but his eyes showed nothing of it. He left the kitchen and went into what must be his bedroom, and came back with a pile of dry clothes. A T-shirt, a pair of jeans, a thick cabled sweater, so thick a yearning rose in me at the thought of so much warmth.

He pulled out the only other chair at the table and set the pile onto it. "You should change or you'll get sick."

The word *sick* automatically conjured an image of my former teacher in the App World, Mrs. Worthington, the way her face used to twist when she'd teach us about the many different ways that being in the real body led to death, one of her favorites being *sickness*. I'd been here for many months and I'd yet to experience such an affliction. I wondered if it was as terrible as she always made it sound, if it made a person feel as awful as the cold racking my body now.

I looked up at the boy. "I'm not changing in front of you."

His eyes flickered away. "I'll go in the other room. I was *already* going to go in the other room," he added.

I glared. "Oh, such a gentleman you are." I raised my shackled wrists from my lap. "Be a real gentleman and unlock these."

He slipped a key from his pocket and with a simple twist my hands were free. I rubbed my wrists, inspecting the deep-red circles etched into my skin. The boy was already heading across the room, not looking back.

"Aren't you worried?" I asked.

He stopped and turned. "Worried?"

I stood and faced him, my eyes darting around the room, taking in every detail, the placement of every window, the door, the entrance that led into his bedroom. "That I'll escape."

"No."

The abrupt simplicity of his answer surprised me. "All right. Then maybe I'll just leave."

"I wouldn't do that if I were you." He went to one of the windows and pulled back the curtain. The snow was so thick it was nearly impossible to see through the panes of glass. The wind shrieked as it swirled around the house. "We're far away from civilization out here, and you would freeze to death before you even managed to travel a mile."

I knew he was right, but I couldn't help making the threat. This place, a cottage more than a house, really an old beach shack, was perched along a remote and barren hillside that overlooked the sea. On his bike as we skirted the cliff, the waves roaring and angry to our left, I'd thought about the ice on the road and how one simple slip would send us tumbling into the frigid waters.

For some reason, my arms were raised now, my hands reaching out, maybe toward the boy, or maybe just toward the stove, with its roaring fire, a source of warmth I honestly didn't have the desire to leave. A wave of exhaustion hit me. They hit a lot lately. Exhaustion would yank me under like the strongest of currents, as strong as the tide surely pulling at the sea right now.

"At some point, the snow will stop," I said to him. "And then what will you do? Cuff me to a piece of furniture?"

The boy shrugged, peering through the center of the glass, the only spot on the window that wasn't covered in snow. "I don't have to worry about that yet. This storm is going to go on for days, at least two, maybe three." He turned to face me once more. The right side of his mouth curled up in that half smile. "This, Skylar Cruz, is what we Real Worlders call a blizzard."

The wind howled all afternoon.

I sat there alone in the kitchen, the wooden chair pulled close to the stove, as close I could get without burning myself. The boy had hidden away in his bedroom ever since he left me alone to change. At first I didn't want to put on some stranger's clothes, and worse, those of a boy who'd snatched me off the street and cuffed me while we sped off on his bike. But then I got so cold my entire body was shaking with it, and the thought of becoming weak with sickness in the middle of nowhere was far worse than peeling off my wet clothes and exchanging them for something dry and warm. I draped my coat, shirt, pants, and socks along the edges of the stove and the back of the other chair. Maybe by nightfall they'd be dry.

The fire snapped and popped, the flame rushing against the little window on the door of the stove, then retreating just as quickly.

I went to work exploring every corner, every nook, everything in this cottage in an attempt to get to know my surroundings, to study them, so when the time came for me to leave, I could do so easily. There wasn't much to see other than the small kitchen open to the living room and a bathroom off to the side with a shower barely big enough to stand in. The only other place I had left to explore was the room where the boy slept.

He'd been right about the storm. It wasn't going to let me go anywhere at the moment. I hated to admit it, but Rain was right, too. It had been stupid of me to go into New Port City seeking Inara. It was too risky, and now I was paying for my recklessness. Then again, a small part of me liked that as my absence stretched on, it would become clear that something had happened, and not something good, and this would make Rain worry. Maybe he'd think he'd lost me for forever, and regret as cold and empty as this stretch of coast would overtake him.

No. Who was I kidding?

Rain wouldn't feel like *he* had lost me for good, but that *they'd* lost me for good. His cause and everyone involved in it. I'd originally thought I was part of their rebellion, that I would have an important role in it. But Rain had kept so much from me, he'd lured me in and played me so well, like he'd been gaming me forever. And I just *let* him. I let my guard down because of a stupid crush.

Stupid.

Even more pathetic, I was trapped by some bounty hunter while my sister got ready to sell my friends, I had no idea where my mother was, and I was *still* mooning over Rain Holt like some pathetic jilted girlfriend.

I got up and went to the window for the tenth time in the last hour.

The storm had grown even fiercer, the sky darker. From the little I could see, it whipped the ocean into a frenzy, great waves rising up and crashing closer and closer to shore, the water nearly white with churning, the surface covered in an angry swirling foam.

Jude must be livid. I'd spoiled her plans once, and now the weather was conspiring to do the same. I bet the Body Tourists were stranded in their hotel. Would the market be shuttered until the snow subsided? That would be at least one small consolation. But then, where were Inara and Sylvia now? Had they been spirited away to somewhere safe? Had the others, too? Or would they lie there freezing, snow drifting across glass boxes and lush red carpet?

There was a rustle to my left and I looked up.

The boy appeared in the doorway of his room. His dark hair stood up on top of his head, the sides short, nearly shaved all around. He wore jeans and a thick braided sweater like the one he'd given me and no shoes, but the checked scarf, worn and nearly in tatters, still encircled his neck. Maybe he slept in it. He stretched his arms high and yawned.

I glared. "You kidnap me in the middle of a storm, and then nap all afternoon?"

"Are you hungry?" was all he replied.

I was. My stomach had been growling for the last two hours. But I crossed my arms and turned my back on him, the fire roaring and crackling next to me. "No."

He let out a loud breath. "Fine," he said. "Have it your way."

In bare feet, he padded across the carpet, then scuffed along the wooden floor, until he reached the kitchen. I watched as he took out a big silver pot and filled it with water, then put it on the stove to heat. Next to it was a block of cheese, which he grated, and what looked like a slab of bacon, which he sliced thinly before chopping it up and throwing it into a saucepan. The smell of it sizzling soon filled the cottage, the comfort of something so basic and elemental as cooking combating the sounds of the storm. Between the warmth of the fire and the anticipation of something delicious to eat, the cottage almost seemed . . . cozy.

If I hadn't been kidnapped, I could even see myself liking it here.

Pasta bubbled in the pot.

My mouth watered.

The boy glanced at me, his strange eyes flashing, that half grin curling up the side of his mouth. This time it seemed less menacing. "I made enough for two. You should eat. Besides, I'm a good cook and you look . . . so very hungry."

I left my place at the window and walked over to the couch, sat down in a heap, and tried to block out the smells of the food. The sky had grown completely dark, and now that I wasn't near the stove, I grew cold. I grabbed the blanket hanging over the arm of the couch and pulled it around me. I thought back to my first days in the Real World, when I'd woken up in the Keeper's house, when she'd cooked for me, how I wasn't allowed outside then either. But the Keeper wanted to protect me, unlike this boy, who planned to turn me over to the one person in this world who hated me most. I was so lost in these thoughts that I didn't hear him approach, didn't notice his proximity until his face was bent close, peering straight into mine.

"Come and eat," he said.

I stared back at him. "Not unless you answer some questions."

"It's going to get cold."

"I don't care."

"Fine," he said. He stood there, watching me, that unreadable look on his face, that scarf of his still circled loosely around his neck. "Ask away."

I blinked. "Are you a New Capitalist?"

"No."

"Were you ever?"

"No.

"What about a Keeper of bodies?"

"No."

"A Keeper of something?"

"No."

"So a bounty hunter. That's all. Nothing else? That's who you are in this world?"

"Yes."

I sighed. "Do you ever give more than one-word answers?"

His eyes flickered a little, and he shifted his head toward the kitchen. He was trying not to smile. "Is that it?"

I got up from the couch and stood in front of him, so we were eye to eye, and his eyes went vacant again, as though he could retreat behind them and disappear at will. I wanted to show him I wasn't afraid. "If you're a bounty hunter, then why take me here? To where you live?"

"This wasn't exactly the plan," he said. "I didn't intend to entertain you as a guest for a few days. But opportunity struck when I saw you there and it happened to strike at the beginning of a blizzard. So I improvised." His fingers stretched at his sides, then relaxed. "I'm going to eat. You can join me or starve."

He walked into the kitchen and piled pasta into a chipped white bowl. It was still hot enough that steam rose from it. My body reacted in that involuntary way that virtual selves never do, that way I was still getting used to, my stomach growling. Each time food enticed me I couldn't help but think of the Sachs family and one of the last conversations I'd had at their dinner table.

And Inara. Inara most of all.

"I can hear your stomach," the boy said.

But I refused to move.

He was already eating, lustily slurping the spaghetti, when I finally gave in, heading to the kitchen and filling my own bowl. I didn't sit with him at the table. I picked up my food and sat on the couch again, my back toward him, and ate hungrily.

Once in a while, though, I could feel his eyes.

My instincts, awake again, alert and watchful, told me this.

By the next morning, the storm had grown worse.

I stretched my arms high, my body still heavy with sleep. The wind moaned and whistled and the cottage groaned and creaked in response. The fire had died during the night and the air had cooled so much I could nearly see my breath. I rose from the couch, pulling the blanket around me, and walked over to the iron stove. There was a pile of wood stacked in the corner of the kitchen and I grabbed one of the thick split branches and added it to the embers still smoldering orange. I'd seen the boy stoking the fire with the long metal rod that leaned against the wall and I did this now, poking at the wood until it started to burn. Soon I felt the warmth and relief of it.

I stood there, holding out my hands.

And I realized something.

I wasn't afraid. There was a kind of peace about being

here during a storm, this place in the middle of nowhere.

And for once, nothing was required of me.

There wasn't a revolution to wage or someone I needed to run from or to or anything I had to fix right this minute. There was literally nothing else I could do aside from just being, just existing. I couldn't even attempt to escape. The blizzard forbade it. There was only the waiting out of things, until the storm subsided and let us slip from its cold and firm grasp, back to the way things were, the way they are, to the reality as icy and harsh and unforgiving as this weather.

But that time was still a ways away.

It was strange to notice how glad this made me. I hadn't realized until this moment that I'd needed a vacation from this world and the responsibilities it had handed me ever since I'd unplugged. I almost laughed for having applied the word *vacation* to my situation, but it was true, it kind of felt like one. That the force of the weather stopped all things, revolution, resistance, maybe even the commerce of the Body Market, was stunning to contemplate.

I almost wanted to give thanks.

I glanced up from the stove toward the boy's bedroom. He was still asleep, I supposed. His door was shut, and I didn't hear any movement behind it. As the wood snapped and shifted, I wondered about him, the way he lived alone out here, about his choice of profession, whether it really was a choice or if, like for so many people in this world, it was something he did merely to survive and because there were few, if any, other options. Where was his family? How long had he been by himself? How does a boy nearly my own age go from being only a boy to becoming a bounty hunter? How do any of us go from being children to becoming the axis around which a revolution in two worlds is turning?

The door of the cabin seemed to bend with the pressure of the snow and wind, grunting and sighing. I went to it, decided to open it a crack, just to see what the outside world was like, if it was really as bad as it sounded. The urge to be in the middle of that kind of natural power, a force that was real and had nothing to do with an App, was irresistible.

I slid aside the bolt. Turned the knob.

Big mistake.

Snow and ice, a shocking amount of it, blew inside the cottage, the harsh wind slicing through the opening, angry and wild. The door flew wide despite my efforts to push it back, using all my strength to try and shut it. I stepped away in shock.

"What are you *doing*?"

Suddenly the boy was in the room, staring at me like I was crazy. He flew to the door and threw all of his weight against it. When the latch clicked, he bolted it shut. His hair was disheveled, sticking up at odd angles, his clothes crumpled, his T-shirt slightly askew. Ice covered one of his arms.

And he was glaring. At me.

"I just . . . ," I started, and stopped. I took a step back. There was something about the look on his face that made me remember our reality: he'd kidnapped me, I was imprisoned here, he was willing to end life as I knew it by handing me over to my sister. The beauty and power of the storm had lulled me into a comfortable stasis, but now my heart skidded frantically. If he decided to hurt me, there was nowhere I could run, nothing I could do but fight back—and a fight in this small space would be ugly. Bloody. Maybe even deadly. I took another few steps away from him, mentally going over where I'd seen the kitchen knives.

The boy's expression softened. "I told you," he began. "I'm not going to hurt you. I'm really not." He ran a hand through his dark hair, taming the spikes. "You were saying something. You just . . . what, Skylar?"

My heart slowed, or at least it began pounding out something else, something unfamiliar. "I was just curious. About the storm. I only wanted to see what it was like to be in it. It's so . . . real."

The boy stared a bit longer, then he started to laugh. He threw back his head with it, his whole body shaking, like he'd been waiting for just the right moment to finally release all of this emotion. "And what did you discover?"

I walked over to the mess on the floor. There was a slanted pile of snow, a triangular arch that nearly reached the dark wooden legs of the couch, and I bent down to touch it. "That it's cold and icy and strong and violent." I looked up at the boy again. Traces of laughter still graced his lips and eyes. He was a different person with so much expression, someone I could see myself liking, who might become a friend, like Adam. I hadn't seen someone laugh like that since I had left the App World, well before Jonathan Holt announced he was closing the borders. But then I remembered how this boy had grabbed me off the street, and I remembered the cold I saw in his eyes sometimes. I was still staring at him when I spoke again. "Kind of like you," I added.

The expression on his face went dormant. "The storm is dangerous. We need to protect ourselves from it. Not invite it inside."

I stood, passing him on my way to the kitchen looking for something to clean up the snow and the puddle it was making on the floor. It was melting fast now that the wood in the stove was burning brightly and filling the cottage with heat. I found a bucket and a pile of washcloths. "Danger doesn't frighten me."

"Lucky you." He extended a hand and lifted one of the washcloths from my arm. "It frightens me."

I glanced at him while I mopped up the icy water. "You don't seem like someone who'd admit that."

He pressed a towel into the floor. "Fear is a normal part of living in the real body. It's healthy to feel it. It's part of how we survive."

The two of us worked piling snow into the bucket. We crouched close, our knees almost touching, arms moving. Goosebumps covered my skin. "But fear can paralyze us," I said. "Instincts, good ones, are essential, much more so than fear, I think."

He stopped sopping the mess and looked at me. His elbow rested on his knee, hand outstretched, like he was hoping I might take it. "I saw you on the cliff that day when you woke up. I saw your escape."

Was I always going to come up against this? Would that day and what happened since always define me? Would my introduction to everyone forever be as the girl meant to open the Body Market?

I curled a little further into myself. Away from the outstretched hand of the boy. "You and everyone else."

"It was pretty amazing," he said softly.

My knees pressed deeper into my ribs.

"I thought you'd be harder to take," he went on, and I could hear a faraway tone enter his voice, a distant pride, as he spoke. "But then there you were yesterday on the street, so lost in thought, so unaware and unprotected.

All I had to do was reach out and suddenly I had you."
His fingers stretched wide, nearly grazing the skin of my
upper arm.

I flinched.

He snatched them back.

I stood, leaving the pile of wet towels in a heap on the
floor. "You lied before."

He looked at me. His eyes weren't impassive now, but
I couldn't read them either. "What are you talking about?"

"You said you weren't going to hurt me, but that isn't
true."

"It is—" he started, but I didn't let him finish.

"You forgot to add *yet*. That you're not going to hurt
me *yet*." I went to the couch and picked up the blanket
again, pulled it tight around my shoulders so it engulfed
my body. "But the minute you hand me over to my sister
you'll be hurting me. So let's not pretend this is anything
else than what it truly is. All right?"

I'd meant my question to be rhetorical.

Then he spoke. "All right," he whispered in agree-
ment.

But his words, they sounded pained.

5

Rain

the high price of betrayal

"I NEED YOUR advice."

Skylar's Keeper looked up from her reading. I stood in the doorway of the room where she was staying. She'd gotten caught here in the storm and couldn't yet return to the mansion. We were all caught at the moment, stuck inside, stir-crazy already. She patted the spot next to her on the couch. A small lamp threw light onto half of her lined face. "Come and sit."

I did as I was told. The Keepers were gentle in voice, but commanding all the same. In just a few days she'd made these rooms her own by fetching a blanket from one place, a few books from another, and nearly always having a pot of tea brewing and a kettle at the ready on the stove.

"You're worried about Skylar," she said.

I didn't move. Didn't confirm or deny this.

"You need to be smart, Rain," she said. "You can't go looking for her in this storm." She laid her book facedown on the coffee table, open to the page where she'd left off. "Skylar will be all right. She's a survivor."

I leaned forward, clasping my hands, elbows digging into my knees. I couldn't sit still, yet the Keeper was like a statue. "What if it's not just the storm that's keeping her away?"

"You're worried that Jude has her again."

My eyes raked over the Keeper's face, searching for signs that she worried about this too, but her expression gave away nothing. "How could I not? The last time Skylar disappeared she was gone for weeks."

"She made it out alive, though."

"Yes," I said, frustrated. The Keeper was being too literal. "But she was never the same afterward."

The Keeper got up and crossed the room to the stove. She turned the flame on underneath the kettle. "Skylar was grieving—*is* grieving. Grief takes a long time to move through us, and she's lost so much." A shadow crossed the Keeper's face, the first sign I'd seen of worry. "We only added to her pain by betraying her trust."

I joined the Keeper in the little kitchen. The light was

dim, and the anonymity it provided was a relief. "I didn't betray her outright."

"That's not how she sees it," the Keeper said. "Withholding the truth is its own betrayal, and we withheld the biggest truth of all."

I hooked my hand onto the back of my neck and pressed it hard into my skin. "It was for her own protection."

The Keeper eyed me skeptically. "You're still telling yourself that?"

"But it's true," I tried again.

"Rain Holt, Skylar was a pawn in your father's game and then in our own—she was a pawn until she proved that she wasn't." The kettle began to shake as the water neared boiling. "Maybe she'll begin to forgive you only after you admit your betrayal openly. Maybe that's what she's been waiting for all of this time."

I stared at the Keeper. Gone was her stillness, replaced by a fiery righteousness as hot as the flame on the stove. I could feel it rolling off her. Could she be right? Could it be that simple, gaining Skylar's forgiveness? "I won't try to find her," was all I said.

"Good."

"I have other things to worry about here," I went on.

"You do."

"That's what I came to discuss," I said, lying once more.

"Of course," the Keeper said, agreeing with me yet again.

We stared at each other in the darkness for a long time, our eyes telling the only truths in the room.

The kettle screamed.

Neither one of us moved to quiet it.

6

Skylar

killer

"I WAS BORN here," the boy said, later on that same evening. "Grew up here."

He offered this information without my asking.

I wondered why. Was he bored? Trying to pretend we could be friends?

It was dark again, the light gone from the stormy sky. The days were shorter in winter, I'd learned, but the blizzard made them shorter still. There was food cooking on the stove again and we were waiting to eat it. I'd given up trying to pretend I wasn't hungry. Besides, I would need my strength once the snow stopped and I made my escape. "Where are your parents? Your family?"

The wind shrieked. The blizzard seemed endless. "I don't have any family."

There was a hitch in his voice. It made me look at him. "What happened to them?"

"They're dead," he said simply. Then he shook his head. His eyes met mine, and I saw in them something new. An opening, a vulnerability, that he matched with his next words. "That's not true. They're not dead. They plugged in years ago."

I stared at him, surprised. "But why are you—"

"Why am I still in the Real World?" he finished. "Because my parents never wanted children, not in this world or any other. So they dropped me off with some Keepers one day, I thought it was only for the afternoon, and then I never saw them again. It turned out they were dropping me off at a special place for children whose parents were plugging in." His eyes fell to his hands and he stared at his palms like they might have answers. "They traded my life for the freedoms of the App World. I was their payment. Their ticket, so to speak." He opened the door to the stove and stoked the wood, the embers sizzling. "Why else do you think I became a bounty hunter? It's fitting, don't you think? I was traded for passage into the App World, used as capital, so why not do the same with others now that I'm no longer a child? I learned very young what a body is worth and I've never forgotten the lesson." He let out a long breath. "I don't know why I'm telling you this."

He nearly sounded apologetic, and the significance of what he'd said felt heavy in the room. I went to the couch, the floorboards creaking, and sat down, doing my best to process what this information meant. But what I said to him out loud was harsh. "If you're trying to make me feel bad for you, or get me to forgive what you're going to do to me, then think again."

Unlike before when I made a cold remark, this time the boy didn't retreat behind that blank look. His eyes were pained, and I suddenly regretted my words.

"I know," he said quietly.

Now I regretted them even more, despite how everything in me screamed against this.

How so very like Trader this boy was, abandoned by his family. How so very like me and so many others in the App World, like a Single, but this time a Single in the Real World. How many orphans would this divide in worlds make? How many children would have to grow up alone, learning to fend for themselves, to harden themselves against abandonment and all the loneliness that goes with it? How cruel this separation between worlds could be.

Is. How cruel it *is.*

And how cruel its people.

The two of us stared at each other, me on the couch,

the boy standing by the iron stove, warming his hands, his mouth nearly hidden underneath his scarf. There was a shift in the air. I felt it, as sure as the instincts woven through my code in the App World that somehow made the transition to my real body. This boy was opening up, telling me his secrets. It meant I had a chance to win him over, that if I did I might get out of this with my life as my own. The storm was giving us time, and I needed to use it to turn us from enemies into friends, or at least something close to this.

I decided to give him some of my own truth, my own deepest pain.

"We're not so different," I said, just as quietly as he'd spoken before. "I was given up to the App World when I was barely five. I grew up as a Single there, a ward of the state, more or less."

He studied me, but I couldn't read him. "Maybe, but your family gave you up so you could have a better future. They gave you up out of love. At least, at first."

"Don't be so quick to jump to that conclusion." My words were bitter. I backtracked. "I suppose that sounds like the truth, but I felt abandoned in the App World. I thought about it year after year, whether it was really love that made my mother and sister give me up, or if they just told themselves it was, when really by plugging me in they'd unloaded a great burden. Regardless of their reasons, I grew up alone in a world that resented its motherless and fatherless children." I got up and joined the boy at the stove, warming my hands next to his, the two of us side by side. Like equals. Maybe even the same. "I spent my life waiting to unplug and find them, to find out the truth, hoping that when I got to this world I'd know once and for all that I was loved—that I'd always been loved. Instead I found out my sister was the leader of a movement dedicated to selling bodies and that mine was to be her first sale. I haven't seen my mother in months and I don't know where she is. And I've never even known the identity of my father." I stopped short of mentioning Emory Specter. It made me sick to think about him.

The boy didn't say anything, but I could feel his eyes shifting my way now and again. The sound of dinner bubbling on the stove was strangely comforting as the two of us stood there. It seemed to cancel out the terrible gravity of our conversation, of our confessions, really, or at least dull it a bit.

"Do you know anything about your parents?" I asked. "Have you sought out their bodies? They must be somewhere." I didn't mention the possibility that they might be part of the Body Market, that they likely would be eventually if not already. It didn't need saying. We both knew this was the deal.

He walked over to the kitchen counter and picked up a wooden spoon, stirring the pot. "No." He stared down into the bubbling stew. "I don't know where they are."

I joined him there, leaning my elbows on the counter, watching as the steam rose up around his face. His dark eyes were big when he wasn't trying to hide them. "Why didn't you plug in on your own? Find a way to?"

He shrugged. "Didn't want to. Didn't need to."

This surprised me. There were always extenuating circumstances behind why someone couldn't plug in—lack of capital, lack of access, too many Real World responsibilities essential to the maintenance of the App World's existence. But to hear someone say they simply didn't want to was unusual. "Why not?"

He shut off the flame and retrieved bowls from the cabinet and spoons from a drawer. He ladled some stew into each dish and carried everything over to the kitchen table. The two of us sat. I studied the food before me, inhaled the rich scent of vegetables and meat. There was something perfect about it, with the cold and the snow outside.

"Maybe I have a death wish," the boy said.

I picked up my spoon. "What's that supposed to mean?"

He seemed to think about this, as though his own words surprised him. "The App World is too safe for me. Too sterilized. There's no risk to living, no cost or consequences. How can you feel anything real, anything big, anything thrilling, if there's never any risk? A life without risk is a life without meaning."

A life without risk is a life without meaning.

Was that true? Did we need to risk our lives for them to be significant?

"I don't know what I think of that," I said. I took a mouthful of the stew. It was delicious. I loved the way it burned going down my throat, warming my insides on the way. I watched as the boy dug into his, occasionally pausing to glance up at me. This whole experience was strange, but our conversation tonight was the strangest thing of all. It was almost . . . intimate. "But you're right about virtual life," I went on. "It's about avoiding risk. About never having to feel real pain or face the fragility of the body." I thought back to the funeral and Emory Specter's proclamation, which seemed so long ago. "Citizens of the App World have been seeking immortality since the beginning and now they've found it."

The boy stopped eating. "I would never want to be immortal."

"Me neither," I agreed.

He put down his spoon and studied me. "You wouldn't? But you're from the App World."

"I am," I started, then corrected myself. "I *was*. When I left, it was mostly to find my family, but it was also because I wanted a choice. I wanted the chance to be in my body and know what it meant to live in it. Maybe I do agree with you, that somehow in life's riskiness, by living in this fragile body instead of giving it up for virtual reality, too scared to live in it at all, we find something far more meaningful."

The boy didn't respond, he just gulped down the last of his stew and began clearing his place. As I finished mine, I noticed he'd stopped moving. He was standing facing the sink, his back to me, his hands gripping the edge of the countertop.

I wished I could see his face.

"Tell me your name," I said suddenly.

He didn't turn around. "You don't need to know my name. It's better if you don't."

"Better for who? You?" Disappointment filled my voice. His answer made him seem like a coward, and suddenly I didn't want him to turn out to be a coward. "So it's easier for you to hand me over and be done with me?"

"I've been doing this a long time. You don't get into this profession if your will is weak." He came over and grabbed my empty bowl and brought it to the counter. Silverware clattered heavily into the sink. "Don't get the wrong idea. Just because you and I had a talk doesn't change anything. We can have dinner, we can spend days trapped here, and we can have a million more discussions about the deepest desires of our hearts." His breaths were coming quickly. He turned around to face me. "I could fall in love with you, Skylar, and it wouldn't make a difference. When this storm is over, I'm turning you in and getting paid. That's just who I am."

My heart was pounding. I could nearly hear it. "If you're that strong-willed, then telling me your name won't change anything." I rose from my chair and it shrieked along the floor. My hands curled into fists. "If you're trying to protect me, then don't. I don't need anyone's protection."

His mouth was a thin line, his lips pressed together hard. Two round spots of red dotted his cheeks. He closed his eyes a moment, then opened them again. "It's Kit. My name is Kit." He dumped the rest of the dishes and the silverware into the sink with a great crash. Without another word, he walked past the stove, and disappeared into his bedroom.

Kit, Kit, went his name in my mind.

Or maybe it was my heart beating it out.

I clutched at my chest.

Then I let go. My will could be just as strong. I was the girl who'd plunged a knife into her sister's eye. And I'd killed and killed again.

As the wind ripped around the house and the snow piled higher, the drifts nearly topping the windows, I considered what Kit said earlier, that he had a death wish. I let it console me as I took the long, sharp blade I'd seen him use to prepare dinner and slipped it safely between the layers of clothing bulking up my arms, hiding it in my sleeve for later, or just in case I decided to use it in the night.

Everything around me was red.

The floor, the ceiling. I pressed my hand against the wall and it yielded, my fingers disappearing into it.

I started to walk, and walk and walk and walk until people appeared, lots of them. They were talking over one another. I joined the stream and let the crowd take me along. It wasn't long before I saw what pulled them.

Long glass cases, like coffins, appeared everywhere.

People walked up to them, peered into them, touching the sides with their hands.

The Body Market.

I was in the Body Market.

I began pushing through everyone, pushing beyond them, running from box to box, searching without even knowing what I was looking for, even though of course I did, my whole body and my entire mind knew it instinctively. It wasn't long before I found her, and she looked exactly the same as she had two days ago.

Inara, beautiful and golden and lit up on a dais.

She was so peaceful.

I banged on the glass with my fists. "Inara, it's me! It's Skylar!" I'd meant to whisper, but for some reason it came out a scream.

That's when I noticed that the walls and the floor and

the ceiling were no longer red and plush but a cold flat gray that echoed my words, throwing them back at me. Throwing them back to the crowd behind me.

Everyone turned.

"That's her!" one of them said.

Whispers became shouts, and people started toward me.

Their thick black boots thudded against the stone floor.

I ran, my pulse ripping through my veins, the aisles of the market a giant maze, a funhouse full of the shiniest glass, glass that reflected everything around it like mirrors. I slid the knife from my sleeve, held it like a dagger. I tore along, and eventually the sound of footsteps faded, so I slowed enough to look at the bodies on either side of the aisle, searching for Sylvia. I didn't stop, wouldn't have ever stopped, but then I recognized another one.

I halted, my lungs heaving, but I heard nothing else. Everyone else had disappeared and I was alone. A great emptiness seemed to surround me. I went to the body in the case. It was a boy. I looked upon him, the way his brown hair curled across his brow. I pressed my hands to the glass, the knife clanking against it. If the boy's eyes were open, I knew they'd be the color of the sea where I loved to swim.

"Rain," I whispered, a sharp pain stabbing my center. Regret and dismay did a dance around me and I gripped the handle of the knife harder. "Why are you here?"

That's when I recognized more than just Rain.

Adam, too. In the glass box to Rain's left.

And right next to him was Parvda.

The Keeper. She was here as well. How? Last I knew they were hidden and safe at the mansion.

But no. No, they weren't.

They were all right in front of me.

Lacy. I even saw Lacy Mills.

And then, then I saw something even worse, someone whose presence made my heart break and fall into a million pieces.

"Mom? Mom!"

I tried to go to the coffin where she lay, lifeless, but for some reason my legs wouldn't move, well, they would, but so slowly it might take forever to reach her. It felt like I was pushing my way through brush as high as my waist in a forest, even though there was nothing but air. I swung the knife like I could cut a path through whatever was holding me back, trying to get there faster, doing whatever I could. The handle of it burned my palm, but not with heat. It seemed made of ice.

With every step forward my mother only got farther away.

My feet began to slow, the knife began to slow.

Everything was so cold.

I was so cold.

I looked down at my feet. There was snow all around me, covering me, rising up my body, and when I turned toward the sky I realized the lights had gone out in the world. My body shivered, my teeth chattering against one another, clicking and clicking, and any bit of warmth left in me seemed to dislodge itself with the sounds.

"Skylar!"

I heard my name shouted. From far away.

But I couldn't turn to it. I couldn't seem to move.

"Skylar! Skylar!"

As the voice got closer I gathered all the strength I had left and raised the knife behind my head, the darkness so complete I couldn't make out my own limbs. When I heard my name one last time, this time so near it was only a whisper away, I plunged the knife into whatever or whomever was upon me.

The next thing I knew I was back in the cottage, but I wasn't in the living room on the couch. I was in a different room, on a bed, and I was sopping wet. My clothing was soaked and my hair was soaked and dripping down my shirt. Everything was so cold. *I* was so cold. I couldn't feel my hands or my feet. I couldn't see them either. They were wrapped up in sweaters.

What in the world had happened?

"You're awake."

I sat up and my whole body groaned in protest. Kit

was standing in the doorway. His eyes said nothing, but his clothing said something else. It was streaked with red.

"You have blood all over you," I said. My voice was hoarse.

He pulled a shirt and pants out of a small chest of drawers. "You need to change out of those wet things. I would've . . . but I didn't want you to think . . ." He placed the clothes next to me on the bed. "Just do it, Skylar," he added, and left me alone.

I looked around again. This must be Kit's bedroom.

I sat there a minute, trying to understand. But then my teeth started to chatter, and I remembered how they'd been chattering before, recently, though I couldn't remember exactly when. I stood up and began to pull off my wet shirt, but my hands were still wrapped in sweaters. I let them unravel and fall to the floor. My hands wouldn't work right. I couldn't feel them. My fingers were curled into hooks, still and useless. Would my feet be the same way? I sat down and kicked and kicked until the sweaters around them fell off. I tried to wiggle my toes. Unsuccessfully.

I took a deep breath and tried to stay calm.

Then I did my best to peel away the rest of my clothing, replacing everything with the dry things Kit left me. The tips of my fingers and toes tingled, like someone was sticking tiny needles lightly into my skin, but not in an unpleasant way.

Not at first.

The tingling spread to my palms and the backs of my hands and my knuckles and the bottoms of my feet and the tips of them, too. Everything started to burn.

The tiny pins and needles became knives.

The pain stole my breath and I wished for the safety of the App World, for the healing power of a download that would take this horrible agony away. Tears poured down my cheeks.

"Can I come in?" Kit asked from behind the door.

"What's happening?" I cried.

Panic flowed through me. Something was deeply wrong with my hands and feet. Hatred for the body, for being in it, being real, followed up the panic. By the time Kit came into the room, the pain was so intense I was blind with it. I didn't even protest when I felt him pick up my legs and move them onto the bed. I didn't resist, either, when I felt his hands around my hands, rubbing them between his own.

Eventually, after what felt like a million years, some of the pain subsided. Kit moved on to rubbing my feet, and they too, began to feel slightly better, and then a whole lot better.

I watched him work.

No one had ever touched me like this before. Held my hands in theirs or my feet, my toes. Well, not with my knowing it. A jumble of feelings tumbled through me. Even though Kit was doing this to warm my skin, my frozen limbs, it felt like . . . like something *more.* I wiped my hand across my face, as much to hide the burning feeling in my cheeks as to dry the tears.

"I'm okay." I wanted to pull away from him. "I think I'm better."

Kit stopped and looked at me. "Is the pain gone?"

"No," I said honestly. "Almost." I tried to move, but he held fast.

"You can't get up. You need to stay here and rest."

"But—"

He took a deep breath. "Don't argue, Skylar." He sounded so tired right then. Absolutely exhausted.

I decided to listen, because I knew he was right. Then I noticed his bloody shirt was gone. "You were bleeding. You were hurt. Why aren't *you* resting?"

"I'm fine," he said.

"What happened?"

"Which part—to your hands and your feet? Or to me?"

"Both," I said.

"Well," he began, *"you* had frostbite, or nearly."

"What's frostbite?" Mrs. Worthington had never taught us about it, which was surprising since she took such pleasure in the various ways the body could make us hurt and undermine our existence.

Kit finally removed his hands from my skin. "Frostbite is a condition you get in the extreme cold, where parts of your body actually freeze."

I shook my head. "But . . . how could that have happened?"

"You don't remember anything?"

I racked my brain, but all I really knew was that I'd been dreaming. "No. Not really."

Kit crossed his legs on the bed. Clasped his hands in his lap. "Skylar, when I found you, you were out in the snow."

"No," I said, trying to think, to understand. "I was . . . I was just dreaming."

"You weren't," he said. "Well, you were, but I guess you were also sleepwalking. Or trying to escape. Though escaping in your bare feet is a questionable idea in a blizzard. And without anything on your hands."

I thought about the snow, how it was piled so high it was nearly impossible to see out of the windows of the cottage. The idea of being outside in it, unaware, unprotected, was terrifying. My hands were still curled like hooks and they were ghostly pale, like the blood couldn't quite pump itself to my fingers yet. "Am I going to be okay? Or am I going to . . . lose them?" I added in a whisper.

Kit inched closer to me on the bed. He reached out his hand for one of mine. "Can I?"

I nodded and let him take it, watching as he inspected my fingers, my palm, even my wrist. The skin still burned, though only a little.

"I think I found you in time," he said after a while.

"But you may notice that you're sensitive to the cold over the next weeks, especially your fingers and your toes. They're always the first to freeze." Kit eyed me. He still had my hand. I wanted to take it back but also, I didn't. "Which is why a person should always wear gloves out in the snow. And shoes. And socks."

"If I was awake, I'd never have been so stupid as to risk my life like that."

"I didn't say you were stupid," he said. "But you could have died." Something unreadable passed over his face. "Listen to me, Skylar, there are some things you just can't fight and win. There are real things more powerful than any human or technology that we can dream up, and when we face down those things, we must show them our respect and back away. This blizzard is one of those things. And right now it's beaten you and you have to let your body heal."

I found myself staring hard at Kit, wanting to see what his eyes told me. Once his eyes began to speak, they revealed so much, far more than with other people's. Maybe that's why he worked so hard not to let them speak at all. Maybe he knew how much they gave away when he wasn't careful.

"I'll be back later to check on you," he said.

I could tell he didn't really want to go. Reluctance— that's what his eyes revealed. I wondered how far that reluctance might extend. I glanced down at his hand, which still held mine.

"Sleep, Skylar," Kit said, sliding it away and getting up.

I stopped him with another question. "The blood I saw earlier. On your shirt."

Kit didn't turn around. "Yes?"

"You didn't tell me what happened," I said, though I was pretty sure I already knew.

He kept his back toward me and didn't speak.

"Was that from . . . from me?"

His fingers curled around the edge of the doorframe. "Yes. You had a kitchen knife. You stabbed me with it."

"Oh," I gasped out. My heart constricted. "I was dreaming," I reminded him.

He looked at me over his shoulder. His eyes were empty again. "I'm sure that was it, Skylar," he said, his voice full of sadness, or maybe regret, and then he closed the door behind him.

I was alone again, in the quiet.

But my instincts nudged me like an insistent child.

I'd been doing this all wrong. Escape, violence, that wasn't how I was going to win in this scenario. Kit was right: my gaming skills were useless, given the storm and the havoc it wrought. I took a deep breath into my lungs and let it out, remembering how the people in this world regarded me, remembering how they focused on my body, how I'd become a symbol to their cause, and therefore I had worth. To Kit, I was something to trade. But last night, at dinner just before he told me his name, he said something that stuck in my mind. It replayed itself now as I sat here on his bed.

I could fall in love with you, Skylar, and it wouldn't make a difference.

But maybe he was wrong.

Maybe it would make a difference. Maybe, just maybe, if he even came close to such a feeling, he would let me go, wouldn't be able to allow himself to give me over to my sister.

I needed to get him to like me.

And I knew, I could tell that he already did like me, at least a little. That's what he kept hiding from his eyes, what he chased away whenever it showed itself. *Interest.* What I needed to do to Kit was the very same thing that Rain did to me. And in getting Kit to fall for me, I'd be doing something I hadn't even known I'd wanted to do until now: I'd be getting back at Rain. Because somewhere, deep down, despite Lacy, despite everything, I knew Rain still had feelings for me.

Just as I did for him.

7

Rain

family

THE APP WENT through my code like a shot of heroin.

My virtual self soaked it up all at once and let out a long sigh of relief. I studied my arms, my hands, to see what new and exciting thing I'd become.

But something was wrong.

I was . . . exactly the same as before.

Unchanged.

That feeling, that sense of joy that spread through me completely, to every bit of my code, vanished as suddenly as it had appeared and I nearly retched.

Where was I?

I looked around.

Strange. I was exactly where I'd thought. In my room

in the Holt family penthouse atop the tallest skyscraper in the City. Across the street, the facade of the Water Tower rippled and curled a bright blue, waves breaking along its surface. Just beyond it I could see into another penthouse. Two girls stood side by side, their virtual hands pressed across the glass.

One of them seemed to look straight at me, as if she wanted to tell me something. They were like ghosts, glowing beyond the glass.

Did I know them?

I turned away, shook off the strange feelings, the way the girl's hand reached for me. The App was the problem. It must be faulty and was messing with my code.

I called up more Apps, more and more until they nearly blocked everything else from view. They chatted me and prodded and caressed my cheek and my shoulders and even my feet. Their presence helped to relax me and I lay back on my bed, hands behind my head, taking in the sweet anticipation of downloading another one, or maybe two or three at once. I was so rich with Apps, I'd always been so rich with them, and this knowledge was an enormous relief. But at the same time, I . . . I hated them for some reason, the way they wouldn't ever leave me alone, or give me a moment's peace. They were like a plague on my existence.

Sometimes I didn't know who I was without them.

No. I definitely didn't.

My father's voice floated down the hall.

Before I could block him from entering my room he'd already appeared, standing in front of me. With a startled, piercing sigh, the Apps around me fell to the floor, dead.

I jolted up from the bed.

I'd never seen them so . . . dead before. They were lifeless, covering every surface, the bed, the pillows, even my legs.

Could an App die?

Could they all?

Were they even alive in the first place?

My father was watching me with that smug look he sometimes got, like when he was about to tell me the latest way in which I'd failed his expectations.

"Hello, son," he said.

I stared at him without speaking. What in both worlds could he want from me now? He never called me *son*.

"I need you to do something for me," he went on.

I waited.

"Something on behalf of this family, on behalf of your duty to the App World."

"No," I said, before he could even reveal what it was. That's when I remembered I had something to tell *him*, something that I'd been thinking about a long, long time. I glanced out the window, looked beyond the Water Tower again, the way it glowed a bright blue in the Moonlight 4.0, searching the skyline for the two girls in the glass, but the girls were gone.

Jonathan Holt's smug look had fallen away. "What do you mean, no?"

"There's something I need to tell you first," I said, my eyes steady on him. "I've decided to unplug."

The moment these words were out of my mouth the Apps everywhere turned to dust.

I sat up and rubbed the back of my neck.

I'd fallen asleep on the floor of the plug facility. I'd been dreaming, just dreaming. The waves flowing into and out of the great dark cavern sounded their comings and goings, despite the storm. The ocean never stilled, never stopped for anything. I breathed deep, taking in the salty, damp air, and turned to the glowing glass case next to me.

My father lay there, plugged in, unmoving.

I got on my knees, the floor hard underneath them, staring at him in the coffin-like case.

And I nearly laughed.

He was the most powerful man in the App World, well, perhaps aside from Emory Specter. But in just a few seconds, if I wanted to, if I decided it would suit my purposes, I could rip him from his existence there and force him into the Real World. He was so very vulnerable, we all were, plugged in, yet every App citizen lived their virtual life like it would never end. Though, with the miracle of virtual technology and the grand plans of Emory Specter, I supposed now it really wouldn't have to.

For a second I was ashamed, having such malicious thoughts about my father. But then, one of the things I'd learned since waking up in the Real World was that I could be ruthless. An image of the knife thrown by Skylar hurtling across the room and sinking into her own sister's eye flashed in my mind. *All* of us could be. Sometimes a person had to be ruthless and even a little bit malicious to survive, and to make something of himself or herself in this life.

Thoughts of Skylar reminded me of my dream, the two girls in the window of the penthouse. The girl I'd been looking at, looking for after she disappeared, was Skylar. In one of her more talkative moments after the night of the fire, she told me about the Sachses' apartment, how she'd loved it, loved its view of the Water Tower, her favorite building in the City. Skylar and I were standing at the edge of the ocean that day, and she was staring out at the New Port City skyline in the distance, the Water Tower spiking the clouds. Her hair whipped and tangled in the breeze.

I couldn't tear my eyes away from her.

And I remember how in that moment I thought to myself:

You're so beautiful. No wonder you inspired your sister to conceive of the Body Market, to think that with you she could change the fate of New Port City. And you will change its fate, but not in the way your sister imagined.

In the way that I have.

The thought started out so sincere and innocent and then grew so sinister. Like something that would cross the mind of my father.

Skylar kept talking, telling me how she'd look out at the view almost nightly at Inara's. I explained to her the exact location of my family's penthouse mansion, and how my room faced the Water Tower as well.

"You were right there all along. Just across the way," she said, the air chilled with the onset of winter, the waves rushing along the sand of the shoreline, then receding again.

"I was," I replied, still unable to take my eyes from her. I even went so far as to suggest that maybe I'd seen her there one evening before I'd unplugged.

Maybe my mind wished for this in the dream, that Skylar had been right there, hand pressed against the glass of Inara's family's apartment the very moment I told my father I was going to unplug, right when I'd decided to take control over my future, only to find out my father had already decided the same fate for me.

Even the decision to unplug, he took away from me.

He was so pleased when he realized that my big plan coincided with his.

"I knew I'd find you here."

I leapt back from the glass. There was Lacy, standing just a few feet away, her face lit up by the glow of the cases lining either side of us.

"You always know where to find me," I said.

"That's because you and I are the same, Rain Holt." Lacy sat down next to me. The two of us stared at the face of my father for a long, long time. I kept my hands in my pockets.

8

Skylar

exchanges

A FEW HOURS later, the power went out in the cottage.

For the rest of the night I'd slept like the dead. When I woke again the world was still white with the raging storm, the light outside bright from the snow coming down sideways, everything inside a dull, filtered gray. I got up from Kit's bed, unprepared for the way my feet weren't quite ready to hold my full weight, and nearly fell. The first days I spent at the Keeper's came roaring back, how I'd stumbled at first, trying to walk, having to hold on to everything in my path. My hands and feet throbbed from my unplanned excursion into the snow, and I felt something like relief that there was nowhere else for me to go right now except into the next room.

So that's where I went, slowly, deliberately.

Cautiously.

I was even more wary of Kit now.

He was standing in the kitchen, staring at the pile of wood stacked against the wall. Or maybe he was contemplating how little wood was left. Three pieces formed a lonely triangle on the floor.

The chill in the air was noticeable. "I guess we burned through it quickly."

Kit kicked the logs that remained with a ferocity so intense I jumped. They flew in different directions, skittering across the floor, one of them coming to rest at my feet.

I went to him and gripped his arm. "Violence isn't going to conjure up more wood."

Kit froze. He stared at the place where my fingers curled across his skin, as though he could see the inner workings of my body, the web of veins and muscle and bone.

Quickly, I retracted my hand. Then I bent down to pick up one of the scattered pieces of wood.

Kit's eyes raged when I met them again. "Let's see if you're still making jokes when you and I are freezing tonight."

"We're not going to freeze," I said, though not at all

sure I was right and he was wrong. "I thought there was more wood. There was a lot left yesterday. Where did it all go?"

He went to the edge of the kitchen where one of the logs had come to rest and retrieved it. He glared at it. "You're smart, Skylar. Where do you think?"

"We burned it, obviously."

"Well, *we* wouldn't have if you hadn't gone on that little excursion in the middle of the night and forced me to use up most of the stores to keep you warm," he snapped.

I swallowed. "Oh."

"Oh? Really? *Oh*. That's all you have to say?"

"I'm not sure what else you want to hear."

Kit turned his glare on me. "Nothing, ideally."

I matched it with a glare of my own. "You're the one who brought me here, so deal with the consequences."

"Don't remind me. And at the moment, I'd prefer to spend the rest of this day in silence."

I crossed my arms. "Fine. We've done enough talking to last me a lifetime."

"Good. I'm glad we agree."

I returned the log to its resting place against the wall in the kitchen. "We do."

Kit piled the other two pieces on top of it. Then he stalked across the cottage to his room and went inside, slamming the door behind him. My hands balled into fists, rage building in me like water rising against a dam, threatening to spill over the edge. I approached the iron stove, noticing how the warmth coming from it was weak. I glanced toward Kit's room, thinking that behind his closed door it could only be colder, wondering if he was sitting there on his bed shivering.

Then again, why should I care if he was?

I went to the window and stared out the tiny circle that was still clear of snow. The storm was still so fierce it blocked any view of the ocean, as though the ocean had ceased to exist. The notion that this thing called a blizzard could eclipse a sea so vast and wide it seemed to stretch on forever was stunning. It was incredible how the Real World could transform itself into something so totally other from one day to the next. One afternoon it might be cold, yet sunny and beautiful and at peace, and the next it was brutal and dangerous, even deadly, the sun blocked from the sky and the ground buried under a blanket of ice and snow. A pinch of sadness stung my skin at the thought of how the App World was stagnant, and I wondered why its leaders would choose an unchanging world for its people over one that had a mind and will of its own as this one did.

Then again, we had Apps to change us.

Maybe this was supposed to be enough.

I went to the stack of books on the shelf and grabbed one and began to flip through it, this time paying attention to what was on its pages, then grabbed another and then another. Each of them held some version of the same story: humanity abandons its planet for another world, or to live in space, because the world becomes uninhabitable. All of the books predated the App World by at least a decade. How ironic. These novels had predicted the future fairly accurately: humanity did abandon the world, at least the real version of it, not because it became uninhabitable but because they'd gotten bored of the real and so enticed by the virtual that the real no longer mattered. It was interesting that Kit had chosen to collect these in particular.

Eventually the weak warmth from the stove died altogether as I read. I considered throwing one of the remaining pieces of wood inside but decided against it. Then I noticed a bin shoved into the corner of the kitchen. The threads of a tattered scarf dangled down the side. I set the books back onto their shelf and went to it. In it I saw the bloodied shirt and a length of checked fabric stained with blood. Guilt pressed into me. I took them over to the sink and soaked them in soap and water, scrubbing them until the thick dark stains began to fade. When they were nearly gone, I hung them to dry.

After another long while, I finally heard the latch click on the door of Kit's room. By then, I was surveying our remaining supplies in the cabinets. My eyes widened when I saw him. "Your face is gray!"

A bright-red mark was spreading across his shoulder.

He swayed on his feet, like he might collapse.

I took his other arm, and together we staggered over to the stove. Gently, I pushed him down into a nearby chair. Then I retrieved two of the three last pieces of wood and shoved them into the dying embers, poking them with the long iron rod until they caught. A fire smoldered and eventually it blazed hot.

A tiny groan escaped Kit's mouth.

Color returned to his cheeks, but only a little.

I watched him, waited as the warmth transformed his body. When life seemed to find him again, he looked up at me, his eyes soft and unfocused. I reached out to him, my fingers grazing the edge of his sleeve. "Can I?"

His eyes flashed, the whites unusually big and bright. "Can you *what*, Skylar?"

The mischievous tone told me that Kit would be okay, at least eventually, so I began peeling back his shirt. But when I did, I gasped. The wound was deep and jagged. The seam at the center gaped wide like a mouth and circling it were angry rings of red and purple and yellow. Mrs. Worthington's lessons raced through my mind, words about infection and amputation and eventual death, yet she'd only ever provided us with warnings and never cures, thrilled only with frightening us.

Kit's head lolled slightly. "Ugly, isn't it?"

"Shut up," I ordered. "I'm trying to think."

Mrs. Worthington may be of no use, but I'd spent years

running through forests while gaming, fighting attackers with swords and knives, left alone to tend my wounds with whatever I could find. Only water from a stream if I was unlucky, but in better circumstances, if I was near a city or even a house . . . I began to open and close all the cabinets in the cottage. When I exhausted those I retreated into Kit's room, ignoring his protests. I found what I was looking for under the bed, a fairly extensive stash of it. The bottle gripped in my hand, pale golden liquid sloshing about, I returned to the place where Kit sat by the fire.

"Now you're talking," he said, reaching for it.

I held the bottle away from him, grabbed a nearby rag, opened the stopper, and soaked the towel in the alcohol.

"Hey!" he protested.

"Take off your shirt so I can clean that cut."

He gave me that lopsided smile of his, and I wondered for a brief second if he was delirious. "It's not a cut you gave me, Skylar. It's a stab wound."

I didn't smile back. "Whatever. Just do it."

"So forward," he murmured, and began pulling the shirt over his head.

"Look who's calling *me* forward," I said, ready to tease him further, but stopping short when Kit's sly smile fell away. As he adjusted his arm to slip his shirt off, the smile was replaced with a look of pain and a groan deep and guttural as a lion's. Two sweeping tattoos covered his upper arms, all the way to his shoulders. On one of them, a series of dark birds rose in flight along his skin. On the other was a curving sliver of moon amid a sky full of stars.

They were beautiful.

So intricate.

The wound cut across the skin covered in night, splitting open several of the stars.

Kit's breathing was shallow. "Do me a favor." He nodded at the bottle in my hand. "Pour me some of that before you use it on my 'cut.' I'm going to need it."

I retrieved a glass from the kitchen and filled it halfway. When Kit shook his head I relented and topped it off until the liquid reached the brim. With his good arm Kit took it and downed the entire thing in a single gulp. Despite my better judgment, I poured him some more, but this time he held the glass in his hand without drinking any.

"Are you ready?" I asked.

He nodded, then closed his eyes.

For one single moment I hesitated.

This could be my chance to escape for real. If I left Kit weakened and dying, when this blizzard finally ended I would be in good shape to get away. But as I stared down at him, so vulnerable, and as I thought about how our stories were so similar, how we both felt abandoned in this life and had done all we could to survive despite this, I knew that I couldn't leave him like this. I had to help him.

It was the right thing to do.

But in my heart I knew I would help him because I wanted to, not simply because it was right.

I'd have to deal with what that meant later.

I began to clean the wound with the rag. Kit managed to remain silent even as I pressed the towel into the deepest parts of the gash. But the way he gritted his teeth and his breaths became uneven told me that the pain was severe.

"I don't know why I'm helping you," I said after the worst of it was over and I'd reached the outer parts of mottled skin. I was careful to keep my attention on the shoulder I was tending, not allowing it to stray to the rest of him.

Kit opened his eyes and they found mine. "I don't know why you are either."

Blood trickled from the edge of the cut, and this time I began to wash the wound with a towel soaked only in water. Soon the rag was as red as the very center of the gash. "If I'd been smarter, I would have helped you only in exchange for something in return."

There came a silence, and for a moment I wondered if Kit had passed out from the shock of the pain. But when I shifted my gaze from the wound, he was watching me.

"I will owe you a favor then," he said.

My eyes narrowed. "And why would you do that?"

He glanced over to the clothing hanging in the kitchen.

"You washed my scarf," he said, trying for a grin.

I shook my head. "That's not why."

His stare was hard. "For the same reason you're helping me, Skylar, which is to say, I have no idea."

I took the bloodstained towels to the sink and ran the water. Red streamed across my fingers and hands into the basin below before draining away. When I turned around again, Kit was struggling to put on his shirt.

"I'm not done yet," I said, and took it away from him. I waited for a lopsided grin and a comment about how if I wanted to see his naked torso any longer I could just ask, but neither response came, so I knew he must still be in pain. I searched the cabinets for something else that might help Kit's shoulder heal and pulled out a pot of honey I found. I grabbed a spoon and smeared the ugly gash with a thick layer of the sticky salve. Then I took a clean, thin rag and bandaged the wound, securing it along his shoulder blade. "There," I said. "You can put your shirt back on." But it was as bloodstained as the rags I'd used. "Wait, let me get you a new one," I said, and went to his room before he could protest.

Now that I wasn't blind with exhaustion, my hands and feet throbbing from frostbite, I noticed how bare and utilitarian everything was, save a tiny glass jar that sat atop a set of drawers.

Sea glass. Kit had a jar full of colorful sea glass.

I picked it up and turned it around in my palm.

A dozen shades of blue and green winked back at me in the lamplight.

I shook my head.

Nothing I knew about Kit added up. He was a bounty hunter who rode a motorcycle in the middle of winter, someone with hardened eyes and a practiced blank expression. Yet he was also someone who walked along the ocean picking up pieces of pretty glass and saving them in this jar.

I returned it to its place and began opening and shutting drawers until I came to one that was full of neatly folded shirts. I grabbed the shirt on top and the entire stack shifted. The corner of something flat—a paper maybe—stuck out from underneath.

No, it was a photograph.

The old kind that people used to take of one another and keep in special boxes and books before technology made it so images only appeared on screens.

I shifted the stack of shirts farther.

The photograph was of a girl.

She was beautiful.

I picked it up and studied it.

Did Kit have a girlfriend?

Her eyes were big and blue and they stared out at whoever was taking the picture, her skin nearly translucent, her hair long and blond and wavy, and cascading down over her left shoulder. She was maybe a year younger than me when the photo was taken.

I put the picture back and in one swift motion I buried it underneath the stack of shirts. I didn't want to look at the girl's wide blue eyes any longer. The drawer shut with a loud bang. I didn't realize how hard I'd pushed it. By the time I returned to the living room, the fire had died and Kit had finished off his second glass of whiskey and was pouring another. He held out the bottle to me. "Want some?"

I dropped the clean shirt into his lap and took the bottle from him, but instead of drinking any I set it on the kitchen counter. "No, thank you."

"And why not?" His tone was a challenge. "It will help keep you warm."

I eyed the last lonely log sitting on the floor. "So will a blanket."

Kit began putting on the shirt I gave him and groaned in pain. For a moment I wondered if he'd faint, but then the life returned to his eyes and they sought out the bottle of whiskey. "Just try it."

Suddenly I wondered, why not? We were snowed in, there was nowhere to go, and maybe a strong drink would keep me from dreams that sent me out to my death. I grabbed a small glass from the cabinet, plunked it on the counter, and filled it, then spun around and poured more into his.

"Thatta girl," Kit said.

I held up my glass to his. "To favors."

His eyes grew wary, but then he nodded. "All right. To favors," he agreed, joining me in my toast.

I took a big gulp and nearly spit it out. Between the fumes that burned so intensely they could likely kill and the feel of it going down my throat, I honestly didn't know if I was up to Kit's challenge of joining him in this drink. "What in both worlds is that made of? Gasoline?"

Kit had a hand on his stomach, laughing, his whole body shaking, occasionally wincing from the pain in his wounded shoulder. "Yes, well, sorry if it's not up to the same standards one might enjoy from a Whiskey App."

I cupped my throat with my hand. It still burned. "What standards? There were standards used when making this? Are you sure?"

Kit winced harder. "Stop making me laugh. The pain is shocking." He took a deep breath, then another. "You were right to use it to clean that gash. Whatever infection was trying to settle in there, that stuff surely burned it off." He let his hand fall from his stomach. It dangled along his side. "Pull up a chair and try again."

First I retrieved the blanket from the couch, and then I dragged the second chair from the kitchen over to Kit, taking the scarf that had been drying across it and draping it around the back of his neck. It was strange to see him without it, and I gained some satisfaction returning it to its rightful place.

He blinked up at me, surprised, maybe by the familiarity of the gesture, or maybe at the affection in it.

I sat down, pulling the blanket over my lap. The liquid in my glass was the same deceptive color as the honey I'd spread into the wound on Kit's shoulder. I tapped the bottle sitting between us. "You were at least right that it would warm me. You didn't mention the part about how it would set my insides on fire, though."

Kit placed his hand flat on the iron stove. It had already grown cool enough to touch. Not a good sign. "You'll be happy to feel that fire in a couple of hours."

"If I'm still drinking this in a couple of hours, I won't be feeling anything."

A smile spread across his face, the most genuine I'd seen so far. Or maybe it was more wistful. "Exactly the idea."

I laughed and we clinked glasses again.

Soon an hour had passed, Kit slowly draining his glass, filling it, and draining it once more, alternating with bigger and bigger gulps of water. His entire demeanor changed, softened, as though in retreat from something, and I asked my question without thinking. "What, exactly, are you trying to escape?"

His expression darkened. "What do you mean?"

"Why else would you want to drink until it renders you unconscious? Until you don't feel anything anymore?"

"To forget the cold for a while," he answered quickly.

"I don't think that's it."

He took a big gulp from his glass and swallowed it easily. Impressive. "You can think whatever you want, Skylar."

I took a small sip from my drink. The fumes still burned my nose, but not as badly as before, and Kit was right, the flame rippling across my throat felt good. The image of the blond girl I'd seen in the picture flashed in my mind. "Is it love that has you running?" I tried to sound playful, but my words sounded far more serious than I wanted so I clarified. "I saw the photograph in your drawer. I wasn't snooping, I was just looking for a clean shirt." Kit didn't answer. "So?" I pressed, after his silence grew long.

"So what?"

"So who's the girl?"

He stared into his glass like it might tell his future. "No one."

My heart squeezed and I took a sip from my own. "So it *is* love."

He looked over at me. The wind shrieked outside and the cottage groaned against it. Sadness danced across his cheeks. "I do love her, but not how you're thinking."

The temperature was dropping, though I hardly felt it. "Then tell me how."

Kit went silent again. It was getting dark inside the house, and barely any light was left around us. His eyes went to the iron stove. He flipped the latch on the door and pulled it open, watching as the last embers, orange and fading, died out. It was growing as cold in here as the snowy air outside. Kit got up without much trouble, the whiskey working its magic numbing his shoulder, and began opening and closing cabinets in the kitchen.

"Tell me what you need and I'll find it," I offered. "You should rest."

Kit took down an armful of candles and set five, no, six of them onto the table, another two onto the stove, and a few more around the room. He began to light them, his back to me. "The girl you saw is my sister. We're twins."

There came a flicker in my chest that seemed to match the flames of the candles. "But you look nothing alike . . . and I thought . . ." I trailed off, trying to figure out what, exactly, I was really thinking.

"Before, when you asked about my family, I didn't mention her."

"Why?"

Kit returned to his chair again and picked up his glass. "Because of everyone, she hurt me the most. So I left that part of my story out."

My mind went to Jude. "Sisters do that," I said with a heavy sigh.

Kit eyed me, then clinked his glass against mine. "I suppose you, of all people, would know." He took a sip. "My parents abandoned us both. Two children in exchange for two adults' passage into the App World. For years it was just Maggie and me—that's her name. We took care of each other, stood by each other's side. But even though she and I are twins we're still so very different, and not just in terms of looks. There's something right about how Maggie is all light—light hair, light skin, light eyes—and I'm all darkness." He laughed a little sadly. "I never wanted to leave the Real World, but she longed for it our entire lives. She hung on to this romantic belief that our parents were waiting for us to join them in the App World so the four of us could live happily and virtually ever after. I never had the heart to tell her the truth."

I pulled the blanket higher. I was starting to shiver. "But didn't she know?"

Kit shook his head. "I lied to her. When I figured out what our parents had done, I was sure it would break her heart, but I worried it might break her altogether. Maggie was the sweetest girl I've ever known, but she was fragile too."

I studied him. "You're talking about her in the past tense. Did she . . ." I trailed off.

"She's not dead," he said, answering my unfinished question and wincing a little. "She's in the App World."

"She plugged in?"

He nodded. "That she did."

"Did she go there to be with your parents?"

Kit was silent a long time before answering. "I've wondered if she's sought them out, though I'm not sure they wanted to be found. But when Maggie plugged in, she did it for herself. She wanted a virtual life so badly."

"So Maggie abandoned you too."

"Everyone does in the end, don't they?"

I didn't answer, didn't want to think through whether or not what Kit said was true. He was shivering alongside me now, and I offered him some of the blanket. I was almost surprised when he took it. As I watched him, I couldn't help but see the face of a boy, one far younger than his years. His vulnerability was striking when it appeared, made all the more so because he typically seemed so hard and cold to everything around him. Something still didn't add up about his sister plugging in, though. "How did she afford it?" I asked. "How did she pay for her passage to the App World?"

Kit shrugged. "Why do you think I became a bounty hunter?"

My jaw fell. "You did it for her."

"I did it for us," he corrected. "Well, that's the lie I sold her. All along it was supposed to be for the two of us. We would save enough and both of us would plug in and be reunited with our parents. She would go first and then I would join her." Kit took a sip of his whiskey, closing his eyes against the burn of it. "But I was never going to join her. I didn't want a virtual life and I never wanted to see our parents again. Besides, it would take forever to save enough money for the both of us, no matter how much we scrimped."

"So you lied to her about that, too."

Kit tried for a grin, but his eyes were hollow. "I'm an excellent liar, Skylar."

"I thought you said she hurt you," I said, ignoring his comment.

"She did. I think she knew all along that I was never going to the App World. She was fragile and sweet, but she wasn't stupid. She could do the math. But she went anyway. Left me here all on my own. When she said good-bye, right before plugging in, I could see it on her face. She knew we would probably never see each other again."

My throat felt thick and knotted. "I'm so sorry."

"Yeah, well, don't be too sorry for me or for her."

Kit picked up the bottle and offered to pour some into my glass. It was empty, so I let him. "Why not?"

"That's why I took you, Skylar," he said. "A body for a body. Yours for my sister's."

I gaped at him. "What are you talking about?"

"My sister was beautiful—*is* beautiful. She plugged in, and now she's one of the prize wares for sale at the Body Market. It would cost a king's ransom to get her back, but get her back I will." He eyed me. "That's where you come in."

My hand tightened around my glass until my knuckles grew white. "So you give me up to my sister, take the money, and buy your own sister back."

Kit looked away. "Yes. It's all very simple."

"Not if you're me."

He sighed. "No, I suppose not."

I shifted underneath the blanket, pulled it tighter, just for something to do. Kit got up from the chair and headed into his bedroom. He returned with another bottle from the stash under his bed. I looked at the one that sat atop the stove, surprised to see that we'd drunk the entire thing.

Then I held out my glass to him and started to laugh.

The corner of Kit's mouth twitched as he filled it. "What, Skylar?"

"The last time I drank, it was the calm before the storm," I said, still laughing, louder now, remembering my first night at the mansion on the beach with everyone, the night before I was taken by Jude's people. "But it's storming out now. Do you think that means this is the storm before the calm? That would be so nice." Kit met this with silence, so I spoke again to fill it, and because somehow a tiny bit of hope had found me in the middle of all this frigid air. "Maybe there's another way," I found myself saying.

Kit's smile vanished. "Don't forget what happens next, Skylar."

The laughter died in my throat. "I didn't," I told him. "How could I? You've made it all very clear."

"Good," he said, his voice sounding so sure.

But his eyes, they weren't sure at all.

9

Rain

reciprocity

"AT LEAST YOUR father cares about you," Lacy said.

I looked at her, sitting there on the floor in the dark, her eyes reflecting the glow of the lit glass boxes all around us. They were full of sadness. When Lacy showed this side of herself, how lost she's been all her life, how alone she still was, I couldn't help thinking that what she said was true: she and I *are* the same.

"My father only cares about me insofar as what I can do for him," I said. "For the Holt family, for our famous and important name in both worlds. He's as bad as Emory Specter, he's so desperate to hold on to his power. It's just that the result of my father's desperation will have a better outcome for everyone than Emory's."

Tiny beads of water clung to Lacy's eyelashes. One of them slipped to the edge and fell onto her freckled cheek. "Maybe. But it's difficult when your only use to people is, well"—she laughed bitterly—"to be used and to use others. It teaches you to be cruel to everyone. Cruel and mean. I've been cruel and mean ever since I was a little girl. Those are hard skills to unlearn, you know?" She sniffled.

It almost made me want to lean forward and kiss her sadness away.

Almost.

I held back. Was this Lacy the actress, or the real Lacy? The App World Lacy never cried, never would even scrunch up her nose so unselfconsciously. The App World Lacy was fiery perfection at all times, ready to burn anyone who came near. Except when she was around me. "Don't cry," I said, deciding to believe her display was real.

She wiped her eyes. "Sometimes I'm so alone, you know? And sometimes I wish I could go back and tell your father *no*." She laughed bitterly again. "Tell *my* father to go to the Real World to his face instead of behind his back."

I nodded. *Go to the Real World* for people at home was basically the same as *go to hell* used to be in this one. "Sometimes I wish I'd done that with my father, too."

This made Lacy smile a little. "See? We are the same."

"Maybe," I admitted. This made her smile brighter.

"My father should never have taken advantage of you like that."

She eyed me. "Rain, you and I both know that Jonathan Holt came to me because you told him how much I hated my parents. He knew if I had the chance to hurt my father I would, and that my father is on Emory Specter's side."

I grimaced. "I'm sorry, Lacy."

She shrugged. "Why?"

"For telling my father your secrets. For giving him the ammunition to get you involved in this situation. It wasn't his business to know your feelings, that you'd be willing to go against your parents out of . . . revenge. I wish I could undo it."

Lacy stared at me. "I go back and forth about being stuck in this world. Sometimes I hate it." She paused. Then she reached out her hand and took mine. "But sometimes I'm glad," she added, her voice barely a whisper.

In the quiet, the wind howled through the caves that led to the ocean. The way the storm held us here, the force of it, made it seem like all that lay ahead might never happen, like the Body Market was all a dream, like there was nothing else we needed to do in this world aside from being and living. I looked at Lacy's long fingers, the way they were intertwined with mine. Her real hands were so delicate. Fragile. And here she was, entrusting them to me. Lacy was full of contradictions and I was finding it difficult to wrap my head around whether this was a good thing or a bad thing overall.

What was I supposed to do here? Should I take my hand back and tell her I didn't want the same thing from her as she wanted from me?

Or did I?

I raised my eyes to meet Lacy's, and as I did, I remembered the first night that Skylar spent with us on the beach, when I'd almost kissed her before she went into her room to sleep. What if I had? Would things have happened differently? Would the fact that I'd lied seem a lesser offense when she found out the truth, or would it have been even worse? I would never know, because that's not what happened. There was no going back.

But here I was now, with a chance to do things differently. Lacy wasn't Skylar, yet she and I had our own history, and it was worth something. Maybe more than I'd ever admitted until now.

Lacy's eyebrows were a high arc of feathery red against pale skin. "Rain," she said wonderingly, like she already knew the thoughts flying through my mind.

Before she could say anything else, I kissed her.

10

Skylar

playing hearts

MY HEAD SWAM.

The whiskey, or whatever it was Kit had in that bottle, was doing a number on my senses. But he was right that it warmed a person through, or at least tricked the body into thinking it was warm. The cottage was so cold by now that when Kit and I spoke, we could see our breath crystallized in the air, our words turned to ice.

Though the mood between us had grown anything but icy.

The colder it got, the more things seemed to thaw, even after the uncomfortable reminder Kit offered about the reality of our situation. Or maybe it was just the drink that was having this effect on us, the way it made everything looser, including our tongues. Well, mine, at least. My tongue and my limbs.

"You have the strangest eyes I've ever seen," I told Kit, and touched the side of his face, as though I needed to emphasize my meaning by physically pointing this out. I could hear him inhale sharply when my fingers met his skin, but I didn't retract my hand. "Has anyone ever told you that?"

"Skylar," he said, but didn't go any further than my name.

"Kit," I said, trying to sound serious but failing. I started to laugh.

He reached up, encircling my wrist. "You're drunk."

"So this is what it's like to be drunk in a real body," I said, still laughing, but my laugh had changed, and my eyes, struggling to focus, somehow zeroed in on the place where Kit's hand met my skin with perfect clarity. I was being reckless, the whiskey dulling my better judgment, but I didn't care. For a moment, I let myself imagine Rain stumbling into the cottage to get out of the storm and finding Kit and me, Rain barging into this moment of intimacy—because that's what this was, I realized, amid the swirl and wooze of my mind. Would a sharp stab of jealousy sting at Rain's middle, just as it had stung mine when I came upon him and Lacy? "I can be vengeful sometimes," I said out of nowhere.

Kit cocked his head, alert. "How so?"

My eyes widened. "Wait, did I say that out loud?"

"You did."

"Oh. I didn't mean to."

He watched me, eyes steady. "Why don't you explain, now that you have."

His fingers pressed into the skin of my wrist, and my hand was still at his temple. Everything seemed to pulse, the blood in my veins, the air in the room, the words as they floated back and forth between us. What came next? How did I answer? Did I tell Kit the truth or did I make up a lie? We seemed poised on the edge of something, maybe the very edge, where I made Kit see me not as someone to trade but as someone essential to the inner workings of his own heart, impossible to give away, impossible to live without. I needed to change his objectives here—his objectives about *me*.

I should kiss him.

That's what Lacy would do in my position. Happily, lustily, and easily.

The floor seemed to rise up and I shied away from it. The drinks were playing tricks on my mind. Or maybe it was Kit I wanted to shy away from. Instead, I leaned a little closer, noticing once again the long, dark lashes that framed his watchful eyes, seeing something unexpected in them. Hope. That Kit was a boy as vulnerable as anyone else.

A sober sensibility overtook me.

No. I wouldn't kiss Kit.

I sat back in my chair. I wasn't Lacy. I'd never be Lacy. I might be able to wield a knife, but my heart was another matter. I didn't like how Rain had played with mine and I wouldn't do it to another person, even if it served me to do so. Moments were fleeting and hearts beat for a lifetime. Playing hearts was too risky a business over the long term. If I was to win Kit over, I would do it without this sort of trick. I would do it for real.

Kit sat there, still, waiting for whatever came next.

"There was someone—*is* someone," I corrected. "Who I care about, who lied to me about a great many things, including his feelings." I drew in a deep breath, daring a glance at Kit. He seemed disappointed with the turn in conversation, as though I had struck him with my hand instead of giving him the kiss he was sure was on the way. I continued, regardless. "I was just imagining that if he came upon us, he might feel jealous. And I was thinking about how his jealousy would make me feel satisfied. That I'd like to make him jealous if I could."

He raised one eyebrow. "And why would you and I, sitting here, make your . . . friend . . . jealous?"

I let out a long breath, thinking to myself, *stupid, stupid Skylar.* In telling Kit the truth about Rain, or at least some of it, I'd revealed the direction of my thoughts about Kit, or rather, my feelings. That they might be interpreted by Rain as romantic meant that they might be interpreted by Kit as romantic, too. I got up from the chair quickly, the blanket falling away and reminding me of the fierce chill in the air. I shivered and stumbled, then righted myself and managed to make it across the room.

I kept my back to Kit when I gave him my answer. "You and I are alone in a cottage in the middle of a storm, sitting so close together and drinking . . . whatever is in that bottle. Anybody might assume there was . . . something more going on between us."

"We're no longer sitting close, though," Kit observed, and I nearly wanted to slap him. "Come back here. You're shivering." When I didn't move, he went on. "I'm serious, Skylar. You need to stay as warm as you can or you'll get sick. And I know you don't want that."

I relented, but before I returned to my place next to Kit, as cozy a spot as I would find in this house under that shared blanket, I spoke again. "Of course, it wouldn't take long for the assumptions someone might make about us to be proven wrong. It would happen easily and quickly and with a mere few words."

Kit eyed me warily. "Oh?"

"You would explain that you are a bounty hunter and I am your captive. That we got caught in a storm and simply decided to do what was necessary to survive it. Nothing more." I returned to my chair and tucked myself under the blanket. "We would only have to tell them the truth," I finished, and Kit looked away.

* * *

The night continued, colder and colder.

Every few minutes, one of us would eye that last lonely piece of wood on the floor. Finally, after what must have been dozens of longing glances, Kit got up and grabbed it. He opened the door to the iron stove and placed the wood gently inside of it, as though it were something precious. The two of us stared at it a moment, grateful it existed, that it was one of the bigger pieces that had been in the pile. This meant it would provide us some heat for longer than usual.

Kit went to work lighting it.

Soon it caught.

Soon it was burning bright.

We drew closer to it.

We drew closer to each other.

We held our hands over the heat emanating outward.

I felt my interest in Rain slipping away, like a wave receding.

Was I so very fickle? Or was it that betrayal is nearly impossible to overcome, to replace with a newfound trust? Does it chip away at our feelings until they are only dust?

"What are you thinking?" Kit asked.

I looked at him. He'd been watching me, without my realizing. I shook my head. Then I spoke. "I was thinking that this warmth is delicious. Too bad it won't last."

"That's not what was on your mind," he said quietly.

His eyes remained steady. I would almost say they were pleading. Kit longed for something. Was it just from me that he wanted it? Or from anyone? Seeing it there made me want to be the only one who could fulfill whatever it was. Once again, I gave him the truth. "No, it wasn't. But I don't want to tell you what I was thinking either. Is that all right?"

He stared at me a beat longer, then nodded. He seemed satisfied with my answer, satisfied that I'd rather withhold my thoughts than reveal them. Maybe this told him just as much as a reply might.

He filled my glass again. The night was passing, full of drink and talk. The wood burned until half of it was ash.

"I would like to call in my favor," I said.

Kit's lips parted with surprise. "Now?"

I sighed. Was this the right time? "Yes," I said, answering my own question and his.

He shifted, wincing with the movement. Even the whiskey couldn't erase a knife wound that festered.

I leaned forward, my hand poised over his shoulder. "You're in pain."

"No," he said.

"You're lying," I said.

The right corner of his mouth ticked up. "Maybe. Ask your favor, Skylar."

I returned my hand to my lap. Thought about the

jar of smooth blue glass in Kit's room and drew courage from this. There was more to him than he gave off. "I said before there might be another way for us . . . to move forward. And the favor is that you consider an alternate plan to your own. For me, I mean. And your sister."

Kit's right brow ticked upward now, to match the corner of his mouth. "Consider but not commit to?"

"Yes," I said.

"That seems like a waste of a favor."

I took a drink of the whiskey. The cold made it so much more palatable. "It all depends on how long the consideration might take." The breath from my words turned to vapor. The wood in the stove was nearly gone already. "What if I'm able to get your sister back for you? Without you handing me over to Jude in exchange?"

A cloud passed across Kit's face. With great effort, he nodded. "I'm listening."

Kit's resolve was faltering, despite his obvious effort to hold it steady. He'd been so confident about his plans for me at first, but our time together was punching holes through it. He wanted an excuse to let it fall away completely. I could see it on him, the hope that we could find another way. "I have friends," I began. "A lot of friends. All of whom are united against my sister and want to dismantle her gruesome market."

"Is one of your . . . friends the person you'd like to make jealous?" Kit asked.

This startled me. It wasn't the first question I expected from him. I nodded. "I think I know a little bit about how you feel. There's someone I need to save from the Body Market, too. It's my fault she's in this situation, therefore my responsibility to fix things. If the entire market comes down in the process, so much the better."

Kit's lips were pressed together. He shook his head. "I don't care about taking down the entire market. I only care about Maggie."

I shifted in my chair. Leaned closer. Looked Kit straight in the eyes. "I don't believe that. I think you care about more than Maggie, but you just don't want to admit it."

His gaze back was steady. "Oh, do you?"

I suddenly felt the weight of two worlds on my shoulders. I had a feeling Kit did, too. "I don't think you're that cold a person. I think you've done what you've needed to survive, just like I have. Just like all of us do." Both of our hands were perched on the cooling iron of the stovetop, and I noticed how close our fingers were. "As part of your . . . *consideration* . . . I'm asking that you return me to where I've been hiding out and to the people plotting against my sister. In doing so, I promise to find a way to get Maggie back."

Kit's composure faltered. "That's too much to ask—" he began.

I didn't let him continue, refused to let him deny me. "And if I fail, I'll turn myself in to you and we go back to your original plan. I told you it was a real favor," I added quickly. "There's also one other possibility," I went on, getting to the part that made me hesitate, the part that maybe revealed more about what I was feeling than I wanted. "You could join us," I said. "If you did, then you would no longer be . . . so alone."

Kit took in a long breath, then let it out, the heat of it clouding the air.

"I'll give you my decision in the morning," he said softly.

11

Rain

beautiful

I STOOD UP, careful not to wake Lacy.

She was still sitting on the floor, sleeping upright, her back resting against one of the long glass boxes, her legs outstretched in the aisle. Her red hair flowed along her shoulders and down past her elbows. It nearly touched the concrete ground. I didn't want to leave her, but I didn't want to wake her either. She looked so peaceful. There was the trace of a smile on her face.

I wondered if she was dreaming about what just happened between us.

I watched her there, her chest slowly rising and falling. After I'd kissed her, she kissed me back, and didn't seem to want to stop. We spent the night listening to the sounds of the storm outside, talking and kissing, Lacy with this happy smile on her face that thawed out my heart. But occasionally I'd see a gleam in her eye, a familiar one, and I was reminded exactly what I was doing and that I was doing it with Lacy Mills. It occurred to me to wonder if she was imagining Skylar in that moment, and how Skylar would feel if she saw us here.

Lacy loved nothing more than to win. I had a feeling she'd consider winning me against Skylar her greatest triumph.

Skylar.

Her name drifted through me like snow caught in the wind, harsh and cold and piercing.

I always thought Skylar would be my first real kiss in this world. But instead I gave it to Lacy.

My heart clenched, like there was a fist wrapped around it.

What was done was done. I made my choice, fully aware of what I was doing. But now that the repercussions were staring me in the face, so was a bright flash of regret. If I ever got to a place again where Skylar and I might have some sort of romantic possibility, I would have to tell her about this night with Lacy before she and I could move forward. It wouldn't be fair otherwise.

I turned my back on Lacy.

Where was Skylar anyway? Was she all right? As these questions pounded at me, I realized Lacy and I weren't alone. Someone was standing at the end of the aisle. She raised her hand in an awkward wave. Quietly, I went to her.

I shoved my hands in my pockets, trying to act casual. "Zeera, what's up?"

Zeera's eyebrows were arched. She gestured at Lacy behind me. "I didn't mean to interrupt."

I shrugged. "You weren't."

Her eyebrows arched higher. "That's not what it looks like to me."

She and Lacy had become friends over the last couple of months. They were the least likely people I imagined connecting, but somehow they had. I don't think Skylar even noticed their friendship, she'd been so out of it. But Lacy and Zeera spent a lot of time together now.

I sighed. "I'll let Lacy give you the details if she wants to."

Zeera's smile was a bit smug. "You two? Finally?"

"I don't know, Zeera," I hissed, trying not to raise my voice and wake her. "Yes. Maybe. We'll see."

"Don't hurt her, Rain Holt," she scolded.

I tilted my head to the side. "Really, Zeera? Did you come here to judge me, or for some other reason?"

She frowned a little. "Follow me."

Zeera led me to the weapons room, a place I'd been avoiding because Lacy was there a lot, visiting Zeera, whispering about what, I didn't know. Zeera punched in the code and pressed her hand to the touchpad on the wall. The great vault of a door opened to let us inside. The room was full of screens, big and small, but only one of them was turned on. The biggest one, a gigantic, thin rectangular panel against the back wall. A single image shone from its surface.

I went to it, transfixed. "Am I seeing what I think I'm seeing?"

Zeera came over and stood next to me. "You are." Her voice was hushed, as though we could be overheard on the other side of it.

The two of us stared. "Is that . . . is that *live*?"

"Yes, it is," she said.

"How did you get this up?"

Zeera's smile was full of pride. "I finally hacked in. I think this storm turned out to be good luck. I haven't worked in such a concentrated way in ages. I caught the one feed that's active and this was what I found." Zeera paused for a breath, the smile dropping from her mouth. "I can't figure out the location for where it's coming from though."

I took this in, then returned my attention to the monitor. "So who is that?"

On the screen a girl was pacing back and forth across a beautiful room. She moved at such an angle that I couldn't get a clear look at her face. But her hair was striking. Long and blond and wavy, buttery like silk. She wore only a slip of a dress, her skin pale, her frame tiny. It wasn't Skylar, that was for sure.

Zeera was shaking her head. "I have no idea. But I've been watching her long enough to know that she's a prisoner, which means she must be important to the New Capitalists. Like, Inara important, like . . ." Zeera trailed off.

Skylar important.

These unspoken words hung in the air.

We were both thinking them.

Cold pierced my heart as another thought followed.

If Jude didn't have Skylar, then who did? I should have felt relieved, but somehow I didn't. I swallowed as the reason came to me.

That Skylar had simply left us for good.

I took a step closer to the screen. Everything around the girl was decorated in shades of blue, patterns of blue, the couch, the rug, the wall hangings, the bedspread. "Doesn't that seem like the room Skylar described, where Jude held her?"

"That's what I thought, too," Zeera said.

"Whoever she is, you're right," I said. "She's not there of her own volition."

The girl froze, midstride, like she'd heard something that startled her. Like maybe she'd even heard us.

Zeera picked up a nearby keyboard and began typing frantically. She shook her head in frustration. "I got the image up but I still haven't figured out the sound."

The girl turned around slowly and for the first time I saw her face.

Her eyes were big and blue and bright, long blond-tipped lashes fanning out from them to match her flaxen hair. Her cheeks were flushed red, the same color as her lips.

She was beautiful.

Zeera's fingers were flying across the keyboard, but still no sound emitted from the speakers. "Come on, come on."

Just then, a second person stepped into the frame. Her back was to the camera.

Zeera stopped typing and looked up. "Is that . . . ?"

The two of us stared at the screen, side by side.

"Yes," I said. "Jude." I took in the sight of them talking, wishing we could hear. The woman kept her back to the feed, but it didn't matter. I was certain it was her.

"You think?" Zeera asked.

"Yes." I pointed to the girl's face on the screen, which told us everything we needed to know. "Don't you see her eyes?" I went on. "The look in them is of terror."

12

Skylar

good-byes

I WOKE TO find my legs tangled with Kit's, my body slumped against his.

I jumped up, startled. I yanked at whatever was encircling my neck and pulled away Kit's scarf. Every part of me shivered.

Kit didn't move. Didn't stir. He slept like the dead. I wondered if he was hungover from too much drink. I draped the scarf over him.

Then I noticed a change in the cottage.

No. Outside of it.

The wind no longer howled. A different-colored light crept inside.

I went to the window.

The storm was over. Pale yellow sunshine crept through the icy glass. The snow was piled higher than I ever could have imagined, but it would rise no longer. When I finally turned around I saw that Kit was in the process of waking up. I waited for his first words of the day, for his decision about what I'd asked of him, but he said nothing about our night.

"We need to get to work," was what he said instead.

"Clearing the snow from the doorway," I surmised.

"Clearing a path so I can chop more firewood. It still may be days before we can get farther down the road than a mile or two. The snow will cover everything, and many feet deep."

My heart sank. *Days more, trapped in this cabin? Alone with Kit?*

A knot pretzeled in my stomach.

A lot could happen in a few days. My relationship with Kit had changed dramatically already, and I wasn't sure what I thought of it changing any more, or what those changes might entail.

I took a deep breath. "How long do you think it will be before they can reopen the market?"

Kit was rummaging through a closet off the side of the kitchen and pulled out two large shovels. "A few days, maybe." He tossed one to me and I caught it. "Not long."

I nodded. A few days was better than nothing.

We went to the door and for the first time since my midnight excursion, we opened it. I thought we would encounter a great wall of snow, but luckily the banks had sloped away from the cottage walls and there was little more than a few inches that covered the ground in front of the house.

The world outside was quiet and soft, asleep under a thick blanket of white. We could see all the way to the ocean, which shimmered under the sun, only the barest of waves rippling the water. I squinted against the bright glare, but I couldn't bring myself to turn away. "The Real World is beautiful," I said in a hush.

"Sometimes, yes," Kit agreed quietly. "It can be many other things, far less pleasant, but it's important to acknowledge when it's beautiful, I think. It's what helps me remember why I'm here."

Maybe I was caught up in the stunning magic of this snow-covered wonderland, or maybe our night of confessions still pulsed in my veins when I professed what came next. "I am going to trust you, Kit," I said. Kit had kidnapped me, but he still had never betrayed me. He'd never masqueraded as something he wasn't, however unpleasant it had been at first.

Unlike Rain. Rain had lied.

Kit turned to me. "I am going to trust you as well, Skylar," he said.

There. I had my answer.

I would get my favor. I knew his answer was yes without him having to tell me directly.

Without another word, shovels in hand, we got to work.

It took two days before we were ready.

Two days of shoveling, of clearing paths, of chopping wood and warming up by the stove, of sipping the terrible-tasting whiskey in the evenings that with each glass went down smoother than the one before, of dressing and redressing the wound on Kit's shoulder, which burned him now, but not with infection, only the soreness of torn skin and muscle. An easy truce settled between us, one full of patience and something else, but I couldn't quite put my finger on what, or maybe I didn't want to. A new Kit emerged during this time, someone quick to smile and quick to laugh, who once, when I was in the middle of a sentence, pelted me with a ball of snow and marveled at the way our footsteps made fresh imprints on the landscape, as though no one before us had ever traversed our path on this earth. I wondered if this was the Kit he'd been when his sister was around, or if he, too, was relieved that the burden of trading one body for another was lifted from his shoulders, even if only temporarily.

The time it took for the world to open itself up to our leaving was shorter than Kit predicted. The sun burned bright and hot from the moment the snow stopped, melting rivers through the drifts all the way to the dirt below. Icicles hung from the trees, the water *drip, drip, dripping* onto the ground, creating circular basins where tiny winter sparrows took their baths. The sky shone a brilliant cold and endless blue and the ocean beyond the cottage shifted and sizzled as the waves washed away the banks of snow they reached. I found myself leaning against the handle of the shovel now and then, sighing at the landscape the storm had brought with it. As Kit and I worked during the daylight hours clearing what snow the sun didn't take on its own, my body reveled in the use of its muscles, enjoying how the movement warmed me to my still-weak fingertips and toes, my face smiling toward the light in the sky. When, at the end of the second day, it was evident that tomorrow we could make our way back toward New Port City, and from there out to Briarwood, I realized something.

I didn't want to go.

I wasn't ready for this . . . *vacation* to end.

"What's the matter, Skylar?" Kit asked me that same evening.

It was late, darkness had fallen, and the iron stove burned warmth throughout the cottage. Kit and I sat across from each other at the kitchen table, the bottle of homemade whiskey between us, our glasses half full. I was the one who'd gone searching for Kit's stash under his bed, returning to the kitchen and plunking our drinks for the evening in front of him, seeing how his eyebrows arched in surprise at the gesture.

"It's been strange to be so cut off from the rest of the world." I looked around the room. The couch with the blanket thrown over its arm. The black stove pumping heat from its belly. The table and chairs, the kitchen, the remnants of dinner, the creaky wood floor and the windows, now clear of snow. The tiny house felt like more of a home after less than a week than any other place in the Real World, more even than the Keeper's quarters.

"This storm was unusual," Kit said. "The longest I've ever known."

"But it was more than the storm," I said. "Being here is so solitary and quiet. There's . . . peace. In the App World, you're always connected to other people. You're never alone. You don't even have to be alone with your own thoughts. Ever."

"And what are your thoughts telling you now?" Kit asked.

"I don't think I should share that information," I said, then regretted that I didn't take more time to consider my answer.

"I think you should."

My hands cupped my chin, elbows on the table, if only to keep myself from guzzling the honey-colored liquid in my glass too quickly. "For a while I've forgotten who I am," I said finally. "And tomorrow it will be time for me to remember."

Kit studied me. The end of his scarf escaped the tight wrapping around his neck. He wore it nearly always, sometimes even in sleep, even when the cottage burned with warmth. Tonight he wore a short-sleeved shirt, and I could see the bottom edge of the tattoos on his arms, of birds taking flight and stars reaching for the moon. "For a while I've forgotten who I am as well," he said darkly.

His tone pierced me. Had I been wrong to trust him these last few days? Would he go back on his promise? Would I? We were both playing a dangerous game. A part of me longed to go back to those fleeting first days in the Real World when I thought my escape on the cliff was a dream and my only objective was to strengthen my colt-like jittery legs so I could find my mother and sister.

"I haven't forgotten who you are, Kit," I returned, just as darkly.

"Maybe you should."

I shot him a look. "What do you mean?"

He shrugged, but his eyes betrayed sadness. "Maybe you should forget me altogether. Forget this ever happened."

It was my turn to study him. The boy I saw in front of me now was so different from the blank-faced bounty hunter who grabbed me off the streets. His hand lay on the table next to his glass, and I found myself wishing that I could take it. "How could I forget?" I replied, intentionally leaving my words open to various interpretations.

"I've always been pretty forgettable," he said. "My parents, then my sister."

Kit's comment made me sad. "I'm going to help you get her back." I swallowed. "One way or another," I added in a whisper.

Kit nodded. Then he said, "I know."

Late, late into the night, when my eyes began to get heavy, I went to the door of the cottage and stepped outside. The winter sky, now clear of all clouds, winked with a million stars.

I thought about the tattoo on Kit's shoulder.

So beautiful.

Like Kit.

I turned around quickly and went inside.

This thought was only the tiniest of whispers.

But my heart, for some reason, could still hear it.

The morning of my departure was sunny, just like every other one since the storm had ended. A sunny sky in winter was different from one in the fall or the summer. The blue of it clearer, the color somehow colder, to match the temperature. The App World was so full of sameness. The standard settings of virtual selves, the weather, the routines of the day. But even the ever-present downloads had a peculiar sort of sameness to them, or at least a predictability. Everything was so controlled there.

Here, everything was so beyond our control.

I glanced at Kit, who'd passed out last night on the couch and was still sleeping.

Or maybe it was just that *I* felt out of control.

And maybe I didn't mind the feeling. Maybe I actually kind of liked it.

I took a deep breath and let it out.

By the time Kit roused I'd spent an hour outside, looking at the sea, standing at the edge of the road where it met a dip just above the sand and rocks. Today the water was tame, like it was taking a nap. The bare tree limbs and tiny thin branches were still covered in a layer of ice that shined where the light hit. The mansion where Rain was, where Adam was, where everyone else was, sat on the edge of the ocean and backed up into a thick forest of trees, but I wondered whether I'd find it as beautiful as this place once I returned.

I watched the sun rise higher in the sky.

Soon it was time to go.

I returned to the cottage and went straight into the bedroom without looking at Kit, who had his back to me anyway, making coffee in the kitchen. His black-and-white checked scarf lay draped across a chair. I picked it up and wound it through my hands. Then I wrapped it around my neck, tucking the end of it away as I'd seen Kit do so many times. I wanted a memory from this place, from this time. If someone had asked a week ago if I would feel such nostalgia about what began as a kidnapping, I would have laughed in their face. But a lot can happen in a week.

When I walked into the kitchen, Kit's eyes went to the scarf, but he didn't say a word. When it came time to leave, I didn't take it off, didn't move to return it, and Kit didn't ask for it.

He wasn't looking at me when he spoke. "Are you ready to go back to your friends, Skylar?"

I nodded. Kit's bike was waiting for us out front. I followed him out of the house, watched as he held the handlebars while I got on. Before he started the engine, he reached out and retucked the end of the scarf that had come loose around my neck, eyeing it and eyeing me. Then the bike roared to life and we were off, speeding away along the coast just like before, except that now, everything was different.

The cold stung my skin and my eyes.

I didn't look back.

Not at the cottage or the ocean.

I couldn't bear to see it disappear behind us.

13

Rain

party

THE SNOW STOPPED two days before, but I'd barely noticed.

I couldn't tear myself from the weapons room. Zeera managed to hack in to another video feed, and now we had a view of the Body Market in addition to the girl in that beautiful room.

But even so, we hadn't learned much.

Until this morning, the market had been closed because of the storm, the glass cases taken to another location, the Body Tourists nowhere to be seen, probably still hiding out in the hotel, staying warm. But now the market was a flurry of activity, mainly of New Capitalists trying to clear out the snow, and returning the bodies, one by one to their displays.

No sign of Skylar though.

I sighed. I couldn't seem to get her out of my head, and if I was honest, the reason I couldn't stop watching the screens was that a part of me kept waiting for her to appear on one of them.

"Why the big sigh?" Zeera asked.

I'd almost forgotten Zeera was with me. "I just wish we could see things from a new angle," I lied. Well, I *had* wished this, but I hadn't been wishing it at the time of Zeera's question. "This feed isn't giving us much to go on."

Now Zeera sighed. "I know. I'm working on it."

I put a hand on her shoulder. "You're great, Zeera. I didn't mean to criticize."

"But you're right. We're not going to get far with such a narrow view."

The two of us turned back to the monitors. "You've given us far more than we had before these two feeds, so I consider it a win. We're getting greedy."

"We're running out of time," Zeera said. "It won't be long before the market starts accepting bids." She shuddered.

The door opened and Lacy appeared. "Can you, like, leave here for a few minutes, or is this your new permanent home?"

"This is important," I said.

She rolled her eyes. "Isn't everything?"

"Lacy," I said, trying not to sound as impatient as I felt.

Zeera glanced at her. "Hi, Lace."

Lacy sauntered over to the monitors and stood between us. She pointed up at the screen that showed the girl. "Well, isn't she just adorable."

The way Lacy said it told me she thought otherwise. "Whoever she is, she's Jude's prisoner."

"Whatever." Lacy turned to Zeera. "Any sign of Sylvia, sweetie?" she asked in a much kinder tone.

"Not yet," Zeera said.

Lacy silently put an arm around Zeera and gave her a squeeze.

I shook my head. Lacy was a cocktail of contradictions.

She watched Zeera, whose attention was still glued to the monitors, and her eyes got a gleam in them. But not a cruel one. "The snow has stopped, and people around here *really* need a break. We should all do something fun." When no one said anything, Lacy gave me a pleading look. "You're the one who's always planning parties to keep people happy, Rain. I think it's time for another."

Then she grabbed my hand.

The three of us stood there, connected by Lacy.

A tear rolled down Zeera's cheek. She'd been working nonstop, hoping to find any sign of Sylvia, and still there was nothing.

"You're absolutely right," I finally said. "Everybody needs a break." I looked at the time. "Lacy, can you get everybody out on the west side of the house by two p.m.?"

Her brow furrowed. "But there's nothing out there aside from . . ." She trailed off as understanding dawned. A smile appeared on her face. She beamed. "Definitely! Perfect. Absolutely perfect." With her other hand she grabbed Zeera and tried pulling us both toward the doorway.

But Zeera stayed put. So did I.

Lacy let go, defeated. "Come *on*, guys."

I waved her away. "I'll be there in just a few minutes."

Lacy pouted. "It's not like anything interesting is going to happen in the next hour, if it hasn't already."

"I'm sure you're right." I turned back to the screens.

There came a great huff and a sigh from Lacy.

Zeera went to her. "I'll go with you," she relented. To me, she said, "We'll see you in a few." Now it was Zeera leading Lacy out the door.

I stared at the monitors, waiting, but honestly, I had no idea what I was waiting for. Aside from that single occurrence when Jude had appeared in the room with the girl, we'd seen nothing other than the girl pacing, sleeping, and sitting, and the bodies being attended by Keepers at the market. It was good we had a view into Jude's world, but there was little to see. And for the last hour, the Body Market had been quiet. Even the New Capitalists had left.

Then, in the very corner of the screen, I saw movement.

At first, I thought it must be one of the New Capitalists. I shifted the view so it amplified just that spot, like Zeera showed me.

"What?" I said, incredulous, to no one. "That can't be . . . that's impossible. . . ."

I got closer to the monitor, as if this would alter what I was seeing.

Or at least, what I *thought* I was seeing.

"Holy . . ."

The screen showed a closeup of a boy. He was maybe twelve. Like everyone else around him, he was in the typical case of the plugged-in, on display at the market.

But unlike everyone else, his eyes blinked open.

Then, I watched as he turned his head toward me and placed his palms flat against the glass.

14

Skylar

real, beautiful things

THE FIRST THING we heard was singing.

The bike's engines were quiet now, and faint voices traveled over the waves and up across the dunes. They came through the trees at the edge of the parking lot. Kit and I stilled, listening. The notes grew stronger and louder. They were haunting one moment, mournful and low, before rising higher until they crested into something happier, joyful, even. At first I thought there must be ten or eleven voices, threading themselves together and dispersing depending on where the song led them, but eventually I realized that there were only three.

Somewhat abruptly, they stopped.

There was clapping, and laughter, and some happy shouts.

I let out a breath. "I've never heard real singing before."

Kit and I got off the bike. "My sister used to sing." He watched me steadily.

"What?" I asked, trying to read his eyes.

He reached up and brushed a thumb across my cheek. "You're crying."

I nearly stepped away, then pulled myself together and shook my head, as though to deny what Kit had said. But I could see that his fingers had come away wet. "Maybe I'm crying a little," I admitted. "The ride," I said with a shrug. "The wind," I added, though I wondered if he knew as well as I that it wasn't either of those things.

The happy voices floating down the beach were like warnings.

Or reminders.

Even though they held joy, hearing them meant that I'd returned—to this group of seventeens, to Rain's plans, to the people who wanted to use me, or who at best thought I should become a seamless member of this rebellion against my sister.

The thing was, despite all that Jude had done, I still loved her.

And for months now, I'd had no sign of my mother. I couldn't help worrying that in a rebellion, a real one, she might get caught in the crossfire. I closed my eyes, pressing against the thought that maybe she hadn't made it out alive the night of the fire. Maybe my tears were about all of these things. Maybe they'd been waiting this whole time and returning to this place drew them out.

I looked at Kit. Saw the way his face seemed to fight all expression. "You're good at hiding your emotions," I said, then thought:

Or maybe my tears are about not wanting to say goodbye.

Kit locked his bike and retrieved the small pack he'd strapped onto it. He hooked it over his good shoulder. "Not always."

"Let's take the back way," I suggested, wanting to get my return here over with. We crossed the parking lot and stepped between two tall pine trees. A bed of needles was just visible under the snow and ice. Someone had shoveled recently. The sun had gone behind the clouds, so the light was gray and filtered by the branches overhead. The shouts and laughter got louder, closer.

Whatever was going on, it was likely Rain's doing.

Or maybe Adam's. Or both.

Two tiny pangs dinged my heart at the thought of them, though the one for Adam was benign. Comforting. Those two boys were constantly scheming to come up with ways to make the seventeens forget they'd been cut off from their virtual homes, left behind like trash, providing some fun amid the very real and very sinister political situation that had caught us between worlds.

"Help me up, help me up!" came a shout.

The voice of Parvda.

I smiled a little. Parvda had become as close a friend as I'd made in the Real World. She was likely calling out to Adam, sounding half scolding, half kidding, but her tone with him was always loving.

A dense thicket of trees still blocked our view of whatever was happening.

"I guess they aren't spending all their time worried about your absence," Kit said from behind me.

For a moment I'd nearly forgotten he was there, his footsteps falling without a sound, perhaps the learned skill of a bounty hunter. I turned around to answer. "Having fun and playing around is part of daily life in this place, no matter what the circumstances," I said, maybe a little defensively, then pushed on through the last of the trees into the clearing, one that was usually dusted with sand and dirt.

I halted at the very edge.

Kit stopped behind me.

Before us was a gigantic basin, a pond really, as big or bigger than the playground at the center of Main Park in the App World. This one had frozen over, the ice shiny and smooth in places, but it was also crisscrossed with sharp lines.

All the seventeens seemed to be on it.

"They're skating," Kit said.

"I know." I remembered ice-skating from home, when Inara and I were little and we'd sometimes receive an invitation that would download us into a skating party with everyone from school. I'd never gotten the hang of skating, though Inara was talented from the beginning, twirling and twisting in the air like it was nothing, laughing and giggling with delight. If she were here, maybe she'd find that her talent would translate easily from our old world into this one, as so many skills seemed to do. "Well, *most* of them are skating," I observed.

Some people simply took a running start in their boots and slid as far as they could go before toppling over. But just about everyone was wearing skates, either black ones for hockey or white boots that laced up past the ankles. There was Parvda, just as I'd thought, on the other edge of the rink, Adam holding her hand, his arm around her back. There was Surry flying around the far curve as though she'd been skating her entire life, and Jason, who stumbled a few steps, like he thought the blades were for walking not gliding, and the countless other seventeens I'd gotten to know since I'd moved out here after the night of the fire.

Kit stood to my right. "You're crying again," he said.

I wiped the back of my hand across my face. "I wish," I began, then hesitated. "I wish I could join them sometimes."

"You could. You can," Kit said quietly. "Isn't that why we're here?"

"No," I corrected. "I've tried before and I've never been able to. Not really. At least, not the way the others do."

Kit and I fell silent again, sheltered enough by the trees that no one had noticed us yet. On the ocean side, where the dunes rose into hills, a series of thick fallen logs served as bleachers, the seventeens crowded around them, the snow still rising to their knees.

And Lacy. There was Lacy.

Her pale freckled cheeks were rosy from the cold, her hair bright against the white of the landscape behind her. She was smiling, sitting close to someone, another girl whose face I couldn't see, their heads bent together in conversation. The other girl turned slightly.

Zeera?

For a split second I wanted to call out her name, to go running and shouting that I'd seen Sylvia, that we could still save her, that I'd already tried to start that process in motion, but Zeera's presence next to Lacy startled and stopped me.

Since when did those two have anything to talk about?

I took a deep breath and let it out.

For Zeera to like Lacy, to talk to her like she might be a friend, said something, that maybe there was more to Lacy. I didn't love the idea of having to admit this about her. The truth was I'd rather find out otherwise, that Lacy was *less*—less nice, less smart, less interesting. Just . . . less.

"There are a lot of you," Kit said over my shoulder.

"There are a lot of *them*," I corrected.

We stood there, watching, and I wondered if anyone would ever notice us. Maybe we could just turn around and walk back the way we came and leave here forever.

Then, "Skylar?" I heard called out from my right.

I looked toward the familiar voice.

Adam was skating our way. "Skylar, you're okay," he shouted gleefully.

Everyone halted then, wherever they were—in the center of the makeshift rink, having just fallen onto the ice, ready to throw themselves into a slide. Conversations around the fallen logs went silent. They turned toward the place where Kit and I were standing at the edge of the clearing. The moment was familiar, *too* familiar, like the first day Rain brought me here and we'd entered the gym, where everyone stopped what they were doing to take me in, the girl they'd seen on display up on the cliff.

But then I saw that Adam's eyes were bright and smiling, and Parvda's shined with relief as she made her way slowly in our direction, trying hard not to fall. I didn't allow myself to look at Lacy. I didn't want to know what her eyes said now that she knew I'd returned.

Adam expertly skidded to a halt in front of us.

Then he scooped me right off the ground and squeezed

me so tight I nearly couldn't breathe. "We thought you might be gone for good," Adam said. "I've been so worried. Don't ever do that again."

I tried to speak but my voice was muffled.

"Sorry," he said, and put me down again, all the while eyeing Kit, and not in a friendly way. "You brought back a friend," he said.

I wasn't sure what Kit and I were at this point, but it had never quite felt like friendship. "Adam, this is Kit," I said. "He was born in this world. He's . . . kind of like a Single here, actually."

Adam's face changed at this, immediately growing less suspicious. "Hello," he said, and extended his hand.

Kit took it. "Nice to meet you."

"Skylar," Parvda said, finally reaching us.

I carefully stepped onto the ice and we hugged. "I missed you."

"I missed you back," she whispered into my ear. Then, "Who's the boy?"

Her tone was curious, and maybe a little hopeful. Parvda was the only person with whom I'd openly discussed my feelings for Rain, and how much his betrayal had hurt me.

"I'll tell you later," I whispered back. "I promise."

"I'm holding you to that," she said, and let me go.

I saw Rain over Parvda's shoulder. He was walking toward us across the ice. I heard Parvda introduce herself to Kit behind me, and an exchange of hellos, but they seemed to occur far off in the distance. I waited for the usual feelings that Rain provoked to come over me, the flutter in my stomach, the static that seemed to rush across my skin, but instead I felt . . . nothing. I almost wanted to pat myself down, to make sure I was still in my real body, so accustomed had I become to the way Rain seemed to send my heart tumbling off a cliff every time I saw him.

Rain stopped a few feet away.

"Skylar is back," Adam said to him, full of enthusiasm.

"Hi," Rain said to me softly.

I reached up to my neck to retuck the end of Kit's scarf. It had started to come loose, and I suddenly wanted to feel it tight against my skin. "Hello, Rain."

Neither one of us moved to hug the other. We stared at each other awkwardly over the ice. A crowd gathered behind Rain a short distance away, Lacy front and center, her hair a soft red flame amid the rest of the seventeens. We might not be in the App World, but the talent Lacy transferred from there to here seemed to involve claiming everyone's attention without having to make even the smallest effort.

Kit stepped forward. "I know you," he said to Rain.

Rain regarded him. "And I know you," he replied. Then he turned to me. "Skylar, he's a bounty hunter.

You've brought a bounty hunter to the mansion."

The other seventeens erupted into chatter at this, and Lacy smirked.

I hadn't expected Rain and Kit to know each other, hadn't thought much about whether bringing Kit here would be a problem, or even cause a scandal. "His name is Kit." I glanced at Kit, but his eyes were locked on Rain. "He's my . . . he's a friend. We got caught in the storm together and . . . we helped each other survive it." None of this was a lie, but it omitted so much of the truth that it came close.

Rain was shaking his head. "Did *Kit*"—he said the name with disgust—"tell you how he works for your sister?"

"I don't work for anyone but myself," Kit snapped.

I swallowed, remembering to breathe. "I know what he does, Rain, and yes, I know that he's traded before with my sister. He told me everything," I added, shushing the part of me that wanted to say things like *unlike you, who left out the most important things until it was too late.*

Rain winced, as though he could hear my thoughts. "He can't stay."

Kit's hands were balled into fists. "You can speak to me directly. I'm right in front of your face. And don't worry, I wasn't planning on staying. I only came to deliver Skylar."

"Kit—" I started, but he was already turning to leave. Then he halted in front of me, his face inches away.

"I'll see you again," he said in a low voice. "At some point." His words became vapor in the cold, puffs of white that faded into nothing.

My lungs seemed unable to pump air. "Our deal," I whispered. "I didn't forget. I would never back out. I made you a promise."

His face changed, his eyes growing sad. "Yes. Our deal."

I blinked. He was so close. "You don't have to go," I said. "I'll talk to him."

"No. I do have to. I'll see you," he said, and started off, brushing past me on his way to the crush of bare-limbed trees and the path that led to the parking lot and his bike.

I thought that this was it, that I'd seen the last of Kit's face after seeing nearly only his face for so many days. My heart constricted, watching him go, but then he stopped and turned around.

"Skylar, I almost forgot," he said.

I went to him, thinking he was going to ask for his scarf. There was a crowd watching from behind me, and I knew Rain was witnessing my every movement. My hand went to the fabric encircling my neck, ready to unravel it.

But Kit unzipped his bag and was digging around inside of it.

He pulled out a small jar. Shades of blue and green glass gleamed from inside of it, caught in the glare of the sun.

He held it out. "I thought you might want to have this. To remember . . ."

I took it from him. The glass was cold in my bare hands. By the time I found it in me to say something, Kit had already disappeared beyond the trees.

PART TWO

15

Skylar

regret

THE GYM WAS empty, so that's where I went.

I chose a knife from the selection on the table by the target. I stared at it in my hand. The blade was short and silver and glinted in the overhead light. It was so different from the kitchen knife I'd used on Kit during my dream, the one that had cut across the stars inked onto his shoulder, the wound from it oddly the turning point in how we regarded each other.

Kit.

In my other hand I held the jar of glass he'd given me.

I set it down on the table. I touched the scarf that was still around my neck.

Then I hurled the knife at the target.

Just before it hit, Emory Specter's face flashed before me, the knife landing in the exact spot that was right between his eyes. The image faded. He was the reason we were all in this mess. He was behind the closing of the border between worlds and the removal of the bodies from the plugs. Well, Emory Specter and my sister.

Was it possible I was related to him?

Could he really be my father?

I went to retrieve the knife.

"You haven't lost your skill."

I stopped midstride.

Rain was standing there, watching me from the doorway. "It's been months since I've seen you pick up a knife. Since I've seen you step foot in this place." His tone was hesitant, but hopeful.

I didn't move. I stood halfway between a table full of knives and the one that stuck out from the target. Bull's-eye. For a second I wondered why I'd come back to Briarwood. I'd felt so different at Kit's cottage, like the old Skylar, the one with ideals and hope and energy, who'd woken up again to possibility, to a future worth living.

Now, being here, I was exhausted all over again.

I sat down suddenly, in the same spot where I'd been standing, between the jar of sea glass and the blade I'd thrown, and placed my head in my hands.

Footsteps came my way.

Rain sat down across from me. I could see his feet and

his knees. The way the bottoms of his boots were caked with snow.

His head dipped low, trying to meet my eyes. "Skylar, talk to me."

"I shouldn't have returned," I whispered. "This was a mistake."

"Skylar," Rain said again. "We should talk about . . . what happened when you were away." He paused a moment. "And your new friend."

I looked up. Stared past Rain to the blue of the wall behind him. "I don't know who I am anymore. Or what I want." I let my gaze slide back to him. "But I know I'm not ready to talk about this last week. Not yet. I need time to think about it myself."

His brow furrowed. "The storm has made all of us pensive, I guess."

My eyebrows arched. I wondered what Rain meant by this, but I was too tired to ask. I got up, leaving Rain sitting there by himself on the floor. I went to retrieve the knife from the target and I could feel his eyes following me, watching as I pulled it out carefully. Then I held the blade in my hand, studying it. "I don't want this anymore." Saying these words made me realize I meant them.

Rain stood. "What? Target practice?"

"No," I said, slowly, thinking through what I hoped to articulate, not sure what it was, exactly. Only that something was churning inside of me that needed out. "The violence. The rebellion. I don't want any part of it. I want to find another way of doing this. Of dealing with my sister. My family." These last words came out a whisper.

Rain's lips parted, but he didn't say anything.

I went to the table and set the knife down, trading it for the jar. The second my hand was around the glass I felt relief. Like I was holding on to something real, something that was more mine than anything I had at Briarwood. Or that could be mine if I let it.

When I turned to leave, Rain was right there, close enough to touch, and I started.

"Skylar," he said, and this time my name had more of an edge to it. His eyes went to the jar of glass, then flickered back to my face. "Before you make any rash decisions, there's something you need to see."

The heavy vault door sighed open.

I hesitated to enter. The first time Rain brought me to the weapons room, I'd imagined encountering a place full of guns and bombs and other sorts of ammunition, and was surprised to find a collection of the devices people used to harness the old kind of technology instead, some of them so small you could hold them in your hand.

Rain beckoned. "Come on."

My feet were like sandbags, heavy and resistant, but I took a step inside. I saw the now familiar screens mounted on the walls and stacked on tables and chairs. They were big and small and medium and every size in between. My hand tightened around the cool glass jar. Way in the back of the room I saw Zeera.

She turned around and smiled. "Hi, Skylar. It's good to see you again."

I thought of all the things I wanted to tell her. And ask. I walked up to her. "You and I should talk." I glanced over at Rain. "Maybe we can go somewhere afterward?"

Zeera's eyes were curious. "Sure. Whenever you want."

I clasped my hand in hers and squeezed. "It's important."

She swallowed. Then she nodded and looked away. Let go of my hand. I wondered if she knew instinctively that it was about Sylvia.

Rain pointed at two large screens on the wall. "This is what you needed to see."

Two of the monitors were lit up. One of them showed an empty room. There was a couch and a rug and a coffee table. The corner of a chair. The screen kept flickering. The second monitor seemed to look out onto a wall. A wrinkled wall, but still a wall.

I looked at Rain. "I don't get it. What's so important?"

"Just wait," he said and nodded up at the screens. "Keep watching."

"I finally hacked into the Wi-Fi in the city," Zeera explained. "The New Capitalists turned the grid on, but so far I've only gotten through into these two feeds.

If I can just get into the server, we'll be able to connect everywhere we go." She pointed to a table full of tiny flat screens. "Everyone will be able to communicate using these. From, like, opposite sides of the city. From anywhere, really."

Lacy appeared in the doorway, her face rosy from the cold outside. She had a pair of ice skates knotted over her shoulder, one white bladed boot hanging down her front and the other down her back. Her eyes were bright and alive, and they were trained on Rain. "I knew I'd find you here." She beamed at him.

He turned to her. "Hi, Lace," he said, sounding sheepish.

She swept into the room and parked herself next to Rain like I wasn't there. Like an Invisible App had erased me from view. "Come back outside and play with us," she said.

Then she grabbed his hand, got on her toes, and gave him a kiss.

On the mouth.

Rain glanced at me right afterward.

And Zeera eyed me sideways.

I tried to act like I hadn't just seen what I'd seen.

A lot can happen in a week, I remembered thinking. A lot could change.

Apparently, not just with me. Quite a bit had happened here, too.

Lacy turned my way. "Hi, Skylar." She waggled her fingers at me. Her nails sparkled as usual. "Welcome back."

I blinked at her. "Thanks."

Everyone fell silent.

Now Rain wouldn't look at me and neither would Zeera.

"Okay!" Lacy said with a loud laugh that made everyone flinch. "Awkward much?" When no one responded, she spoke again. "Well, I'm heading back outside to the party. I hope to see you *all* there soon." She got on her toes to give Rain another kiss. "Bye, darling," she said, and disappeared into the hallway.

I tried to decide how I felt, but couldn't.

Lacy was right. This was awkward.

I wanted to say something to Rain, tell him that it was fine if he was with Lacy, that I didn't care, but I wasn't sure if this was true. What I wouldn't give to be in the App World, where I could download something that would help me find the perfect response, or whisk me away to some other place, or suck the awkward from the room until we were all giggling uncontrollably. Then, luckily, I was saved by Real World events.

"There," Zeera said excitedly, pointing upward.

Rain was pointing now too. "Skylar. Look."

I followed the direction of their fingers. One of the screens had come alive. The wrinkled wall had disappeared. It was a person who'd finally moved away from the camera.

"That's the Body Market." I took a step closer. I recognized the lush red carpet and the glass boxes filled with bodies that appeared to be sleeping. Keepers rushed around, polishing the glass.

"It's been deserted except for the Keepers since the storm," Zeera said.

"So it *was* closed," I said.

She nodded.

Rain stepped closer to the screen. He glanced at Zeera. "Can you make that one section bigger—the one from before?"

Zeera eyed him. "He's gone, isn't he?"

I looked from Zeera to Rain, confused. "Who's gone?"

As Zeera was in the process of enlarging the corner of the monitor, the other screen suddenly came alive. A girl darted across it, then disappeared.

I turned to Rain. "Did you see that?"

"Yes. We've been watching her. We think she's a prisoner."

"A prisoner?"

Rain shifted. Dug his hands in his pockets. "Of the New Capitalists."

"You mean, of my sister."

"Yes," Zeera confirmed.

I gave Zeera a look of gratitude. I'd rather people

be honest than try to sugarcoat everything. I didn't see enough of the girl to get a good look at her, but I saw enough to be certain it wasn't Inara. "Any idea why she's a prisoner and not a part of the Body Market?" I asked carefully.

Any idea why she's special? went my brain. Had I been replaced? Had Jude found another girl to be her symbol? Had she moved on from Inara? My heart sank when a new thought flowed into me. Could this mean Inara had somehow been . . . *sold* already? I took a deep breath and let it out slowly. *No.* I wouldn't allow myself to think that way.

Zeera finished amplifying the corner of the other screen. It was focused on the face of one single body. A boy—young. Maybe twelve. Both Rain and Zeera studied the image.

"It's definitely not him," Zeera said. She sounded astonished.

Rain was nodding. "You're right. He's different."

Zeera zoomed out again. "What do you think it means?"

"I honestly don't know," Rain said.

"What are you guys talking about?" I asked.

"The other day, someone else was in that same case," Rain explained. "The same age. The boys even look sort of similar. But that boy is definitely not the one we're seeing now."

"Maybe he was sold," I said, since this seemed to be

the most logical possibility.

"I don't think so," Rain said. "Before, with the other boy, while we were watching . . . he . . . he seemed to just . . ." Rain trailed off, like he couldn't get his next words out.

"He just woke up," Zeera finished for him. She snapped her fingers. "It was like he just . . . suddenly unplugged!"

Static rushed across my skin. "Maybe someone in the App World was helping him." I thought about Trader, how he'd helped Adam, Lacy, and me, and how he could move between worlds as he pleased. Something else began to tug at me, too, an idea, but one I couldn't quite put my finger on it. It was still too unformed.

"Skylar, what are you thinking?" Rain asked.

There was hunger in his eyes. I paused a beat, staring back at Rain in a way that matched his intensity. I broke our stare and shrugged. "I'm not sure," was all I said, which was the truth. Then I turned on my heel. "I'll be in my room. I'm going to get some rest," I called over my shoulder and walked out.

16

Kit

one minor detail

THE WIND SEEMED icier on my return trip to the cottage, my bag so much lighter without the jar of colored glass. Or maybe I just hadn't noticed the cold with Skylar at my back, her arms wrapped around my waist as I delivered her to her friends.

Then left her there.

For a moment, I'd actually considered staying with her, and seeing what I could offer these people organizing against the New Capitalists, and what they could offer me.

See where more time with Skylar might take us.

I twisted the handlebar and the bike went faster.

Anger choked my throat, but even the speed did nothing to tamp it down. What was wrong with me? I was letting some . . . *girl* mess up my life. Come between me and all my responsibilities. Which generally involved being completely irresponsible with everyone but myself and my sister. The sun burned in the sky and the glare from the snow was nearly blinding as I went into a sharp curve and pulled up alongside the water. I wasn't far from home and I was shivering but for some reason I didn't want to get there.

Skylar's gone.

This knowledge reverberated in my chest. Followed by a name.

Rain Holt.

Of all people, Rain Holt has to be the guy Skylar wanted to make jealous. That made the possibility of my staying with her turn to dust. He was notorious the very moment he stepped into the Real World, like some young version of his father. *Heroic*, people called him, just because of his name and his decision to unplug. He got whatever he wanted whenever he wanted it, half the Keepers bowing down before him because of his mere existence.

Apparently, what he wanted included Skylar.

The look in his eyes when he saw her today . . . and the look he gave me afterward. There was jealousy there. He was jealous that the two of us showed up together.

A smile stretched across my lips at the memory.

Then the cottage appeared on the hill and I sped toward it.

As I pulled up the drive, still dusty with snow from the tall banks on either side, there was a flicker of movement in my peripheral vision. I came to a halt and the sound of the engine died.

That's when I saw him.

The man's arms were crossed over his chest, his thick body standing guard before my front door. He was so tall he nearly cleared the frame.

"Where is she?" he barked. "You made promises."

I walked up the path and stood in front of him, crossing my arms to match his. He might be bigger than me but I wasn't afraid. Fear was a powerful motivator, I'd always thought, but eventually you had to overcome it or you wouldn't survive. "Hello, Jag."

The cold whipped around us, blowing snow into the air. When the crystals were caught by the rays of the sun they gleamed like diamonds. If Skylar was here, she would marvel at the beauty of it all. My heart twisted in my chest.

I was wrong.

I could feel fear. I *did* feel it.

For Skylar.

Jag's eyes narrowed. "Where. Is. She?"

I cocked my head and stared hard at him. "Where's who?"

"Quit messing around. You know exactly what happens if you lie to us."

Everything in my body wanted to flinch but I held steady. "I don't have her," I admitted. Jag's lips curled into a snarl, but before he could respond I spoke again. "But I will. I will soon."

"You'd better. Or you'll never see your sister again."

Jag stepped aside, straight into the snow, cutting through it like it was nothing. He disappeared around the side of the house.

"Bye, Jag," I called after him, forcing a laugh into my voice, acting like the irreverent asshole he expected me to be, as though I wasn't the least bit worried about the situation I'd gotten myself into.

Because of a girl.

Not just any girl, went my brain involuntarily.

There came the sound of a car roaring to life and soon Jag was racing away. Only after he was gone from view was I able to take in a breath. My entire body slumped with the release of so much tension. When I'd told Skylar about my sister, about my plan to get her back, I'd left something out.

Something major.

My sister wasn't simply a part of the Body Market. Getting her back involved more than raising enough capital to purchase her or even stealing her away in a heist.

The head of the New Capitalists was holding my sister.

Jude, in other words.

And the only way she'd let Maggie go was if I handed over Skylar.

A sister for a sister was how Jag, Jude's lackey, had put it.

That was the deal.

That was the trade.

I opened the door and walked into the lonely house.

17

Skylar

beautiful little weapons

THE ROOM WAS just as I left it.

Big sprawling bed. Too big for one person. The drawers full of clothes from the previous owner, clothes I'd co-opted like everyone else in their own rooms. Windows that looked out onto the beach and a big glass door with a set of wooden steps that led to a path over the dunes. Today the sand was swept with drifts of snow rising up over the tall grass and cattails, giving the entire room an eerie, pale-blue glow. This place was beautiful and it had been mine ever since my first visit, but I still missed the tiny cottage perched along the sea. I took the jar of sea glass Kit had given me and set it next to my bed.

Shouts and laughter from the party still sounded

faintly. Soon the sun would set, the darkness bringing with it an icier cold. I wondered how long everyone would last before coming back inside. I sat down on the bed, thoughts tumbling through me about returning here and saying good-bye to Kit, about the boy at the Body Market waking up on his own. The girl in that room and who she could be. How I'd put the knife back in its place on the table and decided right then that I never wanted to throw another. Not even to protect my own life. Not unless . . . not unless someone *else's* life depended on it.

Living in a virtual world had turned our bodies into something like machines, altered our brains so drastically that we could react like video-game warriors, wired to do things instinctively, like *kill*.

I no longer wanted to be a killer.

I didn't want to be a video-game warrior either.

I just wanted to be human. Human and real.

Just a girl. A normal girl with a normal life.

Right.

There came a soft knock on my door.

I sighed. I really didn't feel like answering more questions about what happened while I was away. The knocking continued, more urgently now. I got up and answered the door.

My heart softened when I saw who was standing there. "Hi, Zeera."

She was wringing her hands. "You said—"

"I know, come in." I shut the door behind her. "It's good that you're here."

The two of us went and stood by the tall glass windows, looking out onto the snow-covered dunes. Zeera leaned against the glass. Her tall frame was reflected across it like a ghostly twin that mimicked her every movement. Her mouth tightened into a thin line. "Do you know something about Sylvia?"

I reached out and placed my hand on her arm, saw the way we were connected in the glass. "Yes," I started.

Her eyes flickered to mine. "Just tell me. I can take it."

I nodded. "Well, the good news is, I found her."

Zeera brightened, then immediately wilted again. "But the bad news is, you found her at the Body Market," she guessed. "Am I right?"

"I'm sorry," I whispered. "I wanted to get her out of there that moment. But I put down a deposit. To make sure no one else could take her."

Zeera swallowed. Her face drained of color. "A deposit?"

I bobbed my head once. "I gave the man selling her all the money I had. And I promised him far more than he was asking for when I came to pick her up."

She slumped against the glass of the windows. "How . . . how did she . . . seem?"

"Perfect, Zeera," I assured her quickly. "She seemed utterly healthy and perfect. Peaceful. Like she was having a nice dream," I added, deciding to leave out the part about which section of the Body Market featured Sylvia. Or the skeeviness of the man. I hoped he'd keep his word and she would still be there when I came for her again.

A single tear ran down Zeera's cheek. "What if he sells her to someone else anyway? And then she's gone for good?"

I opened my mouth, but nothing came out. Not at first. "Don't think like that. We're going to get her back. We *are*."

Another tear rolled down Zeera's cheek, followed by a stream of them. "But you don't know that. We can't know that. She might be lost forever."

I put both hands on Zeera's shoulders. "I'm going to do everything in my power to get her back. Just like I'm doing with Inara. And everyone else at the Body Market, for that matter. That much I can promise."

Zeera nodded, but her eyes were swimming. "I'll do whatever I can to help, too."

"So . . . Lacy and Rain, huh," I said after a while.

Zeera raised her shoulders in one big shrug. "He finally gave in, I guess." She studied me a moment. "Are you upset?"

"Honestly, I don't know," I said. "Not as upset as I once might have been."

She nodded.

"More perplexed, maybe, than anything else." Through

the window I watched the tips of the tall grass that stuck up from the snow sway in the wind. "I know they have a long history, and that Lacy's been chasing Rain for years. But he's always resisted—or at least that's what he's told me. And Lacy . . . Lacy's just . . ."

"—not as bad as you think," Zeera cut in.

My eyebrows arched. "No?"

Zeera shook her head. "She really isn't."

"You two have become friendly."

"Yeah. That's been going on awhile though." Now Zeera's eyebrows arched. "This is the first you've noticed?"

I shrugged. "I guess I've been kind of checked out."

"Well . . . are you back now?"

I thought about how to answer. Before I could admit that I wasn't sure how long I'd stay, Zeera spoke first.

"We need you here," she said.

I was shaking my head. "I don't know, Zeera."

"All right," she said, slowly. "So. Tell me what you do know, then."

"Well, I came out of this fog I've been in," I began, thinking through my next words carefully. "There was something about the storm, about everything that happened around it, that made me remember the old Skylar. I feel like myself again. So in that sense, I *am* back. And I want to help. I'm *going* to help."

"But . . . ," Zeera supplied.

"I'm not sure what that means yet. I'm not sure who

I trust anymore." I sighed. "I don't think I belong here. I might need to . . . go my own way. And soon."

"Like, how soon?"

I looked away. Thought about Kit. "Like, immediately?"

Now it was Zeera reaching out to me. "You can trust me, you know."

The light was seeping from the room as the sun set. "Can I?"

"I might be friendly with Lacy, but you can count on me."

I switched on the bedside lamp. "Okay, so, in the vein of counting on you, I have a favor to ask."

"Already?" she said with a small laugh. Then her eyes grew serious. "Anything. I'll do whatever I can, especially if it leads to helping Sylvia. What do you need?"

"Can we discuss those little devices? Those tiny weapons you've got in the vault," I corrected.

She studied me. "Yes," she said, hesitant. "What about them?"

"How long will it be before they're up and running?"

"Not long," Zeera said at first. Her eyes darted around the room. Then guilt flashed on her face and her resolve seemed to crumble. "I mean, I'm not supposed to share this with anyone." She glanced toward the door, as though someone might be on the other side, listening to our conversation. "But they're kind of up and running already."

I rolled my eyes. "And Rain has one, right?"

"Yeah." She started digging around in her pocket. She pulled out a slim, rectangular screen and held it between us. "So do I."

I leaned closer to get a better look. The screen lit up. It glowed blue, and rippled when Zeera touched it. The surface reminded me of the Water Tower in New Port City. "Wow," I said, unable to tear my eyes from it. "It's almost . . . beautiful."

Zeera looked at it with pride. "Isn't it?"

She transferred it to my palm and the light suddenly dimmed. "Oh no! What did I do?"

Zeera laughed. "Nothing, don't worry." She pressed a button at the bottom and the screen came back to life.

"I remember learning about these in Real World History, and all the division they caused between families and loved ones, all the anger and hurt feelings, all the obsession," I said. "But I never thought I'd see one in person, or hold one in my hand."

"I know," Zeera said. "It's kind of crazy."

"It's hard to imagine something so small and so pretty could end up being so . . . destructive. That it would require people to choose between their bodies and virtual life, one or the other." I ran a finger across the smooth surface, wondering if the screen might feel like the ocean, too, or if my skin would sink into it like water. Instead, a bunch of little pictures slid across the screen. "*Now* what did I do?"

Zeera peered over my shoulder. She was smiling like she had a secret. "Skylar, you are never going to guess what those are." I studied the images. "Come on," Zeera pressed. "Think. I bet you can figure it out." Zeera's excitement always returned in the face of technology.

"All right." I turned my attention to what I was seeing on the screen. There was a storm cloud with a lightning bolt through it. There was a fat red heart. There was a cartoonish-looking cat dressed up like a person. There was a square image of a beautiful bedroom. The list went on. I stared and stared, wondering what they could represent, why anyone would have tiny photographs of such random things. There was even what looked like an angel's wing, long feathers fanning out from the center of a blue border. I smiled at that one, reminded of Inara.

Then something clicked.

"No way," I said, astonished.

"Tell me."

"But it's . . . it's crazy what I'm thinking."

Zeera was shaking her head. "I bet it's not."

"Okay, fine." I geared up to spit it out. If Zeera laughed, she laughed. "Are these little things . . . are they . . . some kind of . . . are they Apps?" I barely got that last word out.

Zeera squealed. "Congratulations! You guessed right!"

My jaw dropped. She was being serious.

"You are looking at the original Apps," she said. "Like, Apps 1.0 or Apps 0.5 or something. The prototype of the

App as we eventually experienced it in our virtual lives and in our brains."

I returned my attention to the little icons. They were so static. Nothing at all like the ones at home that would swirl and dance, lunging at you to steal attention away from the others, downloading into your body, changing your physical appearance, your abilities, what happened in your mind. I pressed my finger into the heart, curious what would happen. I pressed and pressed. But . . . *nothing*. "They're broken, I think."

"Kind of," Zeera said. "When I got the device running, the icons were already loaded onto it. They just . . . popped up as I began playing around. Believe me, it took me a while to understand what I was looking at, too. They're just . . . remnants, I think, stored there by the old owner of the device. The images are kind of, like, ghost Apps or something. They no longer have any content. Or, maybe they just can't connect where they're supposed to, because the connection itself is gone."

The two of us stared at the tiny screen, marveling at this piece of ancient technological history we held in our hands. I swiped my finger across it again and the icons disappeared. I turned to Zeera, the edges of an idea forming. The tablet in my hands might be ancient history, but in the Real World, any technology beyond basic electricity was a major advancement. "What if we . . . ," I started, and trailed off, trying to comprehend what was shaping up in my mind. That half-formed idea from earlier—it tugged at me again, harder now.

Ever since Rain, Zeera, and I spoke about the boy who woke up in the market, I'd been thinking about Trader and his power to unplug himself and others, about the App he'd created that allowed us to move between worlds. But the something else nagging at me was something that Jude, of all people, had said to me when I woke up in her mansion and saw her for the first time. It struck me as so strange at the time that I remembered it word for word:

But your body, it just doesn't want to stay under. It's like . . . it's always wanting to shift between states. Between worlds.

Was it possible this young boy didn't want to "stay under" either? That his body or more likely his brain naturally wanted to "shift" between worlds? Is that what had happened to me all those weeks Jude held me captive, weeks that until now seemed like one long, nightmarish dream? I'd thought they just drugged me to keep me unconscious, but maybe they had been trying to plug me back in and my brain was somehow resisting the plugs? I hadn't wanted to go to the App World, had fought going the entire time—that much I knew. But was it possible that my body and mind had simply *refused* to go? That it had overridden the plugs? And if this were true, could we harness that resistance somehow?

Could we . . . code it? Into something downloadable?

"What, Skylar?" Zeera pressed.

"Okay," I began, trying to give words to all that I was thinking. "What if we could invent a *new* App? One that, I don't know, could help us take down the Body Market?"

Zeera's eyes widened. "Tell me more."

"Well, the New Capitalists have turned back on the—what did you call it? Wi-something?"

"Wi-Fi," Zeera supplied.

I nodded. "Yes! The Wi-Fi. And Wi-Fi is the old, Real World way that people used to connect to the virtual, right?"

"Correct," she said.

"So . . . what if we can find a way to use this technology against the New Capitalists? Like . . . what if we created an App that could wake up all the bodies? One that could override the plugs?"

Zeera tapped her chin. "That would be some App."

"It's probably impossible," I said, realizing how ridiculous the idea sounded now that I'd said it out loud.

But Zeera's eyes had come alive with activity. "No . . . maybe not. It's actually pretty intriguing. Maybe we could design something that downloads automatically into the bodies at the market, kind of like a virus, one that would run through the network of plugs the New Capitalists control."

"But a good virus," I said, getting excited again.

"Exactly." Zeera was still tapping her chin. "But we'd

have to be careful—real brains are fragile. They damage easily. Even to create an App like this would require testing and playing around with someone's mind—ideally the mind of the boy we saw wake up. We'd have to dig around and find out if there's something in his code that we could harvest and copy." Zeera sighed long and heavy. "But unless you know where he went, then we're out of luck. Even if we sent out a search party, I doubt we'd find him in time. The boy could be anywhere."

"The Real World is a big place," I agreed.

But what if there was someone else? I thought. *Someone right here, whose brain might hold the key?*

"And," Zeera went on, "I don't know if I could figure this out on my own. What we're talking about is complicated. I wish I wasn't the only one around here who knew how to code."

I nodded. I really needed to find Trader. He kept trying to convince me that things weren't as they seemed, that he hadn't betrayed me. What if he hadn't? Maybe he could help. Besides, I had so many questions for him. "I might know someone. If only I could figure out where he is . . . ," I added, my mind racing.

"Do you really mean that?" Zeera's voice was suddenly full of hope.

"Yes," I said.

Zeera stared at me hard. "I want my Sylvia back, Skylar," she said. "So if you think this person could help, then he's worth the trouble of finding."

"Okay," I said slowly, trying to imagine where in the Real World Trader might be—if he was even still in the Real World at all. "It just might take a couple of days." *Or weeks or years*, I added to myself privately. For all I knew, I'd never see Trader again. But I wanted to remain hopeful and I wanted Zeera to stay that way too.

Zeera's eyes went to the tablet in my hands. She took it from me, lost in thought, and began tapping the screen. A keyboard appeared. As Zeera typed, words formed inside of a bubble. Then she hit a button that said *Send*.

"What are you doing?" I asked.

Zeera swiped her finger across the screen and the bubble disappeared before I could read what was inside of it. "Messaging Rain," she said, as though this was no big deal.

I leaned closer, staring at this seemingly magic object. "So the tablets *do* work!"

With another swipe of her finger, Zeera brought up a stream of bubbles that contained an entire conversation between her and Rain. "Enough to send messages over the Wi-Fi," she explained. Then she held out the tablet so I could get a better look. "See?"

The messages mostly involved updates about the monitors, and an occasional comment about how Lacy was looking for Rain. But I nearly couldn't believe this technology was available and we weren't taking advantage of it. "Zeera, we need to call everyone to a meeting," I said. "As soon as possible."

She eyed me. "To talk about the App? Don't you think that's a bit premature?"

"Not the App." I reached over and took the little tablet back from Zeera. "We store these devices in a place called the weapons room. Maybe it's time we start figuring out how they can live up to their names." The tablet glowed bright, like fireflies were trapped inside of it. "There are so many of us out here and plenty of tablets to go around. If these really are up and running, we need to teach people how to use them. They could change how we do everything. Especially if we find a way to code that App."

"Listen, you know me," Zeera said. "I'm all about taking advantage of technology. But why don't you talk to Rain about it? I'm sure he'll listen to you."

The screen dimmed on the tablet, as though the fireflies were dying. I took a finger and swiped it across the surface as I'd seen Zeera do, and it immediately brightened again. "It's not like Rain told me about the one he's using to communicate with you."

Zeera's eyebrows arched. "Skylar, you just got back! And the first thing Rain did was bring you to see what we've got on the monitors."

"True," I admitted.

"Maybe he didn't want to tell you everything right away. Maybe he's protecting himself."

I laughed. "From what?"

"From getting hurt," she said.

"Getting hurt how?"

Zeera glanced at the shards of blue and green that glinted inside the jar on the bedside table. "Like you don't know. Like you didn't show up with Mr. Mysterious, Dark, and Brooding today."

I rolled my eyes. "Rain has Lacy."

"We'll see how long that lasts," she said.

I yawned, suddenly exhausted. "I guess we will."

Zeera walked over to the door of my room and opened it. "That's my cue to let you rest."

"Don't say anything to Rain about our conversation," I said before she could leave. "Or about the App. Or the meeting. Let me handle it."

"All right," she agreed. "But this is exciting, Skylar. You've given me a lot to think about tonight. Sleep well," she added, then disappeared into the hallway.

After Zeera was gone, I changed into my nightclothes and got into bed, wondering if anything we'd discussed was really possible, and if there might just be something about my brain that could hold the answers.

I shivered, remembering what Zeera said about digging around in that boy's brain, looking for the right code to harvest and copy. The notion of someone literally picking through my brain was chilling. But then, if doing so could help put an end to the Body Market, it would be worth being the guinea pig.

Wouldn't it?

As I tucked myself deeper under the covers of the bed, I thought about my promise to Kit, and touched the scarf around my neck. I'd yet to take it off. It was like it was tethering me.

Yes, I knew right then. It would absolutely be worth it. I would let someone dig around in my brain if doing so could help save Inara and Sylvia and all of those other bodies. I would volunteer to be the guinea pig if that's what was required to keep my word to Kit.

18

Kit

fool for love

I MADE SKYLAR a promise.

I owed her that promise. I owed her a favor. I'd offered one up of my own volition, just as she'd offered to care for my shoulder, without asking anything in return.

Well, not at first.

The wood burning in the stove crackled, then popped loudly. I opened the iron door in its side and poked at it until the wood snapped again. I looked around the cottage, looked at it from every angle, waiting, as though someone might emerge from one of the walls to join me for breakfast. I'd lived alone for a long time and I was used to it, I'd grown used to it out of necessity. I was fine with this—had been fine with it. I typically didn't miss the company of other people. Then I brought a girl here for a few days and suddenly the house felt emptier than ever. *I* felt emptier. Lonely.

Lonely without Skylar.

How had I not noticed this before? How had I lived without her company? I needed to remember so I could do it again. My survival depended on it. Or, at least, my sanity did. And maybe my sister's survival. Maybe that too.

Maggie.

Before Skylar, it had only been Maggie.

My sister and me, against the world.

And then, eventually, it was just me. And that was okay.

Until now, apparently, when it wasn't.

"You'll join me soon," my sister said. She blinked at me with those wide blue, familiar eyes. Eyes that were the negative of my own. "Right?"

"Of course," I told Maggie.

She and I were having our good-bye. She was about to plug in, and I was about to lose her forever. She knew I was lying about joining her in the App World, but neither one of us was acknowledging it. The tears streaming down her pale freckled cheeks revealed more than her words ever could. Maggie never cried—*never*. The last time either one of us shed a tear was when I told her our parents left and I'd lied and said that they wouldn't be gone forever.

Here we were, lying to each other again.

And in such a grand setting.

We were standing in the middle of New Port Station. It was a beautiful place. Tall arched ceiling that soared toward the sky. Stained-glass windows that called the dappled light down upon us. The floors were marble, built during a gilded era long ago when trains took people from city to city. Now it was used as a stage of sorts, a set for Real World loved ones to have their good-byes, engaging in the ritual of coming to the station like people used to in the olden days, kissing a sister or a parent or a girlfriend or a boyfriend and watching them walk away, maybe to leave for a few days or maybe to leave for good. That was what we marked here, what we played out like a movie or an opera.

Maggie and I were the only ones in the entire place.

There was a time when New Port Station had been brimming with people like us, sending one another off to be plugged in, everyone drunk on the anticipation of an entirely new life, an entirely new future, full of laughter and excitement. There was sadness, too, loss and resentment, and even the anger and dismay felt by the family and loved ones left behind. But after the first major exodus to the App World, the numbers of those plugging in dwindled and diminished until it was only a trickle, and eventually, a slow drip.

And now, almost nothing.

The minute hand on the great circular clock high above the gate shifted and it struck eleven a.m. We'd been here since ten fifteen, standing, looking around, waiting for whatever was supposed to happen next, just the two of us. My sister and I listened to the chimes, one after the other, until the last one rang out and faded away.

Maggie took a deep breath. "It's time, right?"

My stomach hurt with the thought of watching her walk through that door and never seeing her again. "It should be," I said, trying to muster up a smile.

Our voices echoed. They bounced against the tall, carved walls. Out of the corner of my eye, I saw movement.

Maggie and I turned to it at the same time.

A Keeper was walking toward us. She had long brown hair that was pulled up rather severely in a knot. Her eyes were big and blue like Maggie's. But unlike Maggie's, they were cold. Everything about her demeanor was icy as winter. She stopped a short distance away from us. "Are you ready?" she asked. She was speaking to Maggie, but she seemed to be questioning both of us.

I glanced at my sister. Rivers flowed down her cheeks. "Just give us a minute," I called back.

"Fine," the woman said. She sounded bored. Annoyed, even.

I wrapped my arms around Maggie. She was so thin, so fragile. "Don't cry," I whispered in her ear.

"I love you, Kit," she said between sobs.

"I love you, too," I told her.

It had been a long, long while since the last time we'd shared these terms of endearment. Our love for each other didn't need words. But today was different. Today was the last time we could say such things to each other, so say them we did.

The Keeper sighed loudly behind us, anxious to fulfill her role and take Maggie away. Soon the preparations would begin, and Maggie's life in the Real World would fade to nothing. When she woke, she would see her virtual self for the very first time.

Maggie might be plugging in alone, but she was not to be a Single in the App World. I made sure she would be well cared for after her arrival. Pretending to save for two people's passage to the App World and then blowing every ounce of capital on only one can buy quite a lot of virtual happiness. At least for a while. Eventually it would be up to Maggie to handle her own life, but I had no doubt my sister was capable of this.

Just as she was capable of saying good-bye to me forever.

The minute hand on the clock kept clicking forward.

It clicked once more. Then again.

I lost count how many times I'd heard that sound since it struck eleven.

There were footsteps behind us. Then two hands pulling us apart.

The Keeper glared at my sister. "If you're this inconsolable about parting with him, then you should've thought twice about plugging in."

Maggie's mouth opened and closed like a fish. Her skin shined wet and her eyes were wide and horrified. No, they were full of guilt. She glanced at me.

I nodded back.

"I'm ready," Maggie said.

The Keeper pointed to the door, beyond which Maggie would be taken to the plugs. "All right. Off you go."

Maggie's brow furrowed deep. "But aren't you supposed to come with me?"

The Keeper rolled her eyes. "I'll be there in a moment. I have a few things to discuss with your brother about the arrangements."

Maggie stood there awhile longer, eyes glassy. Before she turned away, she opened the bag she carried over her shoulder and pulled out her most prized possessions. "So you don't forget about me," she said, holding them out to me.

"How could I?" I replied, taking them from her, my eyes burning now.

Those were the last words we'd ever exchanged.

Then she turned and walked away. I watched her go until the moment she disappeared beyond the door.

There.

It was done.

Just like that. I took a deep breath.

I waited for the Keeper to follow after her.

She didn't.

Instead, she was studying me. "Painful, isn't it," she said. "To watch a sibling abandon you like that."

"Yes," was all I said, all I was capable of croaking from my throat at the time.

"You must feel a little angry." The Keeper cocked an eyebrow. "Or even a lot? She must know what you've done for her. And still she leaves you because the pull of the virtual is oh so powerful."

I shook my head. "I'm not angry."

Her eyebrow arched even higher. "Not even a little?"

"No," I said, though this was a lie. But it hurt too much to admit this out loud. "The love between twins like us runs deep. I'd do anything for my sister."

The Keeper studied me a little longer, a little harder, I think. "Hmmm," she said. Then, "Well, see you soon," she added, and before I could reply, she'd disappeared through the door where Maggie had gone as well.

If I could go back to that day, that moment, I would have told the Keeper how angry I was, how something broke that day in me that I could never repair.

But I couldn't go back.

What was done was done.

Then, I met Skylar.

And the gaping wound inside me started to heal.

19

Skylar

plans

FIRST THING IN the morning, I went to see the Keeper. Her door was opening just as I was raising my hand to knock.

"Skylar. I somehow sensed you were there." A smile crinkled her eyes, but she looked exhausted, tired lines rippling across her forehead. Like she'd aged years in only a week. Maybe she'd been like this for months and I was too in my fog to notice, as I'd failed to notice so many other things. "Come in. I was just going to make some tea."

I followed her inside. "You're always making tea."

She laughed as she poured water from the kettle into a pot to let the leaves steep. Then she went to the couch and patted the space next to her. "I'm glad you're safe," she said. "It's good to see you and I'm happy you came to visit. I'm leaving for New Port City soon. I've already been away from home too long with this storm."

"A lot has happened since I left," I said.

"So I hear." Her brows arched. "But you came back to us."

"I don't know for how long."

The Keeper pursed her lips. She got up and retrieved the pot of tea and two cups, then poured some into each one. The steam rose and curled into the air. She picked hers up and cradled it in her palms. "I'm listening."

"The storm gave me time to think about what I want," I began. "And I want things to be different. I need them to be different." I closed my eyes, thought back to those terrible moments I couldn't get out of my head, the death of a friend, stabbing Jude. The image of the knife sinking into her face haunted me. "There's another way to fight the New Capitalists. I have an idea and I want your advice."

The Keeper watched me over the rim of her cup.

My tea sat untouched. "We could try and deal with the Body Market with brute force, and lose people in the process. Or"—I took a deep breath and let it out—"we could use technology. The entire city was once wired for everything, everyone to connect virtually. The New Capitalists are using it to their benefit, and I think that's exactly where and how we attack. We have enough devices in the weapons room for everybody. If we use them, we'll be able to be in touch with one another no matter where we are. If I'd had one during the blizzard, I could have let everyone here know that I was all right."

The Keeper set her tea down and it rattled in the saucer. When she looked at me this time, her expression was clouded. "Don't underestimate technology, Skylar. It can be just as dangerous as a knife or a gun. Even more so."

I stared at her, unflinching. "I'm done using knives."

The Keeper bobbed her head. "I'm sorry about what happened with your sister." She was the only person who didn't shy away from talking about Jude—and the fact that I disfigured her. "But think long and hard about what technology can do—not just to Jude and her plans, but to everyone else. There's a reason the worlds split in two. Real bodies aren't wired for that kind of abuse."

"I didn't come here so you could talk me out of it," I said. "I came so you could tell me about the dangers we should avoid."

The Keeper frowned. "The technology you're talking about, devices that connect you to the virtual even as you remain in the real body—part of their power comes from the way they entice you," she said. She breathed deep and closed her eyes. "I still remember them from when I was young. They could be so much fun."

I thought about the one Zeera had shown me last night. The Keeper was right about the devices being enticing.

"So what's the problem, then?"

"That's why they're dangerous," she said, opening her eyes again. "They become so addictive, and the escape to the virtual so appealing, that people are willing to abandon the Real World, even their own bodies." She shook her head. "How do you think we got to this place? Even though people's brains weren't plugged in to the tablets, their minds and the technology became fused anyway. Some people became like zombies. I remember my own mother . . ." The Keeper's stare traveled somewhere else, far away. Then she pulled herself back from that other place. "For better or worse, the split between worlds saved us. Those who favored technology could live a permanent virtual life, and those who wanted to wipe the scourge of technology from this earth got our wish. If you unleash it again, and on those who have little sense of history before our time now . . ." She sighed. "None of you truly understand what it was like, but I am old enough to remember."

I shook my head. "You make it sound so fatalistic."

Her eyes were storm clouds. "They were like viruses that infected the mind, Skylar."

Everything about me grew cold at the Keeper's words. Had Zeera and I been wrong to talk of viruses as potentially good? "But using technology could save people from getting hurt. It could help us end the Body Market."

"Skylar, be careful—I beg you," the Keeper said. "Technology changes us. Not just our behaviors, but our brain chemistry, without us even realizing it. So it makes sense that being plugged in would change it even more dramatically. You, of all people, should already know this. But trust me, if you reintroduce the old kind of technology, it will make its mark on our minds once again. The human brain is very malleable and that makes it vulnerable. Just because we can't see it happening, like we would see a bruise on our skin, or feel a bone break in our limb, doesn't mean that the brain isn't affected. Or that the technology isn't hurting us."

I picked up my tea, sipping it, wanting to chase away the chill that had settled over me. Was the Keeper right? Could those tiny slivers of pretty metal and circuitry really turn us into something resembling a zombie? And then, what would be the difference between being plugged in and living unplugged? It sounded like different versions of the same thing: living for the virtual and using the body as a way to do it, or transcending the body altogether for the identical result.

But there was another way to look at things.

"You said that this kind of technology acts like a virus of the mind," I began. "But what if that's how we *need* it to act—like a virus, but a good one. Zeera and I talked about exactly this. I think it's how we're going to free the bodies from the market." I swallowed. "From Jude."

"Skylar, don't kid yourself." The Keeper's face turned even darker. "Just because the technology *might* exist to do something like this, doesn't mean you should use it to." She was shaking and spilled her tea onto the table. She began sopping it up with a napkin.

I placed a hand on her arm. "I didn't mean to upset you."

The Keeper crumpled the stained napkin into her fist, the tea wetting her skin. Her eyes softened as she regarded me. "I know I must sound harsh, but if you go forward with this, I want you to understand the possible consequences."

I hesitated before speaking again. An image of Kit flashed before my eyes. "I have another favor to ask." I took a deep breath and went on. "Take me back with you to New Port City."

The tired lines on the Keeper's face deepened. "What could you need to do in New Port City? It's dangerous for you."

I shook my head. "There's something important I need to do. Someone I need to find."

"Skylar—"

"Please. *Please* take me. Just trust me. I'm not going to do anything stupid."

The Keeper sighed. "All right. But I was planning on leaving tonight and you barely just got back."

"The sooner the better," I said, letting out the air from my lungs, relieved she'd agreed. "Thank you."

The Keeper took my hand into hers. She looked at me

a bit pleadingly. "Rain was so worried about you during the storm."

"Rain has other things on his mind these days," I said quickly.

"Don't let appearances fool you," the Keeper said. "You are number one on it."

I didn't go to see Rain that morning. Not at first.

I lingered in my room, in the shower, as I chose what clothes to wear for when the Keeper and I left, her warnings about technology and its unforeseen consequences still fresh and lingering. Eventually I found myself shutting the door of my room behind me, and descending the series of ramps that led to the cavern below the mansion. The faint rush of the surf along the rocks sounded louder as I got closer. The damp air made me shiver as the change in temperature passed over me.

I went toward the spot where I knew that I'd find him.

I could sense his presence, without even having to see him. In this way, Rain and I always seemed connected. He was kneeling on the ground, his head bent over a single long glass box.

Bent over his father.

I kneeled down next to him. He didn't look at me. "Do you ever talk to him?" I asked.

"He can't hear me."

I stared into the face of Jonathan Holt, saw the

resemblance between him and his son. "Just because he can't hear you doesn't mean you shouldn't say what you need to." I turned my head, taking in Rain's profile. "Besides, he might be able to hear you. When I was in the App World, I heard you sometimes," I reminded him.

Rain's forehead came to rest against the glass. "I know. But you're different."

I pressed my lips into a tight line. I was glad not to be anything like Jonathan Holt. He was the man who set me up to die. I knew Rain loved his father, but it was a terrible and complicated love. Maybe it was similar to the love I still felt for my sister. "Do you visit him here every day?"

"Yes." Rain leaned back on his heels, as though suddenly repelled by the sight of his father's body. He moved across the aisle and sat with his back against one of the empty glass boxes. I joined him, our legs outstretched. "So you're talking to me again?"

"I never stopped talking to you," I said.

"You did."

"No. I stopped telling you everything. There's a difference."

"Why are you here then?" Rain's voice had grown cold.

I lowered my eyes. I nearly wished Lacy would show her face, interrupting the awkwardness that kept settling between Rain and me. "I have an idea about how to put an end to the Body Market and I wanted to discuss it with you."

"I thought we agreed. We're going to steal the bodies."

I shook my head. "I think there's another way."

Rain stared directly ahead, the slope of his father's body glowing across from us. "I'm listening," he said, without inflection.

"I've been thinking about the boy you mentioned, the one who woke up."

"And?" In this one word, a lilt returned to Rain's tone. A slight curiosity.

I inched closer, until my arms were nearly touching his. "What if we could wake up everyone?"

Rain turned toward me. Curiosity gripped him fully now. "How would we do that?"

"When you told me about that boy, it made me think of Trader, how he moves between worlds, and how maybe he could help . . . us." I hesitated on that last word, hesitated to include myself with Rain once again.

"Trader?" Rain scoffed, as though the very name was disgusting in his mouth. "But Trader betrayed you."

I locked eyes with him. Stopped short of reminding Rain that he betrayed me, too. "I'm not so sure if he did. I think it's more complicated than we once thought." I inhaled deeply. "Also, I want to find Trader because I think he and I might be brother and sister," I blurted, finally saying aloud this thing I'd been keeping to myself for so many months.

Rain seemed prepared for many different explanations

from me, minus this one. He worked his jaw, but it was like rubber that refused to take the right shape. Finally, five words emerged from his mouth. "But that would make you . . ."

"Emory Specter's daughter," I said. I drew my knees to my chest to protect my stomach. I nearly wanted to retch.

"Skylar," Rain said, my name an astonished, quivering thing in the air between us. "Why would you think that?"

I pulled my knees tighter, pressed them into my chest and rib cage. My bones felt thin and brittle, like those of a bird. "I've never known anything about my father. My mother never spoke about him. It was like she'd made me out of nothing. But the night of the party at Jude's, Specter was there and he and Jude were talking. She addressed him as 'Daddy.'" I buried my chin in the tops of my knees. Little by little I was making myself smaller.

"But if Emory Specter is your father, that would mean . . ." Rain trailed off. He couldn't seem to continue his sentence.

"So many things," I finished for him. "Including that not only is my sister willing to sacrifice me for the New Capitalists' cause, but so is my father." I shook my head. "Half my family. More than half if you don't count Trader."

"All this time and you've never said a word." Rain's tone had softened.

I turned my head so my cheek rested on my knees. "It's not something I would be proud to admit. If it were true." I blinked up at Rain.

His eyes darted away—down the aisle, toward the floor, the ceiling. Everywhere but me. Eventually they settled. "Skylar, if it's true, what you're saying, it means other things, too. Not all of them bad."

"Oh yeah?" I couldn't restrain the sarcasm. "Tell me one good thing."

Rain reached out his hand. It hung in the air, waiting for my hand to meet it. I didn't reach back and after a moment he let it drop to the floor. "It would mean you and I have something very particular in common, that few others could understand." His voice held an urgency. "We'd both be children of rulers from the App World."

I lifted my head and stared across the aisle at Jonathan Holt. "I don't think it's a good thing to be a child of a ruler, Rain."

"The good part," Rain clarified, "is that we'd share something in common."

"There's something else," I said quickly, wanting to change the topic away from Rain and me, change it back to the issue at hand. "Something my sister said that I can't get out of my head, about people waking up of their own volition. Of *me* waking up of my own volition."

"Go on," Rain said.

I took a deep breath. "The weeks Jude had me captive,

she claimed I wouldn't 'stay under,' that it's as though my body kept wanting to 'shift' between worlds—those were her words. I'd always assumed she'd been drugging me at the mansion, but what if she'd been trying to plug me in and my brain simply refused? What if I *can* shift? What if there's something in my mind that might allow me to move back and forth? What if it's possible to develop the skill to resist the plugs, kind of like all those skills we've developed from gaming? Last night Zeera and I were talking about creating an App that could wake all the bodies, but she said that she needed to code it somehow, and it's made me wonder . . ." I touched a finger to my temple. "If maybe the information we need has been right here all along." I got up and went to one of the empty boxes, staring into all of that gleaming barren glass, staring at the headrest along the bottom and the contoured cradle for the body, with places for the legs, the arms, the hands and feet. The "plugs" were tiny wireless sensors along the cradle that tapped into the body's nerve pathways. That was Marcus Holt's genius. I flipped the latch and opened the top—it rose up so easily, like it was made of nothing. I put one foot over the side.

"Skylar, don't," Rain said.

Quickly, before I could decide otherwise, I slipped inside and lay down, placing my arms and legs and back in the right places. Then I reached up and pulled the top shut. At first I held my eyes closed, but when I was ready,

I let them flutter open. When I'd plugged in as a child, I was asleep. Being unconscious was supposed to ease the transition between worlds.

Could I really just . . . shift myself into the App World? Could anyone?

Rain's face appeared above me. "You shouldn't be in there."

I turned my head from his worried eyes and saw Rain's feet through the glass. His ankles, his calves, his knees, all the way to the middle of his thighs. The glass was crystal clear. I pressed the pads of my fingers into the gleam. When I pulled them away I saw the imprints they left. They marred the antiseptic quality of the chamber.

"Skylar," Rain urged.

I ignored his pleas. I was still taking in the cold hardness at my back, the way it hit every bone, every vertebra. Rain opened the top of the case and cool air rushed inside. I gazed up at him. "I wanted to know what it was like."

Rain got down on his knees and hooked his fingers over the side of the case. His knuckles were white. "You wanted to know what it's like to be plugged in?"

I shook my head. "I wanted to know what it would be like to wake up inside a coffin. Like that boy." I changed position so I was sitting cross-legged, my body penned inside the glass but my head above it, so Rain and I were face-to-face. I clasped my hands in my lap. "I'm thinking of all the bodies in the market, and what they might feel if we found a way to wake them up. The first things they would see. The first things they would fear. They would be disoriented. We would need to be there to help them. It would be a heist, but of a different sort." I took a deep breath and let it out. "There would be so many bodies waking at once, it would be chaos. But the kind that could serve us."

Rain was studying me. Understanding had dawned on his face, followed by a sense of urgency. "The App you mentioned before . . . it would need to be a kind of . . . *Shifting* App, but of the Real World variety."

"Yes," I said, jumping up and stepping outside the box.

Rain started nodding. "I like it, Skylar. And I like even more how we'd be using the New Capitalists' own technology against them."

I smiled at him—I couldn't help myself. It was nice to be understood so completely. "Exactly!" I gestured at the edge of the tablet sticking up from the pocket of Rain's jeans. "And on that note, it's time we started training people how to use weapons other than knives." I blinked, hope surging even higher in me. "What do you think?"

Rain was still nodding, and now he smiled back at me. "All right, Skylar. I'm in. Let's give it a try."

20

Skylar

zombies

"SOME OF THE work may involve testing someone's brain," I explained. "We think there might be coding in certain minds—a kind of skill, like with gaming—that allows a person to plug in and unplug at will. It's just a theory, but if it's right, the implications are significant. It could allow us to take control of the New Capitalists' network of plugs in the Body Market."

Zeera, Rain, Adam, Parvda, and I were standing in a circle by the endless rows of empty glass cases. The ocean *shhh*'d and sighed in the distance. We were discussing liberating the bodies at the market, going back for Sylvia, and saving Inara, too.

Adam seemed horrified. "I thought we had a plan. I

thought the plan was to go in and steal the bodies, and plug them back in here."

I wanted Adam's support. "That's one possibility, but this is an alternative."

Adam was shaking his head. "You want to wake people up? Just . . . unplug them?"

"Yes. And no," I said, trying to think of how to better explain. "I don't want to do anything against anyone's will. What I want is to give people a choice to unplug and reclaim their bodies." I glanced at Rain. Things had begun to thaw between us. "It occurred to me that we could use the emergency broadcast system to announce that we were about to upload an App through the Body Market. Then people would have a chance to decide their futures for themselves. They could allow the App to override the plugs, or deny the download."

Rain was nodding. "I think I can help make the emergency broadcast happen."

"Explain to me again where this App will come from?" Adam still didn't sound convinced.

I eyed Rain again. It was true, he was excited about this plan, but he still didn't like the part that was coming next. "Like I said, someone on this side would have to code what happens to the brain if a person is able to move between worlds at will, so we can create the App. To *my* brain, I mean," I added quickly. "I'm volunteering. My brain might have the skill. That's why I need to find

Trader. He coded the Apps that got us here, once the borders closed. And if he's willing to help us, then he and Zeera can work together."

Adam was staring at Rain, openmouthed. "You agreed to this?"

Rain was still watching me. "It's a good idea Adam."

"A *dangerous* idea," Adam corrected. "We're talking about playing around with Skylar's brain."

Parvda's hand crept toward mine from my left.

I wove my fingers through hers. "Nothing bad is going to happen to me. I'll be all right," I said, though my heart was pounding in my chest. I thought about the day I woke up on the cliff, and those weeks my sister held me captive and unconscious, her scientists poking and prodding me while I dreamed. "I'm used to people studying me. Or at least, I should be by now."

Adam was shaking his head. "As to the rest of it, it sounds like you're planning some sort of zombie apocalypse. These people are going to wake up and be disoriented. They're not going to know what happened. Most of them probably won't even be able to walk!"

Zeera stepped into the center of the circle. "We're going to code the App to take care of that issue."

Parvda's eyebrows arched. "But what if it doesn't work? We need to be there to help them, especially if something goes wrong."

"Of course." I reached into my pocket and pulled out

the small rectangular tablet Zeera gave me before we met this afternoon. "And with the help of a little old-school technology, we will be."

That same afternoon we distributed the tablets to the seventeens at the compound.

To the Keepers with us.

To everyone.

People oohed and aahed at the way the metal shined in the overhead lights. How you could see your face reflected in the surface, a silver shadowy self.

Zeera, Rain, Adam, Parvda, and I had prepared for the meeting by moving aside the targets and the knives and the obstacle courses and training mats in the gym, replacing them with rows of chairs for everyone to sit. We shifted and relocated and restructured until the place nearly looked like App World school, except without the holograms and download pods and, well, all the virtual reality.

Zeera was holding up her tablet at the front of the room. It gleamed next to her ear as she explained how it worked. "Most of the devices are fairly similar, though you'll notice slight differences. If you find this little button," she said, pointing to the spot along the center bottom of her screen, "the tablet will turn on. It may also be located on the side. Now let's everyone look for it and try it. Then we'll see what happens!"

There were murmurs among the rows as people ran their fingers along the edges, searching for the magic button that would transform their tablets into living things. Some of the seventeens worked in groups and pairs, helping those who couldn't find the on switch.

But soon came sighs of delight.

"It's beautiful!"

"Look at the colors. So sharp!"

"When I press my finger to it, it ripples like water!"

Only Lacy sat there looking bored, her eyes seeking Rain's as he hovered along the edge of the room.

The shouts and cries continued until Zeera called everyone to order. She went on with her lesson about messaging, as well as how to understand the earliest version of the Apps each of them saw on their screens, explaining that no matter what they did or how hard they tried, these Apps would never download into their brains and bodies.

This provoked a few murmurs of disappointment.

A message popped up on my own tablet.

Rain.

How do you think it's going?

Rain was only a few feet away from me, but his eyes were elsewhere, on the rows of seventeens. I nearly laughed out loud at the sneakiness of it all, how he was talking to me in full view of everyone—in full view of Lacy—but at the same time he was acting like he wasn't even aware we were in the same room.

Such is the benefit of these devices, I supposed.

They allowed a person, *two* people, to act like they had no connection whatsoever, while in truth, they were connecting intimately in plain view. It reminded me of private chatting to people's minds in the App World. How clever that these tablets made secrecy like that possible.

This would be to our advantage.

But I also began to see how these things could cause division, or at least, conflict.

Betrayal, even.

Was it a betrayal for Rain to talk to me without Lacy knowing?

He was standing in the same spot as before. His fingers twitched along the edge of the tablet as he stared down at it, like it might hold the answers to the future, like it was the most interesting thing he'd ever seen.

Was he that anxious for my response?

My gaze slid to Lacy.

She no longer seemed bored. She, too, was fixated on the little screen in her hands, eyes glued to it. A small smile slowly emerged on her face. She hadn't looked up. Not even once.

Maybe the smile was because of Rain.

Had he messaged her too? Had he messaged us both?

A little something in me caved inward at this thought.

I decided right then I wouldn't answer him. Things might be improving with Rain, but Rain was with Lacy now and I really didn't want to be in the middle of whatever was going on between those two. As I let my attention expand beyond him, beyond Lacy, beyond whatever drama was unfolding between the two of them and the three of us, I saw something rather chilling.

The normally loud, raucous seventeens had grown silent.

There wasn't a comment or a peep or even a sigh of delight as before.

The only sound came from the *tap, tap, tapping* of fingers on little screens.

Everyone was sitting together, sending each other messages I imagined, but no one looked at one another. No one shifted or turned or leaned in to their neighbor. They stared at their tablets, enraptured, their eyes glazed over with fascination. Some people held them high in front of their faces, others were bent over in their chairs to get a closer view. Palm after palm cupped their new devices lovingly, as though they held a delicate flower or a tiny living creature, easily crushed.

I swallowed.

Was the Keeper right? Had this been a mistake? Would we come to regret our decision to pass out such weapons? Had we been too cavalier about their power?

My eyes went to Adam and Parvda, who were sitting off to the side. Even they were hunched over their devices, their full attention on the little screens in their hands. Adam leaned away from Parvda, studying the tablet, and Parvda had a broad smile on her face as she looked down into the glow in her palm, the kind of smile she usually reserved for Adam.

Did we, as humans, fall in love with our technology just as we did with one another? Easily and quickly and wholeheartedly? Could we learn to regard the devices that delivered it to us with as much care as another body? Would all of us soon depend on these hunks of circuitry and metal for our happiness? Or even our survival?

As I took in the rapture on everyone's faces, I thought to myself:

This is really how it started, isn't it?

The divide between worlds. Between people.

Between the virtual and the real.

I glanced at the clock on my own little screen. Soon it would be time to head to New Port City with the Keeper. I crossed the room on my way to the door, and when I reached Zeera, I leaned in and whispered, "I don't know about this. Maybe it wasn't such a good idea to give these out to everyone."

Zeera shook her head. "Don't worry. It's just the initial fascination."

"I hope you're right." Before I could walk away Zeera pressed another two tiny flat screens into my hand.

She eyed me. "Just in case anyone else will be need-ing one."

I shrugged, wondering who she was thinking about. Trader. Or Kit. Both maybe? "Thanks," I said.

I was nearly to the door when she called out to me one more time. "Stay in touch, Skylar. That's what these are for."

I was shoving things into an overnight bag when I heard footsteps approaching my room. I thought it would be the Keeper, pressing us to leave, but it was Rain.

The door was already open and he leaned against the frame. "You're really going away again."

I zipped my bag and slung it over my shoulder. There came the sound of glass clinking inside. "I'm leaving to find Trader. You knew that." Rain's eyes were mostly unreadable, but I could detect at least a trace of sadness. "I won't be gone forever," I added.

He crossed his arms. "Why don't I come with you?"

"What about Lacy?"

"What about her?"

My bag was getting heavy. "She wouldn't like it."

"She would deal."

I rolled my eyes at him. "You're sure about that?"

"Skylar—"

"I'm going to be fine. I'll be with my Keeper."

Rain laughed softly. "Will you, though?"

"Yes," I said.

He shook his head. "You're going to see *him*, aren't you. You just left that part out."

Warmth spread to my cheeks. I pushed past Rain into the hall. "I'll be back before you know it," I called over my shoulder.

"Skylar," Rain said behind me softly.

I halted a moment and considered turning around to hear what else he had to tell me. But instead I hoisted the bag higher onto my shoulder and continued on my way.

21

Kit

tattoo, artist

I WENT TO my room and pulled out a flat wooden box from under my bed. Skylar had unearthed most of what I kept in this cottage—a few books, my stash of homemade whiskey, the jar of sea glass I'd collected during walks on the beach. Even the single photograph I had of Maggie hidden under my clothes in a drawer. But she had not found this, or if she did, she didn't mention it.

I think she would have mentioned it.

The box was gray and battered, the grooves in the wood deep, some of them jagged and sharp. I'd made it for Maggie with driftwood I found washed up on the rocks. It was rectangular and fairly large, though not deep. Big enough to store a few of the old kind of magazines inside.

Big enough for my sister's books.

Maggie was an artist. If we still lived in a world where artistry mattered, she would have had a long and illustrious career as one. She was always with a pencil in her hand, bent over whatever sheets of paper she could find—or that I could find for her. Paper was scarce in the Real World these days.

"What are you working on?" I'd ask Maggie each morning.

She always looked up at me with a dreamy smile. Drawing took her to another place, another world, one that she created from her very own imagination.

Well, sort of.

"My novel," she'd tell me.

"Novels are made of words," I would say back.

"Not mine," was her perennial reply.

Maggie's novels were made of pictures, long thin panels that stretched across the paper before her like stripes on a flag. They were filled with intricate scenes, detailed portraits of the people she loved most to write about, telling the stories of their lives according to her own hopes and dreams for them; her own hopes and dreams for herself, since Maggie loved to insert herself amid the drama she was always creating.

I took out the thin bound books now and opened the one on top.

The face that met me provoked a grimace.

Rain Holt stared back from the very first panel. He stood there with his hands shoved in his pockets, shirt half untucked, eyes wide and full of contempt. Or, more like, he floated in the center of a blackened sky. Tiny App icons hovered around him. In the next panel he was reaching out to one of them, or maybe it was reaching out to him, melding with his mind.

I closed the cover again.

My sister's stories were about life in the App World. The famous people there were famous here, too. There were citizens throughout New Port City who were obsessed with them. People like my sister.

The worlds weren't quite as separate as people thought.

We spent time connecting to them ourselves.

We couldn't seem to help it.

The Holt family was top on everyone's list, of course, especially their son, Rain, who made all the real girls swoon. So were politicians like Emory Specter. Mean girls like Lacy Mills and her wealthy friends.

They became the stuff of legends around here.

People like my sister made them legendary by imagining their charmed virtual lives, by fantasizing about all the adventures they must be having on the Apps and penning them on pages like the ones I held in my hands. Tidbits about them, brief snapshots of gossip, would slip through the cracks between worlds, trickle down to us in a slow but steady *drip, drip, drip.* The annual unplugging of the seventeens was a major source of information, of course. But other news would reach us occasionally, stories about App World citizens and their activities, their minds, their parties. No one knew how, exactly, but reach us it did.

Maggie soaked it all up like a summer rain.

I nearly laughed at the simile I chose.

Rain. Rain Holt.

Maggie sure loved Rain.

So did Skylar, apparently.

How was it that one boy could capture the attention of the only two girls I'd ever cared about? If I'd known that Rain was the person Skylar talked of making jealous, I would have hesitated good and long before I made her that promise. Before I jeopardized my sister's life on behalf of her own.

My heart hurt just thinking about Skylar.

Maybe she'll come through whispered a voice inside of me.

Maybe, despite everything, she would.

Besides, it was also true, hard as this was to admit, that Maggie plugged in fully aware she was abandoning me. And she went anyway.

I shook my head. It was all for nothing. All that waiting, all that hoping, all that money, all that drama. She wasn't even plugged in anymore.

Maggie was as real and awake in this world as I was.

I put the book back into its box and returned it to its hiding place under the bed. I should have been more honest with the Keeper who'd come to take her through the gate. I should have told her the painful truth:

That a little part of me hated Maggie for leaving.

That something in the bond between us broke when she walked away.

I wished—I wished with all my heart—that I had known that day in New Port Station that the woman who watched our good-bye was the head of a new political faction in the Real World, a woman on the cusp of becoming the most powerful leader people had seen since Marcus Holt invented the App World.

How I wished I'd known then that my sister's Keeper was Jude.

Later on that afternoon, I went outside to stare at the sea.

I thought about Skylar. I thought about Maggie.

I wondered what to do next. Who I owed more.

When Skylar asked for my promise, I chose not to tell her that taking down the Body Market wouldn't necessarily get Maggie back.

Why hadn't I told her?

I'd said, early on, that this was to be an exchange: *a body for a body.* One sister for another.

Skylar assumed it was about money.

I didn't correct her. I let her think this was true.

But *a hostage for a hostage* was the more accurate way to put it.

The Body Market's status as opened or closed would have little effect on what happened to Maggie. I didn't know where she was. And I wouldn't know until I handed over Skylar.

When the sun drained from the sky I went into my room and crawled into bed. I tried to sleep, but I couldn't. The hours passed and I tossed and turned, without the relief of rest. I'd yet to sleep since I said good-bye to Skylar. Guilt claimed me as its hostage just as Jude claimed my sister as hers. And it refused to release me.

The next time I saw Skylar, I wouldn't let her out of my sight.

22

Skylar

between worlds

"WHY IS IT you need to be in New Port City?" the Keeper asked. "Can't you just tell me?"

We were nearly to the mansion where she lived. The car bumped along the broken road, and skidded occasionally on the lakes of ice that covered over the biggest of the potholes. The Keeper took every back road she knew. She was worried someone would see me in the passenger side, even though it was dark out.

"Neutral ground," I said, not realizing that this was how I wanted to answer her question until the words were out. The tension I always felt with Rain, and now between Rain and Lacy . . . it was just too much.

She harrumphed. "Neutral ground?" She sounded

astonished by my answer. "You think being in New Port City, where half of Jude's people are looking for you, is neutral?"

I looked at her. "I meant my old room. I think it will be good for me to stay there for a night. If that's okay with you?"

The Keeper turned the wheel slowly. "You can stay as long as you like. You'll always have a room at my house, Skylar." She kept her eyes on the windshield as she said this.

I could hear the affection in her tone. It reminded me of those moments after I'd first woken in this world and her actions toward me were like those of a parent. I reached out and put a hand lightly on her arm. She gripped the wheel so tightly I worried about disturbing her careful concentration, but I wanted her to know I was grateful. I suddenly wanted to return her affection. "Thank you. That's nice."

The Keeper turned onto a long narrow drive. Soon the mansion loomed ahead, ghostly and dark in the snow and the starlight. "Here we are."

We went inside. It had been many months since I'd been to her apartment. It looked the same, as always, neat as a pin and in stark contrast to the opulent decadence of the rest of the gigantic house.

The Keeper gave me a quick hug. "I'm exhausted. See you in the morning?"

"I might be gone early," I said, and waited for her to tell me *no*, for her to express worry, for her to make me regret coming here or even remind me about the downside of staying with someone who felt parental toward me. "And I might be back late. Or not at all," I added.

The Keeper only nodded. "Just be careful," she whispered. "And cover yourself up," she added. "There's a coat for you with a hood." She turned away and disappeared through the doorway that led to her room with tired, heavy steps.

Then I went to the bed where I had spent my first days in the Real World, when I'd been barely able to get up, barely able to speak, when I was barely aware of when I was awake and when I was dreaming. Before I lay down, I took out the jar of sea glass from my bag and set it on the nightstand.

Before there was even a sliver of light in the sky, I set out into the city, cloaked with the coat the Keeper left for me on the couch. The hood was lined with a thick layer of fur, and when I pulled it over my head and around my chin it came nearly to my eyes and covered the edges of my face.

It was perfect.

And it was warm.

I tugged at Kit's scarf around my neck.

The snow made a satisfying crunch under my feet as

I crossed the yard to the old shed that stood against a row of trees. Apps were designed to mimic and heighten the experiences of the Real World beyond anything a body could do, but there were always things they left out. The crunch and slide of snow were among the many things I'd learned to appreciate.

Inside the shed I knew I would find something that would be useful today.

I opened the door, and it was just where I remembered.

A bicycle was propped against the far wall; I'd seen the Keeper use it occasionally. I could ride one in the App World, so I bet I could ride one here, too. I wheeled it out of the shed and down the path to the road beyond the grounds, then I got on. The bike wobbled as I pushed the pedals forward and down, uncertain at first. It nearly toppled when I leaned too much to the right. But soon I got it going fairly steadily, and eventually I was cycling as sure as if I was walking on two feet.

The wind was cold on my face.

I didn't mind.

As I pumped and pushed the bike forward, I nearly forgot my plans for the long day ahead. I laughed as I coasted down a hill and wove my way into town and along deserted streets.

The sun was peeking above the horizon when I reached my destination. The Water Tower rose before me, glowing blue like an ocean lit up against the night.

Blue and shimmery like the old kind of technology. The tiny screens Zeera gave me were stuffed into the pocket of my coat. As I took in the constantly moving facade of the building, I wondered again if the similarities were intentional or if the architect simply was inspired by the proximity of the sea encircling the city.

It seemed like there must be a connection.

The Water Tower was the most otherworldly thing in this very real city.

It stood out like a portal to another place.

I hopped down from the bike and walked it into the lobby, deserted at this early hour. I hid it behind a large metal door that was propped open and took a deep breath. I hadn't been here since the day Inara sold me out to my sister.

Hopefully this visit wouldn't end the same way.

I took the stairs. I made my way slowly, stopping to rest. This building *was* like a portal, a place connecting the past to the future, my virtual existence and my real embodied present. It held memories, both good and terrible. The closer I got to the floor with the viewing platform, the closer I got to seeing if I was wrong—wrong to come here, and wrong about what I thought I might find when I arrived. The higher I rose, the more dilapidated the stairway became, until I had to climb through the hole in a metal gate that warned me to *Keep Out.* Soon I was stepping through total darkness, feeling my way carefully, my hand on the rail. When I reached the last floor I pushed through the door into the lobby of the viewing deck.

And I stopped.

Loneliness swept over me like the wind that swirled and beat against the glass walls of this room. I was a Single from the App World, so by definition I was accustomed to the solitary nature of what this meant. But life since I'd come here had become so complicated, the people around me so conflicted with their various allegiances and agendas, I'd never felt more alone in my life.

An image of Trader flashed in my head.

Maybe, just maybe, I had a brother to get to know.

This thought was followed by another about Kit.

And . . . maybe I had someone that I might. . . I didn't allow this thought to reach its end. I wasn't sure how to finish it.

Right then, something in the viewing deck lobby caught my eye. It glinted bright in the red ray of the morning sun and I went to it. When I was close enough to see what it was I halted.

My stomach turned.

A knife stuck out of the wall—a knife I knew. A knife I'd used once.

It pinned a piece of paper there.

I studied the swirl and shine of its mother-of-pearl handle, the way it seemed to capture the pale blue and beige of the sea's shallow waters. It was a beautiful thing.

I would have marveled at its artistry had the sight of it not provoked such nausea.

Were it not the same knife I'd plunged into the eye of my sister.

I swallowed hard.

Then I wrapped my hand around the end of it. It vibrated in my palm like a living thing. I yanked it from the wall. The paper came away with it, pierced by the blade.

On it, someone had drawn a map. It led out of the city, back toward Briarwood to a spot on the very tip of the island. Alongside the mark were two looping initials. *T. S.*

Trader Specter.

I knew it.

I knew that if I was to find Trader, if *he* was to find *me*, the Water Tower would be the place he'd leave a sign or a message. Where I could leave one for him, and maybe he would get it. It's where Inara came to find me and turn me in to my sister, and Trader had been here that day. I examined the knife in my hand again. Turned it over in my palm, studying the blade, wondering who had taken the time to scrub it clean of my sister's blood. I'd wanted a message from Trader, I just hadn't expected it to come with such a fraught reminder attached.

What did it mean? Why would he do such a thing?

I pocketed the knife in my coat, in the same place that carried the two weapons of the technological variety, then I turned and left the viewing deck. The urge to get out of this building quickly powered my legs and my feet. I wanted to get away as fast as I could, wanted to think more about what Trader's message meant, other than its more obvious intent, which was to show me his whereabouts.

Or to set a trap? Leave a warning?

The knife bounced with each step.

I tried to ignore it.

The pounding in my heart urged me forward. Maybe it made me a little reckless. Or maybe it was the presence of the knife that pushed me on to a second destination, one I'd thought about since I woke this morning but didn't believe I would muster the courage required to actually go to. I'd sworn off knives, yet this one wanted to haunt me, wanted to draw me on to places where I shouldn't be.

Or maybe, just maybe, possessing it made me feel safe.

Like there was an arsenal in my pocket.

23

Skylar

a feeling of flight

THE BICYCLE WAS where I left it.

I wheeled it out of the lobby and started on my way, trying not to think too hard about what I was doing, or about the map crumpled in my pocket and the fact that I was riding in the opposite direction it told me to go.

The sun was high. It warmed the cold world just enough to make it bearable to endure the ride out of the city. My destination was far, at least two hours' worth of legs pumping, at times hard enough to push the bicycle up a steep hill. I did it knowing that once I crested the top I'd feel the relief of flying down the other side. It wasn't long before my body thawed with the exertion, the muscles in my legs burning. As the ocean came up on my left

I slowed, though not because I was tired. I mean, I *was* tired. But something else held me back, as though a long tail of heavy rocks bumped and skidded behind me as I went.

The bicycle careened down the last sloping curve, and now I did nothing to control its speed. I was nearly at my destination. There was no point in slowing things further.

The cottage came into view.

My heart lurched so hard I thought I might go tumbling over the handlebars.

I hit the brakes and hopped to the ground. I walked the bike the rest of the way, the snow rising up to my knees on either side of the road. Single lines of tire tracks blackened it in places. Motorcycle tracks. A giant wave seemed to take me up and hurl me forward, propelling my feet. The ocean gurgled and shushed alongside me, drowning out the sound of my footsteps.

I came up toward the top of the hill and as I did, I saw him.

Kit was standing there next to one of the sprawling trees in the yard surrounding the cottage, the one that stood in front of the little house, between it and the view of the sea. He was slumped against the bare bark of the trunk with his whole body, leg, hip, arm, shoulder, like all the hope had gone out of him. Kit looked exactly the same, but he was also a different person. The jacket he wore when riding his motorcycle dangled from one hand, nearly scuffing the frozen ground, and the collar of his shirt flapped in the wind. There was no scarf around his neck, though he seemed oblivious to the cold. He stared out at the water, but I could tell he saw nothing. He was lost in his head.

He didn't see me coming.

As I continued toward him, a million different impulses fired through me. Take the jacket from his hand and place it around his shoulders. Return the scarf I wore to its rightful place around his neck. Do something, anything, to restore the life to those eyes that I once thought were vacant, yet now knew were the opposite, or could be when something brought the real Kit to the surface from the deep place where he kept himself hidden. I wanted to lead him inside the house, place him in front of the stove, and stuff it with wood that would burn through the cold he must feel in his limbs.

All of these impulses, every one of them, were protective.

It was strange how much I wanted to protect him, a boy I knew was strong and could be ruthless. But it's what I felt as I closed the remaining distance between us.

This is Kit, the boy abandoned.

That was the version of him I was seeing.

I was nearly to the tree when he realized someone was there, and he turned, shifted a little, slowly. It was only when he recognized me that his face changed.

"Skylar?" he said, the last syllable lilting upward like he thought I might be an illusion that would disappear into the wintry air.

I wanted to smile, to make a joke, tried to think of a line that might provoke that wry curl along the side of Kit's mouth. I wanted to act like this was no big deal, my return. But now that I was here, facing Kit, the moment seemed to call for something else.

I took another step closer. "Hello, Kit," I said.

Everything about him changed right then, at the sound of my voice. The Kit I knew came roaring back to life. His eyes brightened, his muscles found their own strength, pushing the tree away, his hands twitching at his sides, like they were seeking something. I thought of the birds in flight on one shoulder and the moon and stars on the other and I could imagine them bursting with color.

A smile rushed to his face. "You came back."

I smiled, too.

What happened next happened fast.

Kit closed the rest of the distance between us. He pulled me into a hug and held me there, his body warm, his arms around me, strong and steady but fragile, too, because they were real and they were human and they were vulnerable. For the first time I felt his heart next to mine, beating, fluttering, so alive I couldn't help remembering that real hearts don't beat forever. The thought was terrifying.

He was trembling, with the cold, with something.

What was it Kit had said, while the blizzard held us in its icy grip?

A life without risk is a life without meaning.

Eventually we went inside.

I took off my coat and hung it up on a hook.

The cottage seemed different somehow.

Utterly the same, but also changed.

I ran my hand over the back of the old couch and heard the creak of the floorboards underneath my feet. The neatly folded blanket was sitting there, as always, just like the books on the shelf in the corner. Kit threw some logs into the belly of the iron stove and soon there came the spiced scent of wood burning.

Neither one of us said anything else.

Maybe the circumstances of my visit had altered things. I'd only just said good-bye to Kit two days ago, but here I was again already and this time of my own volition. Today I wasn't a prisoner or a thing to be bartered. I knew my arrival would make a statement, but I hadn't quite prepared for the welcome Kit might give me. Now that I was with him, I felt like I was hurtling toward the edge of a cliff.

"I can't stay long," I said, trying to stop myself from going over.

Kit was pouring coffee. He handed me the cup, then

he sat down in one of the two chairs next to the stove. They were in the exact same position as we'd left them after my last night at the cottage. I sat in the other one. The coffee was hot and it warmed my hands.

A smile still played at his lips.

"Why are you smiling?" I asked.

"You came back," he said again.

I tried to laugh, like this was no big deal. "I thought we'd already settled that." Kit mumbled something. He stared down into his mug. "What?"

He raised his eyes to mine. They held so many things, but fear was the dominant one among them. "I missed you."

I gulped some coffee, felt the burn of it going down my throat. "You left me. You could've stayed."

Kit shook his head. "No. Not with him there."

"Who? Rain?" I asked, even though I already knew it was Rain he meant.

He nodded.

"What is it you have against him?"

He shrugged, then winced. His shoulder still hurt. "I just don't trust him."

I waited for Kit to say more, but when he didn't, I spoke. "Turns out I couldn't stay there either," I told him, pausing, trying to think what I wanted to say next. "I'm not sure where I belong in this world anymore. Or who I belong with," I added in a whisper.

Kit studied me. His lips parted, and closed again. Then he said, "You could stay here."

"No," I replied immediately. Too quickly. "I have somewhere I can be. For now."

Kit's eyes flickered away. He set his mug on the stove and got up. "Are you hungry?"

"Yes," I said, glad for the change in subject.

He took out a pot from the kitchen cabinet and filled it with water, his back to me.

I wished I could see his face. I wondered if it showed disappointment.

My heart pounded behind my rib cage, like a trapped thing that wanted out.

My feelings for Rain still lingered, still peeked their head up to remind me they were holding on tight, that they wouldn't just go away quietly. But as I sat by the stove watching Kit move around the kitchen, the delicate lines of birds and stars shifting in and out of view under the sleeve of his shirt, my heart wouldn't settle, not anywhere and not even momentarily. It seemed to hover in the air, circling, flitting about, never landing.

It was this that told me the truth about Kit, about what I felt for him.

It's when the heart won't settle at all, when it refuses to alight altogether—whether out of fear or anticipation, excitement or the simple joy of flying—only then can it begin to fall and fall hard and fast into the vast and unknown territory that is love.

"Would you give me a ride somewhere?" I asked before I could think better of it.

Kit froze at my words, nodded, then continued cooking, his back still toward me. But I could sense it to the tips of my fingers and toes that if he turned around to face me the disappointment in his eyes would have vanished.

24

Rain

darkest secret

THE CORRIDORS WERE flecked with evening light, washed out and pale blue, like new-fallen snow. I came to a door at the far end of the mansion, nearly hidden in a dark alcove. This part of the house was neglected and no one ever bothered to visit. I knocked once hard, then three times lightly.

That was the code.

The door opened a crack. Two wide blue eyes blinked at me.

No matter how many times I saw her, the resemblance was always startling. "Don't worry," I said. "I'm alone."

Skylar's mother moved aside to let me through.

The room was lit by a single lamp in the corner. The

heavy drapes were pulled tight so if someone passed by outside they would never know anyone was in here. She motioned toward the round table next to the weak pool of light and the two of us sat down. A book lay open near her elbow. It was too dark to make out the title across the spine. I'd brought her so many I couldn't even guess.

"How are you, Mariela?" I asked.

She sighed. "The same. Fine."

"Is there anything you need?"

Mariela brushed a lock of hair away from her eyes. "That's not why you're here."

I nearly had to turn away. Guilt sprouted every time I looked at her. "No."

"It's not safe for anyone to know where I am." She'd anticipated my question before I could ask it. "My daughter especially. You *know* this. We've discussed it many times."

I shook my head. If Skylar felt betrayed before, how would she feel when she found out that all this time her mother had been only a few feet away here at the mansion?

"I can't keep this a secret much longer," I said. "It's going to crush her."

Her eyes filled with sympathy. "I know you care about her and I know that lying to her isn't easy." She reached across the table and placed a hand on my forearm. "And I'm grateful you came back to get me the night of the fire.

Skylar will be, too, when she finds out you saved my life. She'll forgive you the secret once she understands why it was necessary."

"But will she forgive you?" I wondered aloud. "I've spent far more time with your grown-up daughter than you have at this point, so I'm confident when I say that you're wrong." Mariela winced at my words, but I kept going. "She doesn't forgive easily. Not me and not you either."

Mariela pulled her hand back. She clasped them both in her lap. "Skylar's sister doesn't just want me found, she wants me dead. In the eyes of my eldest, I betrayed her first by choosing Skylar to plug in, and again by not siding with her cause and everything that goes with it. Skylar may not forgive easily, but Jude doesn't forgive ever. And with what I know . . ." Mariela trailed off.

"Jude would kill you without blinking," I finished for her. "And you're worth more alive to us and to Skylar than you'd ever be dead. I get that, and I appreciate your willingness to help. But I think Skylar needs to know that you're here."

Mariela's gaze cut across me. "I only help you if you keep Skylar out of it. I want her safe. That's the only thing I've ever wanted."

I shifted in my chair, the wood creaking, the noise angry and sharp against the quiet. I leaned across the table. "Your daughter is going to involve herself whether you like it or not. Whether *I* like it or not. Do you have any idea where she's been?" I didn't wait for Mariela to guess. "First, Skylar went to the Body Market. The *Body Market*. She wanted to find Inara." Mariela's eyes grew wide. "Then she was gone for almost a week—I actually thought she might never come back. She showed up finally with a *bounty hunter*. No explanation. And she won't talk about what happened either."

Mariela ran her hands down her face. "Is she all right?" she asked in a whisper.

"She's fine. Or at least she seems fine."

"But you *said*—" Mariela started.

"I know what I told you before," I interrupted. "And for a long time, Skylar kept to herself. Ever since the night of the fire she'd been . . . different, like she'd lost her will to fight, or really to do anything." I stared at Mariela hard. "But it's back, stronger than ever, and your daughter . . . she has all kinds of ideas about the Body Market."

Mariela got up and crossed the room. She faced the wall. "What kinds of ideas?"

"Intriguing ones, honestly," I said. "Good ones. Though some of the ones she has about herself are rather . . . unexpected."

She spun to face me. "Unexpected how?"

"There's something I need to know," I said.

Mariela hesitated. "What?"

I took a deep breath. "Skylar thinks her father might

be Emory Specter and that her brother is Trader. Is any of this true?"

She was shaking her head. "I should never have said anything. I thought it might be the last time we ever saw each other. . . ."

I inhaled a sharp breath. "So it *is* true?"

Mariela didn't respond.

"Emory Specter is . . . is her *father*?" I pressed.

"Where is she now?" she asked, as though this was an answer.

"Gone."

"Gone?" she croaked. "Where?"

I sighed. "To New Port City with her Keeper."

"But it's not safe for her there!"

"Well." I got up from the table and crossed my arms. "If she knew *you* were here, maybe she wouldn't have left."

Mariela sat down again in a heap. She cradled her head in her hands. "You need to get her back. She's so vulnerable. Her sister . . ."

I stared down at Skylar's mother. "If there's one thing I've learned about Skylar since she showed up in this world, it's that she can take care of herself."

She looked up at me. "I hope you're right."

"I need to go. I'll be back again as soon as I have more information. Consider what I said about letting Skylar know that you're here."

She nodded, but her eyes were elsewhere.

I left her there, not sure what else I could say, and closed the door of her room behind me softly. When I emerged from the alcove, someone was standing there, blocking the hall.

We nearly crashed into each other.

Lacy tilted her head, red hair cascading like flames along her left side. She ran a single finger down my cheek. "Rain Holt, what are you hiding?"

25

Skylar

siblings

I TOOK THE crumpled map from my pocket.

As I slipped it out of my coat, one of the tablets tumbled onto the ground with a loud thud. I bent down to retrieve it, worried that it might be broken, but it seemed fine. No cracks or dents.

Kit was suddenly at my side. He stared at the shiny metal device like he couldn't believe what he was seeing. "Where did you get that?"

"Out at Briarwood." I held it out to him. "You can look at it if you want."

He took it from me. "I haven't seen one of these in ages."

"You've seen one before?"

He nodded. "My parents had them. My mother was obsessed with hers. They were illegal contraband back then, but over the years they seemed to disappear from the Real World, either destroyed or hidden away. Eventually they were useless, because there was nothing to connect to."

I followed Kit back to our chairs by the stove and was immediately greeted by a welcome surge of warmth. The air in the cottage was chilly except right next to the fire. "Apparently my sister has found a way to turn the Wi-Fi back on in this city. And Zeera, the tech whiz I know, found a way to tap into the network so these"—I tapped the on button Zeera showed me—"are functioning again, at least for sending messages."

The tablet came to life, the blue of it projecting a glow onto Kit's face. He swiped a finger across the screen and began tapping away, immediately at ease with the device.

"You know how to use it?" I asked.

"Yeah." He sounded sad. "My mother would give me hers to play with sometimes." He glanced up from it. "This is a nice one. Solar powered. That was one of the last advancements before these got banned." He angled it so I could see the tiny black panels striping the back of it. "And see these?" He ran a finger along the silver edge of the tablet. It was perforated with holes so tiny they formed a kind of metal mesh. "Better for the environment to harness the sun and the wind."

I hadn't thought to ask Zeera about this. "Wow. Clever."

"Maybe," Kit said, but rather darkly. "Or *desperate* might be a better way of putting it." He tossed the device high into the air and caught it. "Before they figured out how to power these with the environment, the batteries would run down fast and people would go crazy when they couldn't get their fix. They'd do anything to charge them up again, even keep their small children in sweltering-hot cars or just abandon their kids altogether to go in search of a charging station." Kit looked at me. He sounded like he was speaking from experience. "The sun and the wind made it so there was endless energy to keep them going and, poof, problem solved."

"Kind of like the way they figured out how to use the sea to power the plugs," I said, making the connection.

"Exactly like that," he said, nodding.

I thought about this, trying to decide if this energy source was more clever or desperate, as Kit said. "It's a bit ironic," I began.

"What is?" Kit pressed.

"Having to rely so much on the ocean and the sun and the wind and the body to access the virtual," I went on. "No matter what the technicians and scientists do, or how hard people try to escape dependence, the Real World and all its natural resources are necessary for the App version to exist. Well, until now," I added. "Until they figured out how to leave behind the body altogether."

Kit tapped the screen a few more times, then peered closely at whatever was on it. "I wonder where the virtual sphere is going to exist, you know, in space and time, once all the bodies are gone."

I nearly laughed. "For that we'd need a physicist. But to me, it seems eerie to disconnect entirely from the Real World. People are making a huge gamble, to think that virtual living can continue on totally disconnected from reality. What if everyone is wrong, and it just, I don't know, blinked out?"

Kit didn't answer. He was busy studying the tablet. Eventually he handed it back to me. "You have a lot of messages," he said absently. Then he got up and took our plates over to the sink.

I looked down at the screen.

He was right. People had been trying to contact me ever since I left Briarwood. Well, Zeera and Rain had. *Skylar! Zeera here. Now we're connected. Just reply and I'll get the message*, said one of the ones from Zeera. *Skylar? I gave you this so you would use it. Write me back and let me know you're okay*, said another. Mostly, the messages were from Rain. One after the other, they ran down the entire screen and beyond it.

Skylar, are you okay?

Skylar, please let me know that you're all right.

When will you be back? Do you know?

Skylar, seriously. There's a reason why we decided to use

these. They're pointless if you don't stay in touch.

We miss you out here.

Zeera says hello. She's busy working on the tech necessary for your plan. Making progress too. Come back soon.

The last message was the one that sent color flaming across my skin.

That bounty hunter? He is NOT to be trusted.

Had Kit scrolled down that far? I didn't reply to any of them—not yet. Instead, I slipped the tablet back into my coat pocket and picked up the map again. Kit stopped washing dishes and came over to me.

He studied the map over my shoulder. "I know where this is."

I eyed him. "So you'll take me?"

He glanced up from the paper. "What's there that you need to see? Or is it a who?" His last words were careful. If I had to bet, he was thinking about Rain.

"It's a who." I took a deep breath. "It's someone I know from the App World. I think he might be my brother."

Kit looked at me with surprise. "You have a brother?"

I lifted my shoulders. "Maybe. That's what I want to find out."

Slowly, he folded the paper in half, then in half again, lost in thought. He held the map out to me absently.

I took it. "We're going to get your sister back," I said, wondering if my mention of a possible brother turned his thoughts to his twin.

He nodded. But his eyes drifted away.

"Tell me what's going through your mind, Kit."

He crossed the short distance to the wall where our coats were hanging on hooks. He began putting on his jacket. "That if you want to go today, we should leave before it gets dark."

"Okay," I agreed, though I felt reluctant to go so soon after I'd arrived, to leave the now familiar comfort of this remote haven by the sea. I went to Kit and stood in front of him. "I know you're worried about Maggie. I understand—I really do. I'm worried about the people I care about too. Thank you for keeping your promise."

Kit wouldn't meet my eyes. He bobbed his head once.

I grabbed my coat and put it on. Kit's neck was still bare. I started to unravel his scarf so I could return it.

He stopped me with his hand. "Keep it," he said.

The place he touched my skin was warm. When he let go, I dug around in my pocket and came up with the other tablet. "I almost forgot. I brought one of these for you."

Kit's eyebrows arched. "Thank you," he said carefully. "But I don't need one. Or want one."

I pushed it toward him. "Why not take it? Just in case?"

He studied me like I should already know. "The only person I need to communicate with is standing right here," he said. Then he opened the door to the cottage and walked outside. I followed him, the roar of the nearby sea crashing across the questions in my mind, smoothing them over like the round rocks that tumble along the ocean's edge.

The air was cold but I didn't feel it.

Kit steered the motorcycle along the coast and over a bridge, then another one. My hands gripped his waist and I leaned into him, peering over his shoulder. His eyes were hidden behind his sunglasses. This was my third time on the bike, and each time felt more normal, like maybe I belonged here. A haze of clouds filled the sky and the temperature began to drop. The noise of the engine was occasionally cut by the sound of a particularly big wave hitting the beach as we raced by.

The trip was quiet and beautiful.

And it was empty of human life. The Real World beyond the city was nearly abandoned.

Virtual life was appealing, but was it really so appealing that this many of us were willing to never lay eyes on the real version again? That we'd forfeit knowing the power of the sea and feeling the crunch of snow under our feet as I had this morning? I tightened my grip around Kit's waist and pressed into his back, sensing the way his body shifted as we leaned into a curve. The smell of leather mingled with the salt in the air and I closed my eyes. Was virtual life worth giving up the opportunity to be this close to someone else's real body?

The motorcycle came around a bend and slowed.

Kit pulled up to the only house for what must be miles. It was so close to the ocean it was practically nestled into the rocks. There was a flat expanse between them just big enough for a cottage. I got off the bike, and as I took in the sight before us, I laughed.

"What's so funny?" Kit asked.

I shook my head. "This just . . . this looks like a place where Trader might live."

The roof sagged, and in the upper right-hand corner it had fallen off altogether. The windows were so covered in grime it was impossible to see through them, and they were broken in places, like someone held batting practice here on occasion. The front steps had nearly crumbled away and a brick chimney along the left side of the house tumbled toward the ground. The facade looked to have once been painted a cheerful blue to match the seaside, but the color had faded to gray in some places and peeled away completely in others. It reminded me of Trader's house in Loner Town, the only difference being that this one was real.

Kit stood there, taking in the broken-down house alongside me. "This doesn't look like a place anyone would be living. Or should be. I bet it's empty." Kit pulled out the map again. "But this is definitely the location."

I picked my way over the rocks and went to the front door, careful not to slip on the ice slicked across them. I knocked and waited. Meanwhile, Kit cupped his hands against one of the windows that wasn't broken, trying to see through the grime.

"I don't think anyone is home," he said. "Or has been here in a long while."

This close to the water, the rhythmic crash of the waves was nearly deafening.

I tried the knob on the door. It creaked open.

"Skylar—" Kit protested.

I went inside anyway. It was the same as outside: crumbling plaster, the floorboards sticking up and splintered in places, a chair that tilted to the side because it was missing one of its legs. The place was freezing, yet the air was humid somehow, with droplets of the sea. Everything was damp. I listened for any sign of life, but all I heard was the roar and sigh of the waves. A thick door that looked to be made of driftwood was cut into the wall at the back of the room. At first when I pushed against it, it didn't move, but eventually it started to budge.

And I yelped in surprise.

"Skylar?" Kit called out from behind me.

I stared and stared.

Beyond it was a single room, nearly sunk into the rocks, simple and spare and clean. There were wires and monitors and tools on a long black counter. It was like a miniature version of Zeera's work space, sleek and humming. In so many ways this place would be unremarkable, if it didn't stand in such sharp contrast to the rest of the house.

And were it not for the single object at its center.

The cradle that served as the plug to the App World, only without the glass box around it.

Trader lay across it, as though sleeping.

I went to him and knelt down. He seemed so peaceful. But I knew better.

Trader was virtually alive and awake and engaged in . . . something. Probably something illegal.

"Trader? Trader? It's Skylar."

Kit was suddenly next to me, kneeling on the floor, staring at me like I was crazy. "I don't think he can hear you."

I shook my head. "I think he can," I told Kit. "Or that there's a way to break through to him. When I was still in the App World, someone in the Real World communicated with me once."

"But I thought that was—"

"Impossible? I know. Me, too." I turned back to Trader. "Apparently there's a lot that we don't know about plugging in and how it all works." This time, before I spoke to Trader, I reached out and grasped his hand, then nearly snatched it back. His skin was cold, like death. "Trader, it's Skylar." I squeezed his cold fingers.

Then I waited.

My hand in Trader's cold one, my face bent over his own.

Meanwhile, Kit got up quietly and went to investigate the counter and its tools. While I sat there, watching for a sign that Trader could hear me, I realized how much I hoped that he could help us. If we could code an App that gave each individual control over their comings and goings between worlds, and over their real brains and bodies, the power structure both here and in the App World would change dramatically. No longer would just a few politicians have control over people's decisions, or be able to force anyone to choose one world over the other. The borders would cease to matter altogether.

People could live in both places.

Kind of like they used to when technology and the virtual was something you could hold in the palm of your hand and connect to and disconnect to at will.

Though that was the problem, wasn't it?

Nobody wanted to lose control over things. Not Jonathan Holt, not Emory Specter, and certainly not my sister and her New Capitalists. Until now, plugging in was astronomically costly and the process itself was shrouded in secrecy, just as the process of unplugging was.

But this would be a game changer.

Well, if we could find a way to code this App it would.

I peered closer to Trader. "Where are you? What illegal thing are you doing right now that is so important that you can't come back from it to see me! The Body Market is going to open again soon and we don't have any more time to waste!"

I sat back on my heels in a slump.

After another long while, I felt a hand on my shoulder and I looked up.

"It's getting dark," Kit said softly. "We can come back first thing in the morning."

I nodded, defeat battling against the hope that maybe tomorrow things would be different.

"I'll wait for you out front," Kit said, and disappeared into the other room.

I was about to get up and follow him when I stopped and reached for Trader's hand, leaned over his face. "Trader, it's Skylar," I tried one last time. "I think I might be your sister," I added in a whisper. "Please answer me."

I was about to give up when something changed.

A rush of warmth shot through Trader's hand, the blood returning, circulating underneath his skin.

I squeezed tighter. "Trader? Trader, can you hear me?" As I sat there, staring at his face, I watched as the breath suddenly returned to his lungs, like a dead body coming back to life. His chest rose and fell, rose and fell, as if he was running.

Then, with a gasp, his lips parted.

Trader's eyes fluttered open and he sat up.

For a moment, neither one of us spoke.

Trader regarded me as though I was something out of a dream, something he didn't quite believe was real, a ghost hovering before him. But then he seemed to shake the feeling away and, finally, he spoke two words to me.

"Hello, sister."

26

Skylar

shifty

"SO IT'S TRUE." I watched as Trader stretched his arms and legs like he was waking from a very long nap. Which I suppose he was.

"You found my note," he replied vaguely.

I pulled the knife out of my pocket and held it in the palm of my hand. "Obviously. But why was this with it?"

Trader stood up. "I didn't have any tape. Or a thumbtack."

I got up and followed him across the room. "Are you really going to joke right now?"

Trader was sorting through the things on the counter of his workstation, one after the other. "I'm not joking. It's what was available. Well, that and I thought it would get your attention. It felt so . . . symbolic."

I pressed my hands into the cold surface. "You definitely have my attention. I'm listening."

Just then, Kit appeared in the doorway. "Hey," he said to me, expressionless, but his attention was on Trader. "Everything okay?"

"Yes," I said. "Really."

Trader's eyebrows arched. "New boyfriend?"

I glared. "None of your business."

"Ooh!" Trader laughed. "Did Rain get pushed out of contention? I wouldn't feel bad if that were the case."

I moved so I was blocking his view of Kit. "Trader," I warned. "I'm not here to discuss my love life."

He was smirking. I wanted to hit him.

Maybe this was what it felt like to have a brother.

"Skylar," Kit said from behind me, saving me from finding out. "I'll be in the other room. Just yell if you need anything."

I didn't turn around. "Will do," I called back. To Trader I prompted, "You were saying?"

He picked up a tiny device from the table, half the size of the ones in my pocket, powered it up, and set it onto the counter again. "Honestly, I'm not sure where to begin. So much has happened since we last saw each other," he added wryly.

I studied Trader. Again I searched for a sign in his face that would confirm beyond a reasonable doubt that we were siblings, but I saw no resemblance. In fact, I saw only traces of Emory there, just as I had the first time Trader and I met in the App World. "You called me sister," I prompted.

Trader peered over the screen. Something beeped. He seemed so unconcerned. "I did," he said. "But you said it first. So I guess now you know."

That sinkhole pulled at my stomach again. My brain couldn't seem to comprehend this could be true. "Emory Specter is my father, just as he's yours."

Trader bobbed his head once. "Sadly for both of us, yes."

"And your mother?" I asked next. "Is she the same as mine?"

Trader's expression faltered. "I don't know who my mother is. In that, you are lucky."

I went to approach him, but he moved away. I still couldn't wrap my mind around the notion that not only did I have a brother, but that brother was Trader. "Why didn't you tell me when we were in the App World?" I asked. "You had so many chances."

"I wasn't sure back then," he said. "I had my suspicions, but . . ." He trailed off, his attention going to the little screen on the counter again. He peered over it.

"But what?" I pressed.

He closed his eyes a moment, seeming exhausted suddenly. Then he took a deep breath. "I didn't want to do that to you, if it wasn't true. I hate my father, and when you and I met, you already hated him too. You had this idealistic hope for a family who loved and missed you in the Real World and I didn't want to upend it. It's nice to feel idealistic." The smug amusement I was used to seeing in Trader returned and he cocked an eyebrow at me. "Still feeling idealistic these days?"

I laughed, but bitterly. "Obviously not. I mean, could it get any worse?"

"It depends on how you look at it." His tone sounded light. "At least you now have a brother with no interest in profiting off you. That's one positive, right?"

My eyes narrowed. "I have a brother who helped my best friend from the App World turn me over to my sister, Jude. To *our* sister, Jude."

Trader's expression darkened. "Either choice I made in that situation was a bad one. But I was always going to help get you out, Skylar. I was never going to let our dear sister sell you to the highest bidder." He walked over to a set of chairs on the other side of the room. They were metal and seemed functional but uncomfortable, like everything else in this place. They faced a tall panel of glass that looked out onto the rocks and the ocean. Trader gripped the back of one of them and gestured for me to take the other. "Listen, I wasn't sure if you were my sister until the night of the party."

I sat down and Trader took his place next to me.

"Well, now we're both sure." I wondered where in our DNA we shared similarities, and what those similarities were. "Does Emory Specter know that I'm his . . . daughter?" I nearly couldn't even articulate this, it made me so repulsed.

Trader nodded. "I'm afraid so."

I stared out the window. A wave crested and crashed onto the rocks, followed by another. The wide and flat ones closer to the house were coated in a layer of ice. Winter could be brutal in the Real World, but there was something comforting about being by the sea, no matter the weather. "And he knows about you, right?"

"Yup," Trader said. "But as I explained when we first met, if you happen to be Emory's illegitimate son, it's best to stay off his radar. Dear ol' Dad sees his children as useful pawns."

I huffed. "Like father, like sister, apparently. At least where Jude is concerned."

Trader's eyes gleamed. "Oh, I'm sure Jude will find out soon enough that she's another pawn in Daddy's plans, too."

"I don't know about that," I said.

"I do." He sounded so sure. "But let's talk about me and you, Skylar. That's what you came here to discuss, right?"

I turned away from the view of the sea and let my eyes settle on Trader. "All those years in the App World I lived as a Single, when I had a brother nearby." I thought about Kit and Maggie, and the bond he spoke of between them, about how strong it was. "We could have helped each other. We could have kept each other company."

"I might not be the best company for you. Or anyone," Trader added.

"Why not?"

Trader shifted in his chair so he was leaning as far away from me as he could get. "I don't like relying on anyone else, and I don't like it when they rely on me either. Unless it's for the right price."

Those words seemed like something I'd hear from Kit. But I didn't believe it—not entirely. I'd seen how Inara and Trader were together. She meant something to him. "I don't know if I buy that."

Trader stared at the waves as they crashed against the rocks. "I don't care if you buy it or not. It's just how it is."

I let out a frustrated breath. "Listen, if it's our father who's facilitated the selling of bodies via the App World and our sister who came up with the idea, don't you think we share some of the responsibility to fix what they've done?"

Trader laughed. "First of all, absolutely not, and second of all, I'm not sure it's that simple, Skylar. Just because they're family doesn't make us responsible. Besides, there are citizens in both worlds who agree that what they're doing is not only okay, but makes sense. Lots of people."

I shook my head. "Maybe. But citizens in the App World only know half the story."

"Trust me," Trader said. "My entire life I've trafficked people back and forth, and I've lived in Loner Town. Most App World citizens plug in and never want to look back. They don't care about what's going on over here."

I wrapped my fingers around the seat of the chair, squeezing hard. My knuckles turned white. "But what if they found out their body wasn't going to be destroyed, and instead would be, I don't know, sold for parts? Or used so that someone else's personality and memories could be downloaded into their brain? Don't you think that might make them pause? Maybe reconsider whether they wanted to hang on to their bodies? Or, at least, reserve the right to decide what happens once they're removed from the plugs?"

"Glad to see you've retained some of your idealism." Trader stood and opened a tiny window high up in the wall. Cold air rushed over us, but it felt good, and it smelled like the sea. Trader sat back down. "Some of them might want that right, but I think a lot wouldn't care. They won't even notice their body is gone, so how could they miss it?"

"We'll tell them!"

"And how do you propose we do that?" Trader was shaking his head. "Besides, you don't just pull people back from living their cushy little virtual lives to inform them of something so utterly sinister, do you? Maybe they'd rather not know."

I was shaking my head. "Maybe not everyone cares what happens to their body, because they've moved on. But I do think everybody deserves a choice about what happens to it, that every single person, whether plugged in or not, has the right to decide about their body's fate. And to make that choice, somebody needs to inform them of what Jude and"—I swallowed, my next words getting stuck in my throat—"our father plan to do."

Trader rolled his eyes. "I stand corrected. You've retained *all* of your idealism."

"But don't you think that's fair?" Now it was my turn to roll my eyes. "Or I suppose you only help people for money. I'm sure Rain could sweeten the deal for you."

Trader shifted uncomfortably. He suddenly couldn't stop fidgeting. Bouncing his knee. Tapping his leg. "There is one person I owe. And who wants no part in the Body Market."

My eyes flickered back to him. "Oh?"

"Inara," he admitted quietly.

"I knew you cared about her," I said. "We share that in common then."

Trader leaned back in his chair, staring at the ceiling. "We do."

I studied him a long while. "Are you in love with her?" I asked carefully.

He sat up again. Then he shrugged. "Maybe," he said. Then he put his head in his hands. "Yes," he mumbled into them, this one word from his mouth full of anguish.

"Tell me," I prodded, gently.

At first Trader was silent, but eventually he began to talk. "Remember when she showed up while you were unplugging?"

"Yes," I said. How could I forget?

"She was so distraught that somehow I found myself wanting to make her feel better, to take all that pain away." He raised his head again. "So I promised her I'd help her unplug to go and see you, if she wanted."

My jaw gaped open. "Seriously?"

The expression on Trader's face was sad. "I'm not always a mercenary, Skylar."

"Go on."

"But I also didn't want her to get herself killed, so I made her wait."

My eyebrows arched. "I'm glad you cared about the well-being of at least one of us."

Trader looked defensive. "I knew you'd survive, Skylar. I figured if we shared the same genes then there was no way you wouldn't make it through." He waited for me to respond, but when I didn't, he went on. "It wasn't long before our sister got to Inara and her family, and she didn't have a choice but to unplug so she could get to you and turn you in to Jude. So I promised I'd go with her and protect her, which is how I ended up here." He smiled a little. "I don't know what it is about her, but I can't help caring what happens to her."

"I understand," I said. "I feel the same way." I reached over and placed my palm gently on his shoulder. "We'll get her back. We have to. I can't accept the alternative. I *won't* accept it."

The two of us were quiet, the only sound the muffled crash and roar of the ocean outside.

After a while, Trader turned to me. "Why did you really come here? It wasn't just for a reunion with your long-lost brother."

"Well . . . ," I started.

He laughed. "See, we all have agendas." Now he was smirking. "Even you."

"Yeah, so if my agenda happens to help you get Inara back, are you still going to complain about it?"

His smile faltered. "I always planned on getting her back. I just hadn't gotten that far yet. The App World keeps spinning regardless of what happens here."

"When I walked into this room today, that's where you were, right? The App World?"

He nodded.

Something occurred to me. "Have you tried looking for Inara there?"

Trader covered his face with his hands again. It was strange to see him so anguished. "I can't find her. I've looked everywhere. No one knows where she is. Her parents are worried sick."

The rhythm of the sea outside the window was worsening as nausea spread through me. "But I thought that the people who were part of the Body Market were still plugged in to the App World. That's what Jude promised."

He let his hands fall to his side. "Well, she lied. Or maybe Inara is a special case where both of us are concerned, and Jude is only doing this to Inara to punish us."

I stood so I could shut the little window. The chill in the room was becoming unbearable. "I have an idea where she might be." Trader looked at me hopefully. "But I'm going to need your help, which brings me to the other thing I came here to ask. How do you go back and forth between worlds?"

"I'm good with coding," he said, then seemed to hover on the edge of something else.

"And?" I prompted.

Trader shrugged. "I've just always been able to."

"Do you think other people can too? Maybe even on their own?"

Trader looked interested. "Explain."

"Well," I began. "Jude claimed that my body didn't want to stay plugged in, that I was able to resist the plugs and 'shift.' Then there was this boy in the Body Market who just . . . woke up." My heart beat a little faster. "Being plugged in changes our brains and gives us new skills and abilities—that much we know for sure. So is it possible that someone would develop the skill to . . . move back and forth between worlds at will?"

Trader got up. "That's an interesting theory, Skylar."

I stood, too. My heart pounded harder. "But is it just a theory?"

Trader walked over to the cradle at the center of the room and I followed him. Now that it was empty I could really study it. It wasn't as sleek as the ones in the cavern under Briarwood, but all that mattered was that it worked.

He crouched down next to it. Ran a hand across the headrest. "There's a glitch that runs through the App World. It operates almost like a wormhole. I learned how to exploit it, so I could move back and forth. I've long suspected that other people might find it, even by accident, and develop the ability to travel between worlds on their own. I bet that's how the boy woke up—maybe he was dreaming about being in the Real World and tapped into the glitch. That's how you get to it. It's probably what allowed your body to resist the plug at Jude's mansion." Trader looked up at me. "It's interesting she used that word to describe it—*shift*."

I crouched next to Trader so we were eye to eye. "Why?"

"Because that's the word *I've* always used—I call it shifting. I wonder what Jude knows about the glitch . . . *if* she knows . . ." Trader trailed off.

I reached out and touched the makeshift cradle, the part that held the torso in place. "Is it dangerous to use it—this glitch? Has it ever . . . hurt you?"

Trader turned to me. "Why?"

I inhaled deeply. "Because I'd like exploit it, too. I want to know if somehow I've developed this ability to go between worlds." I met his eyes. "Let's see if I'm able to shift."

He watched me intently. "Because you want to go back to the App World and tell people about the Body Market."

"I think it's what's right," I began. "But I also want the chance to search for Inara." I paused. "And I think that finding that glitch and figuring out how shifting works might be the key to liberating everyone's bodies. Can you help me?" I searched Trader's face for signs of willingness. "What do you think? There's money if you—"

Trader put up a hand to stop me. "Forget about the money. Inara's a priority in this plan, right?"

"Absolutely."

Trader's eyes brightened a little. "All right then," he said. "Count me in."

27

Rain

lies

"DID YOU FOLLOW me, Lacy?" I asked.

Lacy put on her best *Who, me?* face, which on the real Lacy looked far more innocent than the one I'd grown used to in the App World. "So what if I did? I have a right to know what's going on with you, Rain."

I walked away without looking back.

She caught up. "Who's in that room?"

"Nobody," I lied. "It's just storage."

"I heard voices."

"I was talking to myself."

Lacy got in front of me and halted. She crossed her arms. "Do you have a secret girlfriend or something?"

I shook my head and laughed. "Absolutely not."

"Because if you did, it's my right that you tell me."

"You have a lot of rights where I'm concerned these days, Lacy."

She cocked her head. "Shouldn't I?"

"I don't know. Why do you think you do?"

Lacy exhaled a frustrated breath. Her eyes were murderous. "As your *girlfriend*, I believe I have rights."

My heart softened. "I'm sorry you're upset. You have nothing to worry about on that front."

A triumphant smile crept across her face. "So you agree, I am your girlfriend."

I didn't answer, and instead stepped around her, walking faster this time, wishing we weren't in such a deserted part of the mansion. The relief of running into someone else would be welcome. Though ever since we'd passed out the tablets to everyone, people spent a lot more time by themselves in their rooms.

Lacy caught up once again. "I've seen you sending messages."

I glanced over at her. "I've seen you sending messages too."

"Yeah, but I'm not messaging someone I'm in love with."

I stared straight ahead. "I'm not in love with Skylar."

Her eyes didn't move from my face as she walked. "Just saying that practically confirms that you do."

Now I halted. "Stop worrying about her, Lacy."

"Why?" she huffed. "You never do. And besides, all I suggested was that you were in love with someone, but not the *who*. You're the one who supplied Skylar to fit the description."

"Let this go. Please."

She leaned against the wall and studied her nails. They got longer and longer and she never trimmed them. "Tell me who's in that room and I will."

"No."

"Tell me, Rain."

"No," I said more forcefully this time.

Lacy narrowed her pretty green eyes. Whenever she did this, the innocence on her freckled face disappeared. She abandoned her nails to twist a lock of red hair. "If you don't tell me who's in that room . . ." She paused, dropped the lock of hair, and dug around in her jeans pocket. She came up with her tablet. "I'll message Skylar right now that you're skulking around keeping secrets from every-one."

My heart raced. I grabbed it out of her hand. "Don't you dare."

She snatched it right back, and this time clutched it firm, her nails clicking against it. "Answer me. And even if you take this one"—she held up the tablet, daring me to take it again—"that doesn't mean I can't just get another. Zeera would gladly give me a new one if I asked."

I stepped back from her, disgusted. "There are moments

when I think you've changed, Lacy, when I think you're better than people give you credit for. But then you always remind me you're the same mean, spoiled brat I knew in the App World."

All the triumph in Lacy's face fell away. Hurt filled her eyes, followed by tears. They left trails down her cheeks, one after the other.

I'd gone too far. I reached out to take her hand, but she moved aside before I could. "Lacy," I pleaded. She started to walk. Now I was the one following her. "Lacy, I'm sorry. I shouldn't have said that. Any of it. I care about you. I really do."

She spun around. She was crying hard now, but she looked angry too. Her arms were rigid at her sides. "Sometimes you forget that I'm human, Rain. I *am*, you know. I'm not invincible."

"You're right. I do forget." Lacy sniffled. Seeing the pain on her face killed me. "And then I say hurtful things as though you can't be hurt."

She wiped her eyes with the back of her hand. "Has it all been a lie?"

I studied her. "Has what been?"

She pointed a finger between us. "You and me. Everything that's happened since the blizzard."

I drew her to me and put my arms around her. "No," I whispered.

When the crying subsided, Lacy lifted her head, her

pale-green eyes so wide and hopeful, still glassy with tears. "Then for once be honest with me, Rain. Pick me, not Skylar, to tell your secrets to. Trust *me*. Please? Tell me who was in that room."

I stared down at her for a long while, debating.

Then I took her hand and led her to a place where we could talk.

28

Skylar

awake and dreaming

"IT'S ALL ABOUT state of mind—finding the *right* state of mind," Trader said. "That's how you exploit the glitch in order to shift."

He and I were standing before the cradle at the center of the room. The light had faded from the sky and the room had grown dark.

Kit had joined us again. He stood on my other side, tension rolling off him, focused on every word Trader uttered.

"Do you know how to meditate?" Trader asked me.

I shook my head. "No."

"Pity," Trader sighed. "Finding your way into the

glitch is all about control—mind over virtual. The App World is designed so that everything happens without pause. People go from one thing to the next without stopping to think, by *never* stopping to think." He chuckled. "It's amazing what's possible with a little patience and control. There's so much power to be gained."

"You would know," I said wryly. "But I've never meditated, so what other advice do you have for me?"

"Let's see . . ." Trader studied the floor for a moment. "Okay . . . Have you ever had a lucid dream? You know, a dream you can control?"

I thought about the night when I walked straight out into a blizzard while barefoot, which ended when I stabbed Kit in the shoulder. "I've had a lot of dreams where I'm *out* of control," I began. "The day I unplugged and found myself up on that cliff, I thought that was a dream because it seemed like I could do anything, like I had all of these powers that I would in a game." Trader nodded. "If I hadn't believed it was a dream, I probably wouldn't have tried to save myself at all. I would've given up."

Trader leaned back onto his heels. "Well, shifting can start with falling into a dream. Remember how I told you that the glitch operates like a wormhole? The key is taking control of it, once you're in it. Everyone dreams when they're plugging in and when they're unplugging, but what alters the process is that element of taking control—of knowing you can and then actually finding a way to do it. Normally it's the virtual that takes control of you, but you can't allow this to happen. Instead, you refuse to surrender to the chaos of it. You decide that *you're* in charge. I'm not sure if everyone can shift or just certain people. If you are one of those people, it will take some practice, but once you do it, you'll learn how to go back and forth, and eventually you'll be able to slip into the state that takes you from one world to the other at will."

I stared down at the cradle on the floor. "But that sounds almost . . . easy."

Trader nudged the contraption with his foot. "It is and it isn't. You'll understand once you try it. Or, you won't," he added with a shrug.

I took out the rubber band in my pocket and pulled my hair into a ponytail. "All right then, I may as well see if I can do this."

Kit moved to stand in front of me. "Skylar, are you sure you want to do this right now?"

I fought the urge to grab his hand. "I'll be fine. I'm not afraid."

"Maybe you should be afraid," he said. "What if something happens to you?"

"Don't worry. I've survived worse," I said.

Kit stepped aside. "Fine. But I'll be waiting right here when you get back."

"How valiant," Trader said with a chuckle.

"Shut up," I said.

Trader laughed harder. "Is that any way to talk to your brother?"

I wanted to punch him. Maybe a desire for physical violence and exchanging barbs was also normal for a sibling relationship. Trader and I seemed to be sliding into one seamlessly. "Can we focus? Or did you forget that if I actually get to the App World I'm going to search for Inara?"

The amusement drained from Trader's face. "I haven't forgotten."

"Good." I breathed deep and then settled into the cradle. I lay back until I was looking up at Trader. It was time. "Okay. Tell me what to do."

"When I turn the cradle on, it will start a download into your brain, just like an App," Trader explained. "The plugging-in process will begin and you'll automatically be sent into a dream state—you know what it's like since you've been through it before. Things will be confusing and strange for a while, but eventually, when something appears that's familiar to you, something that you can hang on to, grab at it as hard as you can, almost like it's a rope. It might be a person, or a place, or even a smell. Whatever it is, follow it until things start to settle. And when you feel good and in control, when you know exactly where you are and you remember your purpose in the dream, I want you to picture a door. Once you've got it, once you can see the door clearly, I want you to decide that on the other side of that door is the App World."

I twisted around in the cradle to face Trader. "A door? I just get my bearings, conjure a door, and decide that it goes to the App World?" I laughed. "And where does this door lead in the App World exactly? Do I get to decide that too?"

Trader's eyes narrowed. "Listen, you asked me to tell you how I do it, so I am. If you don't want to believe me, that's your choice."

I tried to expel my skepticism. "You're right."

"For me," Trader went on, "the door leads to my place in Loner Town, which is convenient since it's away from the City center. I suggest you decide that's where you want to go as well. You've been there before, so for now, if you'll oblige me, dear sister, make my place your App World destination while we're still in the practice stage."

"That sounds reasonable," I said, and let myself relax against the headrest.

Trader was standing over me. "But before you go storming into the App World, let's just see if you can get to the door. If you can, I don't want you to go through it yet. Don't even touch it. Don't go near it. I want you to stop, turn around, and return the way you came until you find yourself dreaming in the Real World again. Then, if you're able to wake yourself on your own like you saw me do earlier, that means you're able to shift, too. Then, we'll try again and have you go all the way through."

I tried to process this. "How will I know I'm back in the Real World?"

Trader shrugged. "It's difficult to explain until you're in it. Just trust me, you'll know when you're there. You'll see a signpost of sorts, something important to you that anchors you here."

Kit stood up and crossed the room. "And what happens if she can't get back? If she's not able to shift at all?"

Trader shrugged. "I'll pull her out. I'm going to be monitoring her the entire time."

Kit crouched on my other side. "You're sure you want to do this?"

I nodded. "Yes." My skin tingled with static. I was anxious to get going. "I'm ready."

Trader bent over me, scrutinizing my face. "Don't go through the door. I mean it, Skylar."

"I won't, I promise," I told him. "And I'll look for the signpost to get back." I tilted my head slightly and saw that Trader held the tiny device in his hands again. He was typing away at the screen.

He glanced at me. "Here we go, Skylar."

I closed my eyes now, and waited.

And waited.

Nothing happened.

"When are you—" I said, trying to open my eyes.

But they were so heavy I couldn't.

"Skylar, are you all right? Your face is so pale."

Kit's voice. Urgent, but far away.

"Skylar, you're scaring me. Maybe you shouldn't do this. I'm going to—"

His words were cut off.

Everything grew cold. Freezing, really.

Someone should shut the windows, I thought.

There were voices all around me.

"Skylar. Skyyylllaaarrrr?"

My name echoed everywhere.

I couldn't see anyone.

"What did you do to her?"

"Why do you care so much?"

I was in a black hole, suspended in a sea of nothing. I shivered and shivered. I couldn't seem to warm up.

"I just do" was the last thing I heard before the cold pulled me down, down further into the nothingness.

I was running.

My breath came in gasps.

There was snow everywhere.

My feet kicked it up into the air and it sparkled like stars.

Stars.

I stopped and watched them shine in the light.

The cold faded, and with it the fear.

Where had I seen so many stars before?

Something nudged at me.

A thought, a memory?

Was I supposed to remember something?

I saw a flash of skin, of eyes.

A tattoo.

I was lying in the sand.

The sun shone above my face.

I was warm and happy and safe.

The ocean shushed nearby and a cool rush of water tickled my toes before receding. I lifted my head and opened my eyes. The beach was wide and curved, like a sliver of moon, and I had it all to myself. I smiled. The sea was the color of bright-blue glass, and so clean that when the waves rose and rippled toward the shore they were transparent. I wore a grass-green bathing suit. I lifted my knees and wiggled my toes in the wet sand. Then I let my head fall backward and closed my eyes again, soaking up the soothing warmth. Maybe in a bit I'd go swimming.

I could stay here forever, I thought.

I could die happy.

I lay there, listening to the sounds of the surf, at peace in the quiet of this place, my favorite of all places in all possible worlds. Eventually I heard a voice, very faint, so faint, at first, that I thought I might have imagined it.

"Skylar . . ."

Goosebumps covered my skin. I lifted my head and looked around.

"Skylar . . . Skylar, concentrate. Remember."

Remember? Remember what?

"Skylar, remember the door. Find the door. The door."

I got to my feet and brushed off the sand from my legs and arms. A heavy cloud passed in front of the sun and the light went gray. Raindrops began to patter the ground. The sea turned a dark blue, whitecaps dotting across it, the waves becoming angrier. Thunder rumbled across the sky.

I needed to go.

Soon there would be lightning.

"Conjure a door."

A door.

I spun around, looking for the source of the voice.

There was no one.

A great bolt of lightning split the sky in two.

The crack of it made me jump.

I put my hands to my head. It hurt so badly, I thought it might break in two. I had to get out of here, but the beach only seemed to grow longer and wider as I stood there looking for a path inland. My heart sped. Lightning descended once more, zigzagging toward the ground.

Something tugged at my brain, nagging at it, the voice, and a memory.

My vision blurred, my head pounded, but then for a

single blissful second everything cleared.

Yes, I had to conjure a door, just like the voice told me.

A door to where, though?

A door that would bring me to safety?

Beaches don't have doors.

Lightning cracked again, bright and fast and two feet away from where I stood. I screamed, the smell of burning immediately everywhere. I turned around and around, willing myself from this place, willing myself anywhere, willing the appearance of a door that would lead me out of this dream that was becoming a nightmare.

Dreaming. I was dreaming.

This wasn't real.

But . . . I could make myself real if I wanted, couldn't I? I could gain control of this, something deep inside my mind was telling me. I needed to gain control. The fear subsided little by little, despite the lightning, the thunder, the rain that pounded my skin. My heart relaxed until it beat normally.

I started to walk.

Bolts of lightning streaked around me, like I was gaming and they were trying to tag me out. Permanently. Gingerly, I stepped to avoid them. Ignored the pain searing through my brain.

I would search for that door until I found it.

29

Kit

S.O.S.

SKYLAR LAY THERE, so still.

I wouldn't call it peaceful. I was used to seeing her up and about, her eyes bright and alive. It was strange to see her like this. So lifeless. So . . . fragile. Why would anyone want to do this to their body for years at a time? How could my sister have wanted an existence that entailed giving up so much?

Giving up me?

This thought was brief but sharp, and I inhaled a painful breath.

Trader hovered over Skylar, watching, like he was waiting for something to happen.

Or to go wrong.

His head snapped up. "Stop glaring at me," he said. "She's going to be fine. She's plucky, my sister."

I stood. "Good, because if something goes wrong, you and I are going to have problems."

A smirk appeared on his face. "What's going on between you and Skylar?"

I decided to give him the literal truth. "Nothing."

"I don't believe you."

"I don't care what you believe."

Trader shook his head, then went back to watching Skylar.

She started to shake.

"What's wrong with her?" I barked.

Skylar's eyes squeezed tight, like she was in terrible pain.

I stepped around the cradle so I was standing in front of Trader. "Wake. Skylar. Up." I shoved his shoulder when he refused to look at me. "Something's wrong!"

He glared at me now. "Calm down. This happens sometimes." He tilted his head, as though amused. "Get out of my way."

"You don't care about her at all, do you?" I spat. Then I ran to the coat Skylar left draped on the worktable and dug around inside its pockets. I came up with her tablet and powered it on, scrolling through the messages.

There were dozens more, all of them worried, most of them from Rain. A couple were from some guy named Adam, a few were from that girl Zeera, and there were others from someone named Parvda. There were a lot of *Skylar, please*'s and *Skylar, where are you*'s? There was only one message from a girl named Lacy, but hers was rather unfriendly. *You're no match for Rain. You can't ever trust him. He'll betray you again and again. Leave him for someone who can play at his game and play it well.*

I glanced over at Trader.

He was frantically tapping his fingers across that little screen that controlled the plug, his calm replaced by urgency. Then he was leaning over Skylar and mumbling things that I couldn't quite make out. Skylar had at least stopped shaking. "What are you doing now?"

"None of your business," he said.

"If it has to do with Skylar, it's my business. You're communicating with her aren't you? Can you reach her? Is she okay?"

He chuckled. "A few minutes ago, you told me there was nothing going on between you two. Now she's your business. What changed?"

"She's important to me. I want her safe."

"Why?"

"I have my reasons."

"Give me one of them and maybe I'll consider telling you what's going on."

I thought about dangling a tidbit about my sister but decided against it. Then Skylar convulsed before growing still—deathly still. Trader sighed with relief at this, but I didn't trust him. Not one bit. I looked down at Skylar's messages again. I didn't trust any of these people either, but I knew Skylar did, and I didn't like that she'd put her life in Trader's hands and his hands only. I tapped out a reply to everyone who'd messaged Skylar, even the girl named Lacy.

Even Rain.

If he really cared about her, he'd come to help.

Dear friends of Skylar, it began. *You seem as worried about her well-being as I am. I took her to see someone named Trader. She's right now plugged in and possibly headed into the App World and things don't look so good here. Both for her safety and that of everyone else, I think she needs you. Below are the directions to our location.*

I tapped these in as clear as I could make them.

Come soon, I finished, hit *Send*, and set the tablet aside.

Skylar seemed exactly the same as before, or I thought so at first. Then I noticed something slightly different.

Her cheeks had grown rosy.

Seeing her skin flushed with life was better than the opposite.

I sat down in one of the chairs and determined to be patient.

Skylar came back to me once already.

She'd come back to me again.

30

Skylar

familiar choices

I WALKED AND walked and suddenly I was surrounded by doors.

One, two, three, four . . .

Eleven. I counted eleven.

I didn't see the landscape shift or notice the exact moment when everything changed. All I knew was that it did.

The room with the doors seemed to be in a house, or maybe a mansion. It was long and narrow and the floors were marble. Elaborate gilded crown molding lined the walls at the top and the bottom. The ceiling was ornately decorated with frescoes of women in flowing coral gowns and scholars convening with their books. Angels flew overhead between each scene and great crystal chandeliers threw light over everything. A breeze flowed from somewhere, causing the tiny glass crystals to chime against one another.

I'd been here before.

But when? And where was it?

A feeling crept across my skin.

Dread. It was dread.

My vision blurred again, then it cleared.

I walked from one end of the room to the other, trying to figure out why this place was familiar. It was so long that in a way it was more of a hallway than a room, but one wide enough to host a dinner party and elaborately decorated enough to host something fancy. The doors weren't ordinary doors either. They didn't match, and not just in terms of paint color. Their sizes, their frames, their styles were all so vastly distinct that they seemed to belong to different worlds altogether.

Different worlds.

One of them led to a different world.

The App World.

Exactly where I was meant to go. My reason for being here.

Everything came rushing back, and the clarity I'd sought and the knowledge of why I was here came with it. I'd plugged in and I was between worlds.

Trader was monitoring me right now.

Kit, too. Kit was waiting for me to wake up again.

Trader instructed that once I took control of the dream, I needed to conjure a door, which I had, obviously. He just didn't say anything about conjuring this many doors. Oh well. It was still a dreaming state, if a lucid one. Maybe this was just the sort of thing that happened. But which door would lead to the App World?

The tallest, narrowest one was made of a polished metal, so much so that it gleamed in the light. Another was covered in mirrors, and I caught various flashes of my reflection in it as I passed by, a knee, my hand, the side of my face. There was a carved wooden door, with bright-red paint lacquered across it; one that seemed to be made for a child, with a rainbow-colored hot air balloon adorning it; and another that looked like it might be solid gold. I stopped before this one.

Could this be it?

Something was definitely on the other side.

I heard muffled voices and put my ear to the golden surface. I was tempted to push through it but then I heard something that chilled me and I leapt back, stumbling.

I righted myself.

Slowly, I returned to the golden door. Pressed my ear against it one more time.

"You promised me this would work!"

"I believed it would—"

"Well, it hasn't!"

"If you give it time—"

"I don't have time! The buying has already been delayed for days!"

"But the girl—"

"—means nothing to us, obviously!"

I jerked backward.

One of the voices was a man's and I didn't know it.

But the other one I knew as well as my own.

Jude. It was Jude's.

My heart pounded behind my ribs. My chest shook with it.

This is just a dream, I reminded myself. *It's not real.*

I'm in control here, I thought next.

But was I? Was this really just a dream? Something born of my imagination?

Right then, a sharp pain seared through my head.

I blinked. I breathed.

Tried to bring everything into focus.

I looked around again, finally realizing why this room was familiar. Aside from all of the strange doors, it was exactly like one of the rooms I'd walked through in Jude's mansion. Why, of all places, would my brain conjure this one?

Technology altered our chemistry, this was a fact. It altered our brains in ways we could not predict or control.

This was also a fact.

But . . .

I breathed deep once more. Shook away the thoughts firing through my head. I'd come here with a very specific task and I'd gotten sidetracked. I could puzzle about this later on with Trader.

My eyes fell on another door, one I hadn't yet reached. It was way at the end of the room.

I started toward it and then felt pulled along, like it was a wave that wanted to draw me under. The second I was close enough to see it, to really take it in, I knew that this was the door I was looking for, the one I was meant to conjure. It was boarded up, the wood splintered and graying. The sharp ends of nails stuck out of it in places and it looked ready to fall apart.

I smiled.

Only a door that led to Trader's house in Loner Town would look like this.

On the other side of it was the App World.

My heart leapt, my limbs were light, like they might float, all the pain of before dissipating. My brain seemed full of champagne. It took me a minute to realize what I was feeling.

Excitement.

I was *excited* to go to the App World.

Home.

I was excited to go *home.*

This word lifted through me as though caught on a

breeze. I grasped at it, took it, held it in my hand, and then that hand was actually reaching for the door, ready to pull back those boards that stood in my way of doing just this. Right now.

I was so very close.

But then I yanked my hand back.

I promised Trader I wouldn't go through. Not yet. But the door, it was like a magnet that drew me in, or an App designed just for me, poking my shoulder, buzzing around my head, daring me to download it.

I took a heavy step backward, my feet like lead.

Then another.

With each step my entire body got a little bit lighter.

I'm in control of this, I reminded myself.

It was time to go back to the Real World.

The farther I got the quicker I could walk, and soon I was turning around and the room I remembered from Jude's mansion faded until the landscape changed and I was by the ocean again, but this time the coast was rocky and I was following a road, one that rose up a hill, at the top of which was a tiny cottage. A single tree stood in the front yard, barren of its leaves, its branches sharp against the backdrop of the horizon.

Here it was. The Real World. Trader said I would know it when I saw it and he was right. The signpost had appeared to me as Kit's house. I went straight up to the front door and didn't stop to knock, didn't wait or even hesitate. I reached for the knob, turned it, and went right on inside.

"Kit?" I called out as I went. "I'm home."

I was gasping. Everything was dark.

"Kit?" I called out again.

My voice sounded far away. My eyes were heavy, my limbs were heavy. My torso felt like it was pinned down by something. Like I was being held underwater.

Something had my hand.

Maybe I'd made a mistake.

Maybe this was still a dream.

What if I couldn't find my way out? What if I couldn't find my way back?

"Kit?"

I worked my eyes, pushed them as tight as they could close and then did my best to slide them back open. Finally, finally, I could see. At first it was blurry, but eventually my sight cleared.

Kit blinked back at me.

Those dark eyes were full of . . . everything.

He held my hand.

"You came back," he said, just like before, but different this time, too.

I just wasn't sure how.

31

Skylar

stepping through

THE ROOM HAD grown dark, but not so much that I couldn't make out the other faces all around me.

So many faces.

Slowly, I sat up.

There was Kit, of course. He still had my hand.

Trader, too.

But others had appeared in my absence. Adam and Parvda, Zeera and Rain. And Lacy. She looked slightly disappointed. Maybe she hoped I'd never wake again.

Rain was staring at my hand clasped in Kit's.

Kit eyed me another moment, then let go. "Are you all right? You didn't seem like it for a while there."

"You couldn't wait for us, Skylar?" Rain asked, before

I could answer him. There was anger in Rain's voice—anger and jealousy. All the goodwill that built up between us before I left Briarwood seemed to have vanished. "You had to do this immediately?"

I rubbed the back of my neck. It ached. My forehead throbbed. "It's not like we have time to waste," I countered. "Everything was right here, ready." I glanced at Trader. "And I had a teacher eager to help."

Trader's eyebrows arched. "Teacher?" he repeated, sounding skeptical. But a smile played at his lips. "You did it, Skylar, didn't you?"

"I did," I told him. "At least I think so."

Trader's smile grew. "It must be in our genes, sis."

I smiled back, despite the fact that every part of my body ached. Maybe Trader would turn out to be the sibling with whom I could have the relationship I'd always longed for. If he was in love with my best friend from home, then maybe this was possible.

Zeera sat down on the floor next to the cradle, and Parvda joined her.

"What was it like?" Parvda asked.

Zeera pulled her long hair back from her face. "Were you able to cross the border?"

When I shook my head no the room began to spin and I wanted to retch. "I didn't even try. Trader made me promise not to."

Trader reached up and pulled a long string that

hung from the ceiling. A light went on and a soft glow fell across everyone. "Now that you know your beloved girl"—he was looking at Rain as he said this—"is alive and well, can you give her some space? I have a debriefing to conduct so she can go back." He went to his workstation to look for something.

Adam's eyes widened. "Go back? Right now?"

Lacy snickered. "Just let Skylar do what she wants. Seriously. She will anyway."

I twisted around in the cradle to look at Adam. "I need to. We have to figure out how this works and if we can somehow code the process for the App." I stretched my arms, then bent them a couple of times at the elbows. Why was I so sore?

Meanwhile, Zeera was talking animatedly to Trader. They were studying the tiny tablet Trader used when I'd plugged in. Zeera took the device into her hands and tapped the screen. Then she came over to me, her eyes bright. "I know how to do this, Skylar. Your idea is going to work. When you plug in again, your brain is going to give me all the coding we need for the App." She held up the device. "This not only measures your vitals and your brain waves, it records them. The technology is amazing!"

I laughed at her enthusiasm.

"And Trader knows how to make the App download so it works like a virus through the market," she went on.

He came and stood next to Zeera. He looked down at

me. "Before you go running over the border to the App World, Skylar, why don't we talk about what happened first. Did you see the door I told you about?"

Everyone else in the room quieted at this.

Trader held out his hand and I took it. Gingerly, I lifted myself from the cradle. My limbs groaned. Another wave of dizziness passed over me. Shifting between worlds seemed really hard on the body. When I was standing again Trader let go. "It took me a while to take control of the dream," I began.

"That happens," Trader said. "Each time, you'll get better at it."

"But eventually I found the door. Your door, I'm sure of it. It was boarded up and falling apart." Trader nodded, a bit smug. I nearly rolled my eyes. He was obviously proud of his dilapidated lodgings. "Here's the thing," I went on, thinking back to the long narrow room in which I'd found myself. "I didn't just see one door, I saw lots of doors."

Trader's brow furrowed. "What do you mean?"

"I mean exactly what I said. You told me to conjure a door, but I guess I conjured a whole bunch to be safe?" When Trader didn't nod, or seem to understand, I did my best to clarify. "I ended up in a room full of doors. I counted eleven." Trader was shaking his head. "What? Is that weird? Did I do something wrong?"

He seemed unable to process this. "For all the years

I've been shifting, there's only been one door. You decide your destination, and that is the destination that becomes available to you. Only that one. Conjuring the one door is difficult enough, never mind conjuring eleven."

Slowly, I brought my right knee up to my chest, then my left, massaging the muscles in my thighs. "Well, you're basically walking through a dream, right? That's what you said. And dreams are strange."

Trader considered this. "I suppose." A shiver ran through him. "There are just . . . rules to shifting. The process is always the same and there's always only a *single* door." He looked at me sharply. "You swear you didn't go through any of the others, right? So you don't have any idea where they led?"

I shook my head. "No. I already told you I didn't."

"Good," Trader said. "Only go to mine. The others could be dangerous. You have no idea where they might take you."

"Well," I began, "I did put my ear to one of them."

Trader's eyes rolled toward the ceiling. "Skylar! I told you not to even touch the door, never mind a different one."

"I know. They're, like, magnetized or something. They want to pull you through all on their own. They're difficult to resist."

Trader looked exasperated. "Exactly why I told you not to get close."

"Don't you guys want to know what I heard?" I asked everyone else.

"I do," Kit said quietly.

"Me, too," Parvda said. She nudged Adam.

"Tell us, Skylar," Adam said.

I caught Trader's eye. "I overheard someone having a conversation. It was Jude."

"There's no way," he said.

"I know my sister's voice. *Our* sister," I corrected.

A murmur went across the room at this.

"But Jude's in the Real World," Zeera said.

Rain had been hanging back in the shadows, but now he stepped into the light. "As far as we know she is, but maybe that circumstance has changed." He looked from me to Trader, back to me again. "What if Jude knows about the glitch? There's no reason to think that she wouldn't. She's a powerful person with powerful connections. What if you found a door that leads to Jude in the App World?"

A little part of me shrunk, considering all of this. "Maybe," I whispered.

Trader was nodding. It was surprising to see him agree with something that came out of Rain's mouth. "If Rain is right, and you happened to catch Jude while she was in the App World, then maybe if you go back things will have changed. There'll be fewer doors available."

"Or more," Zeera offered. "Depending on what Skylar's subconscious conjures."

"Or more," Trader agreed.

Rain met my eyes. "I suppose you need to go back and find out, Skylar."

Adam stared in disbelief at Rain. "So now you're on his side?" He gestured at Trader.

"I think she should go, too," Zeera said. She held up the device that connected to the cradle. "The sooner the better, so we can get going on this App."

Everything about me was so tired. All I wanted to do was to crawl into a bed and sleep, but I knew they were right. The moment I was in front of that door, my heart had fluttered with the excitement of going through it, of being in the App World again. The feeling flashed through me again now like an electric jolt into my body, readying me to go. "I can do it."

"Skylar," Kit said, his voice full of warning. "This is a bad idea. You didn't see yourself while you were plugged in. But *I* did."

I turned to him. "I'll be fine."

Zeera stuck a tiny black disc to the underside of the headrest on the cradle. "This is going to download your brain waves so we can start coding the App," she explained. She didn't seem worried that I was going to try and shift again so soon, and this heartened me. Then Zeera began to confer with Trader again. The two of them kept typing things into the handheld device. Meanwhile, everyone else dispersed around the room. Lacy sat on one of the chairs, a bored expression on her face. Parvda and Adam seemed like they were arguing in the corner. Rain was by the windows glancing my way, like he wanted to talk to me, but just when he'd opened his mouth to say something, Lacy got up, grabbed his arm, and dragged him over to the chair next to hers. I went to say something else to Kit, something to reassure him, but he turned his back on me and walked to the other side of the room.

I joined him there. Got in front of him so he had to look at me. "Hi."

He stared, but didn't say anything.

"Are you not speaking to me now?" I asked.

He shrugged. "You're taking a huge risk."

"Oh? This from the bounty hunter who wants to turn me in to my sister?"

Kit shifted uncomfortably. "I didn't do it, though, did I?"

"Not yet," I reminded him. "But you will if I don't come through."

Before Kit could respond, Trader called out to me. "Skylar, get over here. It's time."

"Coming," I called back.

My eyes hadn't yet left Kit. I could just make out the bottom of his tattoos along the edge of his shirt sleeves. There was a lost look about him. I wanted to fix whatever it was he was feeling, and I didn't want to leave again without doing this.

"They're waiting for you," Kit said.

"I'll tell you something." I forced myself to keep my gaze steady, forced myself not to look away. "Remember how Trader told me I'd just 'know' when I was in the Real World again? That I'd find a signpost that would tell me it was safe to wake up, and that I was home?"

The lost look in Kit's eyes faded slightly, and interest nudged its way into them. "Yeah. I remember."

"It was your house," I said.

He seemed confused. "My house?"

I nodded. "When I was trying to find my way back, I ended up at your cottage." I took a deep breath and said the rest of what had been swirling around in my mind since I'd woken up to find my hand held in his. "The signpost for the Real World," I went on. "It was you."

This time, my trip through the dreamscape was far quicker. There were a few moments of confusion, but I took control fast, and it wasn't long before I found myself in the room with the doors. I looked around, taking it in.

Trader was right.

The number of doors had changed.

Instead of eleven, there were fourteen.

I searched the room for the golden one, but it was gone.

Could Rain have been right, too? Did Jude move back and forth between worlds? And if she did, how long had she been doing it? Longer than a year? That would mean she'd been to the App World when I lived there as a Single and had never come to see me, never even tried to.

My breaths came quickly.

Ice began to creep over everything in the room. It crawled down the metal door that shined like silver and the one lacquered in red. Soon it covered one of the new doors that had appeared, one that was encrusted in barnacles and shells and that smelled of the sea. Eventually the ice reached the floor where I stood, nearing my toes.

I wrapped my arms around my body and I began shivering uncontrollably.

What was wrong? What had I done?

My teeth chattered, a constant clicking inside my head. I could no longer think, could nearly no longer breathe. The pumping of my heart began to slow and I fought the urge to collapse into a ball.

I'd lost control of the dream.

Fear took over as the ice crawled over my feet and surrounded my ankles, rooting me there. Snow began to fall in the room and piled up fast, unnaturally so. It reached all the way to my waist before I found a way to quell the terror storming around me.

I used every last ounce of energy and conjured an iron stove, the same one I'd grown to love at Kit's house.

Soon a fire roared inside of it.

A bottle of honey-colored liquid sat on top of it.

I grabbed it and took a swig.

It burned going all the way down.

My heart seemed to jump-start itself again and the ice covering my legs began to melt, enough so that I could walk. Once again, thoughts of Kit had saved me.

I didn't waste any more time wondering what this meant.

The snow was still drifting around me as I pushed my way to the door I was sure led to Trader's house in Loner Town. With a strength I didn't know I had left I began pulling away the boards nailed over it, feeling the App World getting closer and closer with every second that passed. The moment I reached the handle I twisted it and threw my body against the door, shoving as hard as I could.

It gave way and I tumbled on through.

PART THREE

32

Skylar

home sweet home

I LIFTED MY head and looked around.

I was lying on the floor, my heel wedged in a gap between the boards. A cracked mirror hung on the wall and the door to the room swung precariously by its hinges. The atmosphere was thick with must. A moth-eaten, mouse-eaten couch missing one of its legs sat, tilted and sagging, against the wall. This was definitely Trader's house. Even in the dark, the room seemed so bright it hurt my head. I used my hand to shield my eyes and pulled myself up until I was sitting. The furniture was broken and falling apart, but it also seemed to sparkle with magic, like someone had taken an enchanted paintbrush and run it over everything so that the entire room, the entire house, this entire *world* was surreal and strange.

The App World. I'd made it across the border.

I was home!

A surge of something unidentifiable went through me, beginning somewhere in my brain and rippling out toward the tips of all my limbs, literally like a wave scrolling across me, hoping to find sand at the end of its efforts. I laughed.

The wave was ticklish.

But the sound of my laughter was . . . off. Hollow and echoey, like my mouth was pressed against the opening of a great empty shell, and my voice had traveled toward the far edges and then bounced back.

I scrambled to my feet.

The palms of my hands were caked with a pale sort of dust. I rubbed them against each other, but it was no use, the white layer of grime stayed put. I lifted up my hands to inspect them and see what was clinging there, and I swallowed hard. A shudder rolled through me again, like a tremor that began at the top of my head and eventually reached my toes.

No, it rolled through my code.

Because that's all I was now.

A virtual projection.

A basic App World self.

And that's exactly what was wrong. The grime wasn't grime at all, yet my hands . . . they were so . . . not mine.

They were pale, the color of those cottony clouds that brush across a bold blue sky as though to erase it of pigment. It had been a long time since I'd seen Caucasian 4.0, the standard skin color of all citizens in the App World, and I'd nearly forgotten what it looked like. I rubbed at my forearms, at my shins, at the backs of my hands and even my knees.

It was no use.

Here, I was pale, like an apparition. No matter how hard or how long I raked my hand over my skin, the color would not return to it. My brain seemed to squeeze inside my head. This was such a lie. My virtual self was a lie. One of the first things I'd learned when I woke up in the Real World was that my real skin was the same hue as freshly made honey, a golden brown made even richer by the sun.

I went over to the cracked mirror hanging on the wall and took in the virtual girl blinking back at me.

Skylar Cruz, a Single from the App World.

Or, at least, I imagined that I blinked back, because in the deepest parts of my code I knew this was just a trick, that virtual selves don't blink, that they don't need to, just like they don't need to eat or to breathe. It was all for show, for the purpose of the ritual itself. Only the real body needs such movements and gestures, the virtual self mimicking it as closely as possible, so people felt as alive and real as possible.

Here, now, I was myself but I wasn't; I was the person I'd been for my entire life, yet this person turned out not to be like the real me at all. Maybe this was why people shouldn't go back and forth between the virtual and the real. It might make them crazy. In the mirror I saw a version of the eyes I'd always known, the shape of the face, the length of the hair, but everything was duller and less defined. As dull as the blank color of my virtual body. Washed out.

Why was the App World created to do this to us?

I already knew the rules, already knew the reasoning.

They'd told us over and over again in school.

The features of the standard self are designed to be enough like the real version so as to render the person recognizable, but ultimately, to provide the perfect blank canvas so the download of an App can be experienced and shown to its best advantage. They'd made us memorize this statement. It was part of the constitution of the City and it was stored in my code. *Each App is like an artwork with its own palette and style. The miracle is in the transformation of the blank canvas into something far more spectacular. Apps provide the meaning and color of our existence. Everything else is secondary.*

I tried to remember the benefits of this.

Knowledge could be downloaded directly into the brain and stored there. The virtual self was lighter, nearly weightless, as flexible as rubber and impervious to physical harm, capable of transforming into an infinite number of creatures and looks and personalities. And the virtual self could always be restored to its original settings, made good as new, even after losing a limb or breaking every bone until the self was limp as rags. The App World was safer. Indestructible. And so were we, its citizens.

But there was no denying this either:

I wanted my body back, *my* body, the real one, with form and shape and color and flesh that could wither and muscle that could tear and organs that could rupture and skin that would wrinkle as I got older. Despite the heat in the summer and the cold in the winter and the frostbite I'd felt on my fingers and toes. Now that I'd had time in the real body again and regardless of everything wrong with the Real World, I wanted it back like I'd never wanted anything in my life. The real body came with a host of risks, but with those risks came so much that was lush and lovely and varied. I nearly felt the arms of Kit reaching around me, his head buried in my neck.

What if something goes wrong? What if I can't make it back?

I took a deep breath of the atmosphere into my lungs, or I pretended to, and reminded myself that Trader and everyone else was sitting there, waiting for me to shift, and if I somehow wasn't able to, they'd pull me back themselves.

But then I heard voices.

So many voices.

They were coming from outside the house.

It didn't make any sense. Loner Town was always dark and empty and dreary and frightening. The only people who came here were the ones who didn't want to talk to anyone else, who kept to themselves, and who lost themselves in Apping without ceasing, as though life was merely a constant download.

But no, there was definitely shouting. Or maybe it was more like chanting.

I went to the window. A moth-eaten curtain lay limp and thick across it, and I peered through one of the bigger holes.

I took a step back, sure I was imagining things.

Maybe I was still dreaming.

I returned to the window and looked outside once more.

People were streaming down the streets of Loner Town, avoiding potholes as they went, virtual selves awake and alert and marching in unison. It was as populated as the toniest street of the City. I put my ear to the hole in the curtain so I could hear what they were saying.

"Set us free!"

"Open our borders!"

"Our bodies, our selves!"

"My body is *my* body!"

"Plugs need bodies!"

It was a protest! From the sound of it, against not only the border closing, but against the removal of bodies. Police lined the sidewalks as the protestors walked down the center of Loner Town's broken streets. Things in the App World had changed since I unplugged. I watched the people go by for a while longer and realized something else.

Not a single one of them had downloaded any Apps.

They were a sea of pale ghosts moving together, all of them their basic, virtual selves, unaffected by any downloads.

Was this part of their protest?

A boycott of Apps?

The code that threaded the veins of my virtual self grew static with energy. *Wait till I tell the others.* Liberating the Body Market was more important than ever. There were people in the App World who were trapped here, fighting against the changes Emory Specter had forced on everyone.

That my father had forced on all of us.

I turned away from the window. As much as I wanted to continue watching the protest, there was something important I needed to do before I could go back to the Real World again. Something I had to find out.

My eyes scanned the walls of the room until I found what I was looking for, a hole as big as my fist and as deep as my arm. I went to it and shoved my hand inside and began routing around.

"When you get to my house," Trader had whispered to me as Zeera was sticking more round black discs onto the headrest of the cradle, "there's a stash of capital hidden there for emergencies." He looked at me meaningfully. "You can use it for whatever you need."

I could nearly see a reflection of Inara hovering in his eyes, but I looked at him like he was crazy. "What does that even mean? Capital is accessed through the mind."

"You'll see when you find it," he said. Then he smiled. "Remember, I'm a virtual genius. I can code anything."

My arm was nearly shoulder deep in the hole in the wall, but still I found nothing. Then suddenly I reached a pocket of static, something electric, like a lightning bolt.

I retracted my hand and stumbled backward, just in time before a long chain of Apps shot out of the hole and gathered like a swarm of bees around my head. As I took in the sight, I had to give Trader credit. He was clever. It was his own personal App Store, but everything was pre-paid. All I had to do was touch whatever I wanted and it would download immediately.

I glanced longingly at the door that had spit me out into this world.

Soon, I thought. Soon I'd go back. I would.

Just not yet.

A tiny App in the shape of a truffle zoomed past my

lips. It left a trail of sweet chocolate dust in its wake and it took all the will in me not to bite down into it for a taste.

So my brother had emergency sweets in his stash.

That was a fun new fact.

I tried to see through the swarm to pick out the App I wanted. I knew it was here somewhere.

Then, far, far up at the very edge of the moving, swirling mass, I saw it.

The icon for Odyssey.

I waded through the rest of them, swatting away the most aggressive Apps with my hands until there was nothing left between me and the one I needed. I reached out a single finger and touched it. As I did, my entire virtual self sighed with the relief of the download pouring into me like a cold rain after an eternity in the desert. *The Real World is a desert of pain and loss,* went my brain, my code, the part of me that was made to be here and to love this place, to long for it. *I was home, this was home, there was no place like home and no feeling like a download,* it went on. This was only the second-to-last thought that went through my code before I blinked out of the atmosphere and into the game.

The very last one was *Inara.*

I shielded my eyes from the glare of the sun.

It was bright. Brighter than normal, the kind of

sunshine that burned skin and turned it red and angry and blistery.

Something wasn't right.

But the place definitely was. I stood at the end of a long curving stretch of beach, one I'd been to before, on my last full day in this world. I inhaled deeply, expecting the tangy, briny scent of the sea to fill my senses, waiting for it to draw me forward, but instead my entire virtual body recoiled and I took a step backward. There was only the brackish smell of kelp and the foul one of rotted fish. Now that I looked at my surroundings a bit more closely, the sand was more brown than white, and sharp bits of shell and narrow pins of mica were tossed through it, ready to cut the bottoms of careless feet.

This couldn't be Inara's landscape I'd tapped into.

Could it?

I started toward the other end, watching where I stepped, wanting to run but obliging myself to tread cautiously over this treacherous ground. Eventually I crested the tall dunes, expecting to see a single sailboat waiting for me, one small sign that this wasn't a fool's journey, that Inara was somewhere close. That she'd known exactly where to wait for me all this time.

My hand went to my eyes again, curved like a visor.

I *did* see a sailboat.

But there were two instead of one, and neither was in any shape for travel. I descended the hill, my feet sinking into the coarse sand, sharp bits stinging my skin. The closer I got, the more broken the tiny boats looked, as if they'd been battered by a terrible storm. There were holes laced through their hulls. The sails were shredded and the masts were bent in ways that were irreparable.

If both boats were here, then where was Inara?

I looked behind me, next to me, everywhere around me.

The only other thing I saw in this landscape was the island. Like before, it rose up out of the water in the distance. A great gray cloud heavy with rain hung directly above it. I walked up to the tide's edge and stripped off my tunic. Slowly, I waded into the water, my eyes searching the bottom, wondering what unfriendly creatures lurked in the depths of this foreboding place, but the farther in I got, the rougher the waves became, kicking up the sand and making it impossible to see anything. When a great gray wall curled up to at least twice my height, I dove underneath before it could break and began to swim as fast as my arms and legs could take me. Slimy, slithery things darted across my skin but I didn't slow down, not even when, as I came up for air, I spied a pair of triangular fins skimming the surface a little ways off. I kept going until the island grew bigger and bigger, so big that it nearly eclipsed my view of the sea. The harder I pushed, the clearer my mind became and the more confident I was that despite the nightmare landscape around me, I would be rewarded by finding Inara when I reached the shore ahead. Fear was right now filling Inara's mind like a relentless demon, I was sure of it, because Inara-specific kinds of fears were governing this version of Odyssey.

There was no other explanation for these circumstances.

But if Inara really was here in the App World, she should be living her normal life just like Jude promised she would, that everyone would, both before and after their bodies were removed from the plugs. Inara shouldn't even remember what happened to her in the Real World.

None of this made any sense.

I swam harder, until finally my toes grazed the rocky bottom and the water was shallow enough for me to walk. Something sharp pinched my big toe and I shook it off, going faster now, not caring whether my feet got cut and scraped in the process. I wanted out of this angry sea as quick as my legs could take me. Raindrops began falling here and there, quickly turning into a steady torrent that pattered the surface of the ocean and dripped down my face. I wiped my eyes and tried my best to see through the mist and the gray. The island was mostly beach, but at the center of it was a thick cluster of trees. I headed toward them, first at a walk, but as the rain came down harder I picked up the pace until I was running.

"Inara?" I called through the din. "Inara, are you out there? It's me, Skylar!" I strained to hear something other than the pounding of the drops hitting the plants and the wilted flowers hanging on to their stems, but there was nothing. "Inara! Inara! I'm here!" I was screaming. I ran and ran, hands in front of my face, unable to see through the wall of water falling down around me, until I reached a place where the rain no longer drenched my skin and I stopped. I wiped my palm across my eyes, trying to dry them enough so my vision cleared, and looked up. A canopy of palms stretched overhead, a sturdy protective roof.

I took another couple of steps forward, turning all around.

A weak voice sounded nearby, close to the ground.

"Skylar?"

I turned again.

There, just a little ways off, eyes wide and terrified and disbelieving, was Inara, curled into a ball at the base of one of the trees.

33

Rain

likeness

"THERE HAS TO be another way," Kit was saying to Trader.

I didn't hear Trader's response because I was too busy staring at Kit. It was as though each time he moved, I got a glimpse of something, the ghost of someone, like the flash of silver that catches the sunlight, then dims immediately. My brain kept trying to hold on to it, that sense of familiarity, to prod and to shape it until whatever it was I could name out loud.

Kit turned to glare at me. "What are you looking at?"

I glared back. "Nothing much at all."

Kit shrugged, then returned to his conversation with Trader and Zeera.

I walked up to Adam and Parvda. She was sitting on the floor next to Skylar, monitoring her. Her deep-brown hand was holding Skylar's golden-brown one, and she leaned into Adam, who sat next to her.

"Do you guys notice anything familiar about Kit?"

Adam looked up at me and shrugged. "He has an attitude similar to yours?"

I rolled my eyes. "Funny."

"I wasn't necessarily kidding," he muttered.

"I keep seeing something in his face," I went on, undeterred, "something I've seen before, but I don't know where. I'm right on the edge of it and then it slips away."

Parvda shook her head. "Honestly, I've been so focused on Skylar I haven't paid much attention to him."

I walked over to Zeera, who was tapping the screen linked to Skylar's mind, trying to capture the data needed for shifting. Kit leaned against a nearby wall, watching Zeera's every move. She was so engrossed she barely noticed I was there.

"Zeera," I prompted.

When she finally looked up, her eyes were glassy. Dark circles were forming underneath them. "Huh?"

"Can you focus for a minute?"

A shiver ran through her. "Um. Yeah. Yes." She nodded.

I turned her around so she was staring at Kit. "Do you see anything in his face that you've seen somewhere else?

Like, on somebody else?"

Zeera was quiet. She blinked quickly. "You know," she started, but then stopped.

"What?" I prompted, wanting someone to solve the mystery of this nagging feeling.

But she only shook her head. "Nah, nothing," she said, and went back to work.

An hour passed, my mind picking through every other face I'd ever seen in both worlds and coming up with nothing.

It was Lacy who finally figured it out, Lacy, who wasn't even trying.

She walked straight up to Kit, looked him full in the face in that demanding, entitled way that only someone like Lacy could, and pronounced the very thing my mind had been reaching for ever since I arrived at this broken-down house.

"You," she began. She got up on her toes to peer closer into his eyes, the left side of his face, then the right side, inspecting Kit like he was a statue and not a living, breathing person standing in front of her. "You look like that girl being held prisoner on the monitor in the weapons room."

I stared at Kit again and a light in my mind went on.

Kit took a step backward, as though he'd been struck.

Lacy came off her toes and turned to me. "I mean, not

exactly like her, but I'm not the only one who sees the resemblance, am I?"

"No," I replied, shaking my head in wonder. "You aren't."

34

Skylar

aching

I CAME TO from the App World, gasping.

Morning light streamed through the windows of Trader's house.

Everything in my body ached, this time worse than before. My head throbbed like I'd been banging it against something hard and metal.

I sat up and looked around. My mind spun.

I waited for it to settle.

Parvda and Adam were lying on the floor. Rain and Lacy were nowhere to be found, probably off somewhere on their own. Zeera and Trader were standing at his workstation, their fingers flying quickly across the screens in their hands, so bleary-eyed they didn't even notice I was back. No matter which way I turned the person I most wanted to see was nowhere to be found.

Kit was gone.

Everything about my body throbbed and groaned and this suddenly seemed right. My heart had fled, leaving a gaping hole in my center. *Maybe he's in the other room*, I thought. *Out front. Sitting on his bike in the wintry air.* I knew this shouldn't be my first concern, that there were other things so much more important than Kit's whereabouts.

But how does a person do anything when their heart is gone from their chest?

"You're back," Trader said, suddenly next to me.

I was slow to react, like when I'd first woken at the Keeper's house and my words wouldn't come. I blinked at Trader, trying to speak. What finally came out of my mouth in reply to his comment was, "Where is everyone?"

Trader's dark eyebrows arched. "By everyone, you mean your two boyfriends? They left together to go back to Rain's grandpa's mansion."

With great effort, I sat up and swung my legs around off the cradle so my feet touched the floor. The movement produced a dizzy feeling, but then it passed. "Kit left with Rain?"

Trader nodded.

I dragged myself to a standing position and limped over to the window, flicking it open. Cold air washed over me and I tried to breathe. Kit hadn't even waited to see if I'd woken up alive or never came to again.

Maybe he didn't care as much as I thought.

Maybe I shouldn't care as much as I did.

I slumped a little.

Trader crossed his arms. "Well? How did it go?"

I pushed my thoughts about Kit aside. "I found Inara," I said.

His eyes widened. "She's okay?" he whispered.

"Inara is alive," I corrected. "I don't know if okay is the right way to describe her virtual state at the moment."

Worry filled Trader's bottomless black eyes. "Just alive?"

I hesitated. "She's hanging on. She knows we're coming."

"Tell me, Skylar. Tell me the truth."

I shifted from one foot to the other, my muscles straining, my body unsteady without a heart to anchor my center. I took a deep breath and told him everything I knew. "She's hiding out in Odyssey because she's afraid for her parents, and for herself. She knows too much."

"But I thought—"

"—that she'd have forgotten everything?" I shook my head. "Sadly, no. Inara remembers it all. That mind-wipe never came about, as Jude promised. Or at the very least, it didn't work."

"She's all alone."

"Inara is stronger than you think," I said, sounding more confident than I felt after seeing my friend huddled under a tree on that deserted island. The best I could manage before I left her again was to ease her mind enough that the landscape shifted for the better. The rain stopped, the sun peeked out from behind the thick gray clouds, and the smell of rotting fish had dissipated some. "We're going to get her back."

"This is my fault."

"No, it's mine," I said, truly confident this time. "Jude is punishing Inara for my escape. But the good news is, Inara isn't willing to do Jude's bidding anymore, and she wants to fight back. She's had a lot of time to think and said she can't bear the thought of someone in the Real World taking over her body, or using it for parts. She wants to make her own decisions about her body's fate." I placed a hand onto Trader's arm. "Inara doesn't want to lose the possibility of being with you, Trader, even if here is where you want to live. She misses you. She's worried about you."

Trader made a pained sound, then shook his head. "She's worried about *me*?"

I nodded. Then my knees nearly buckled.

Trader caught me before I could fall. He looked at me knowingly. "Shifting is hard on a body."

I stretched out one leg, then the other, concerned I might collapse or pass out. "You didn't mention that before. Then again, you seemed fine after you shifted."

"You get used to it," he said. "Also, I didn't do it twice in such a short time."

I tilted my head up to the cold air filtering down from the window.

Zeera came over to join us. She leaned in to give me a quick hug. "Welcome back."

"How did things go on your end?" I asked her, once the spots had faded.

She glanced over at Trader. She seemed nervous. "I think we got everything we needed."

I eyed the two of them. "You think or you know?"

"Yes," she said.

Zeera didn't sound as excited as I'd expected. "Which one is it?"

"We need to head back to Briarwood," she said carefully, ignoring my question.

If Kit was at Briarwood, I wouldn't mind going there myself. Then maybe I'd find out what could be so important that he would just up and leave me here.

Adam and Parvda stirred across the room. The two of them stood and ambled over. Adam still looked half asleep. "Did it work?" he asked Zeera. "Did you get what you needed for the App?"

She nodded, but then busied herself with the tablet in her hand.

Parvda gave me a worried look. "Skylar, you seem exhausted."

"I'm okay," I lied. "I could shift another twenty times today, no sweat."

Parvda narrowed her eyes. "I don't believe that one bit."

Adam slipped one of his long arms around me. "I'm glad you're alive. Though I still think your plan is crazy."

Adam's comment reminded me of the other thing I wanted to tell everyone. "Speaking of crazy," I began, "there were protests outside of Trader's house, protests in Loner Town. They're against the border closing and the removal of the bodies. There were police lining the streets. People care. Well, at least some of them do," I added.

Trader seemed thoughtful. "It makes sense they'd be in Loner Town."

I shot him a quizzical look. "Why do you say that?"

"Think about it," he said. "I bet the government funneled them there, so the more desirable folk don't have to witness the unrest, or think about whether any of the protestors might have a point."

"That actually seems reasonable," Adam said.

Zeera was still absorbed in whatever was on the screen before her. "Let's go back to Briarwood like Zeera said," I said, watching her. "I don't want to wait around any longer."

Parvda slipped a jacket over her thin shoulders. Then she waved an arm in the air, gesturing for all of us to follow. "All right. I'm driving."

One by one, we shrugged on our own coats and disappeared after her.

I fell into a dreamless sleep on the way there. The next time I opened my eyes I was curled into a chair. I rubbed my temples in slow circles, trying to get my bearings. My body was stiff and exhausted. I sat up, my muscles groaning against the movement, and looked around.

I was in the weapons room.

So were Lacy, Zeera, Rain, and Trader.

And Kit. Kit, too.

A surge of anger went through my tired limbs. He'd left me at Trader's to come here with Rain. What could be so important that Kit would agree to do anything with someone he hated that much?

Trader was tapping away on the little tablet he'd brought with him from his house, but everyone else had their eyes glued to the monitor that showed the girl.

Kit, in particular, seemed fascinated by it.

I got out of the chair to go and join them, my legs unsteady.

Rain was the first one to notice I was awake. "Skylar," he said, when he turned and saw me there. "I was starting to worry."

I shrugged. "I'm fine," I said, but this was a lie. The pain in my body warred with my confusion about Kit's actions. I left Rain and went and stood next to Kit now, but he didn't look at me, or refused to. A sickening feeling gnawed at my stomach.

His eyes were all for the girl up on the screen.

I stared from Kit to the girl and back to Kit again.

"Oh," I gasped, in sudden understanding.

Kit turned to me then, as though he'd just realized I was standing there. "Skylar," he said, his voice strangled. He blinked his eyes quickly, and a tear fell down his cheek as he told me what I'd just figured out without a shadow of doubt. "It's Maggie up on that screen."

35

Skylar

the bad news

"KIT, I'M SO sorry," I told him, and reached out for his hand right as Maggie disappeared from the screen. "My sister . . ." I trailed off, at a loss for words to describe the things my sister did.

"It's one thing to know that Maggie is a prisoner and it's another to have to see it, live," he said, and went back to watching the screen.

But before he did, he wasn't able to hide the helplessness in his eyes.

Lacy smirked as she took this in, Kit and I together, our fingers intertwined. "I'm the one who figured it out," she said to me. She sounded accusatory, like I hadn't done my job by realizing this girl was Kit's twin any sooner. "Didn't I, Rain?" she added, and went and pressed herself against him, resting her head on Rain's shoulder with a smile.

And wasn't Lacy right? Shouldn't I have known? I'd seen Maggie's picture at Kit's cottage. Now that I'd made the connection, the resemblance was obvious.

I tried to catch Rain's eyes, wondering what he thought about all of this, but he was avoiding my gaze. Then I glanced at the monitor showing the Body Market, almost hoping to find I was wrong, that Maggie was there instead, as if that would be a better fate somehow than being Jude's prisoner, but the screen had gone dark.

Zeera's eyes went to the same place. "Yeah. We lost that feed."

Something in me tightened with worry. "You can't get it back?"

She shook her head. "Not so far."

I swallowed. "That's not good, is it?"

"It's not ideal, no."

I turned my attention to the monitor that showed Maggie again, waiting for another sign of Kit's sister, or even for a sign of mine. For the longest time, there was nothing. Lacy fidgeted, but Rain stayed silent, while Zeera and Trader worked quietly together. Then out of nowhere, a girl darted across the screen, blond hair flowing behind her.

Kit hissed next to me, a sharp intake of breath. "Maggie?"

Zeera joined us.

We waited for Maggie to appear again.

When she did, it was like she knew we were watching, like she could sense her brother was waiting there. She walked straight up to the camera and stared directly into the lens. Directly at us. Maybe she'd just discovered it. She looked away, then at it once more, as though debating something. Then, she seemed to make a decision. She took a step back and dug around in her pocket before drawing out a small slip of paper. She held it up to the camera. On it she'd scrawled two words.

HELP ME.

"Where is she?" Kit asked in a voice that was strangled.

Zeera tapped frantically on her tablet. "I've been trying to pinpoint her location for days, but it's scrambled." She sighed and glanced over at Kit. "I don't have time to figure this out right now. I've got to get everything ready or else the Body Market will reopen without even an attempt at interference from us."

Rain nodded. "You've tried long enough," he said to Zeera. Then he turned to Kit. "After tomorrow is over we'll help you find your sister."

Kit's eyes went blank, like a shade pulled down to block out the light. "I'll find her myself." He wouldn't even look at me. "But I appreciate knowing she's alive," he added quietly, before turning and walking out of the room, leaving my hand empty and grasping.

I found him outside in the hallway. "I made you a promise and I'm going to keep it."

Kit was shaking his head. "Back at Trader's house, when you were plugged in, I decided that I can't ask you to." He looked at me fiercely now. "I'm never going to ask it of you, okay? Our deal is off."

My lips parted in surprise. "But—"

"You have enough to deal with," he said before I could finish. "You don't even know yet, do you?" There was a desperate quality to the look in his eyes.

"Know what?"

He pulled me back inside the weapons room and led me straight to Zeera. "Tell Skylar the bad news," he said.

Zeera looked like she was caught doing something she wasn't supposed to. She hurried to the other side of the room, checking on one of her other screens.

Kit called after her. "Tell Skylar the truth about what she's gotten herself into."

This must be the something Zeera had left out this morning. "Just say it, Zeera."

But it was Trader who started talking. "We ran into a problem, coding the Shifting App," he began. "Let's call it a power problem."

Zeera was wringing her hands. "More like a brain-power problem."

"What do you mean?" I asked.

"Well," Zeera went on, "the Shifting App will only work if you shift at the same time as everyone at the market. We, um, need your brain to run it."

I took this in and thought about it. It wasn't ideal, but it wasn't horrible. It would mean I wouldn't be awake when they got people out of the Body Market, but Rain and everyone else could handle things. The plan would still work. "So what you're saying is, I'll need to be plugged in to wake up the others. That doesn't seem so bad. There are plenty of plugs downstairs. Right here."

"Yes," Zeera said slowly.

Kit crossed his arms. "Somebody tell her the rest of it."

"Listen, sis." Trader stepped in once again. "What you said is correct, you need to be plugged in. But the really unfortunate part is that, for the App to function like you want, you know, for it to actually override the plugs the New Capitalists control in the market, you're going to have to be kind of close to the market."

I stared at Trader. "How close?"

Rain joined our group. "Inside the market itself," he said. "On one of the plugs in their network."

My mouth went dry. "But how—"

"We're going to have to swap one of the bodies so we can replace it with yours," Rain finished.

My head spun with the force of these implications. I grabbed the nearest chair and sat down. I thought I might vomit. "I need to be one of the bodies in the market?" I looked over at Zeera, who nodded. Why was it that whatever happened in this world, it somehow always involved me on display? Kit was tapping his foot, like he was waiting for them to keep going. "Just get the rest over with already," I said.

Zeera crouched down in front of me. She put her hands on my knees and peered up into my face. "You're going to have to wait to shift back as long as you possibly can. The second you wake up in the Real World again, the App will stop working. Anyone still transitioning will get left behind." She took a deep breath. "We're going to have an entire team monitoring you, ready to help get you out when everyone else is safe."

"There's no other way?"

"No," she whispered.

"And this is happening tomorrow, right?"

"That's when the market is slated to reopen, so yes," she confirmed.

Kit was glaring at Rain, like this was all his idea. Then to me he said, "You don't have to do this. It's too dangerous."

Rain shook his head. "Skylar can do this. She's been through worse."

Kit snickered. "What, now that you're dating someone else, you're willing to risk her life?"

"Hey, don't bring me into it," Lacy protested. "It wasn't my plan."

Kit eyed Trader. "Why can't you be the one to do it? You can shift, too."

Zeera stood. "That's the thing. I need Trader helping me orchestrate this. I can't do it without him." She sounded regretful. Guilty, too.

I pulled myself out of the chair. "It's okay," I told Zeera. "Really." I knew she always had Sylvia in the back of her mind and I wanted to reassure her, even as my own hope for survival wilted. Shifting had already taken such a toll on my body, and the worst of it was right when I woke up. If I was to be the last person left in the market, there was no way I'd get to safety. I'd end up back in the hands of my sister. I tried to laugh. "This was my idea, I may as well be the last one to clear out!" With the rise of my voice came more dizziness.

Rain's hand shot out to steady me. "You need something to eat." He looked around the weapons room. "We all do."

I nodded. Even after all this time, I still occasionally forgot that real bodies needed food. "Good idea." Kit walked over to the monitor again, his eyes watching for his sister to appear once more. "Do you want to come with us?" I asked him.

He shook his head, his forehead creased with worry.

I placed a tablet directly into his hand and curled his fingers around it. "This is for you, just in case you want to be in touch and we're not together."

He stared down at it.

I didn't wait for him to reply. Instead, I hurried to rejoin the others. We were already headed through the door when Kit called out.

"Don't leave without me today, Skylar," he said.

I turned back. Kit was looking at me, those eyes of his full of worry, his hand still curled around the device I'd given him. "I wouldn't dream of it."

When we got to the cafeteria, no one noticed me enter, and at first I felt a rush of relief. Even after months of living here, people's looks would linger a bit too long when I entered the room, or when I passed them by, their eyes shifting away from their plates and their lunch companions until they landed on my face.

But today, the mood had changed dramatically, and as I realized why, the relief drained away.

Gone was the laughter that darted between tables, gone was talk altogether. People seemed to have forgotten one another. The cafeteria was like a tomb for the walking dead, the silence only occasionally interrupted when two people crashed into each other, each one rubbing their knees or their elbows, their arms or their sides, barely looking up to see the object of their assault. Everyone had their heads bent over their tablets, their fingers *tap, tap, tapping* away. Their eyes were all and only for those little glowing screens, sending messages, I supposed. If they smiled, it was on behalf of whatever they saw happening in their palms. They seemed like they were in a trance.

When we'd first given people the devices, I remembered how everything grew quiet in the room, everyone suddenly engrossed by their tiny glowing displays.

"Don't worry," Zeera had said at the time. "It's just the initial fascination."

So when did that initial fascination wear off? Or did it ever?

Even when I ran into Adam while I was getting my food, his head was bent over his tablet. I wondered whom he could be messaging, since Parvda was just a little ways off, getting her drink.

I looked around nervously, then nudged him.

"Huh?" he said, distracted.

I elbowed him harder. "Adam!"

His head popped up and he blinked at me quickly. "Sorry. Skylar! What's up? You're awake again!"

"I am," I said, then added, "This is what's up," tapping the screen in his hand.

"Oh." He sounded sheepish. "Yeah, these are kind of addictive."

I lined up behind him to get some water. "I can see that. How's that going to affect tomorrow? We can't have people absorbed by what's in their hands instead of paying attention to what we're about to do."

Adam looked around, surveying the scene in the cafeteria. Then he nodded. "Don't worry."

"No?"

"They've gotten really good at using their tablets, really fast."

"Obviously," I said. "But what about the part of the plan where everyone has to deal with what's happening with the people around them?"

"I'm going to handle it myself this afternoon," Adam promised. "I'll call a meeting and make sure everyone knows what they're doing. No one's going to let anyone down, Skylar," he reassured me again, this time in a whisper. Everything was eerily quiet. "Least of all me," he went on. "If you're going to risk your life, everyone here is going to back you up. People will rise to the occasion."

I nodded, trying to convince myself this time. "I hope you're right."

At some point during lunch, a message from Kit appeared on my tablet.

Come stay with me at the cottage tonight.

For the rest of the afternoon, as meetings were held and plans were finalized, I considered his proposal. Maybe if things had been otherwise, if my role tomorrow was going to be different, if things weren't going to be so risky, I would have told Kit no, maybe another time. But this could be my last night in this world, or my last night of freedom, at least, depending on what happened at the Body Market. I thought about my almost-kiss with Rain last summer, how I'd held back—how we'd both held back—as though we would have all the time in the world after things slowed down. When really, it seemed, we'd missed our chance altogether.

In my mind, I conjured an image of Kit, his eyes, the intensity in the way he stared, those tattoos on his arms I'd grown to love, the sound of his voice and the touch of his hand in mine. I'd grown to love our long nights by the iron stove, talking, too. My heart fluttered and my body seemed to feel these memories everywhere.

I might've missed my chance with Rain.

But I didn't have to miss my chance with Kit.

So I found myself typing out three letters in response:

Yes.

36

Rain

responsible

THE SOUNDS OF the nearby ocean were deceptively soothing.

I stared down at my father, my hands balled into fists. Every time I came to visit, he seemed so peaceful, like he hadn't a care in the world, yet he was responsible for so much chaos and grief. *We* were responsible, my entire family, starting with my grandfather, Marcus, who split our world in two.

But a small part of me felt sympathy for Jude and her cause. However misguided, she was doing what she could to keep what was left of this Real World economy afloat, and the people who depended on it as well. Jude was simply taking advantage of the situation in which she found herself.

My father, in her position, would do exactly the same. I was certain of it.

Like always, I pressed my hand against the glass, and like always, this gesture made me imagine a life where my father was just this, *my father*. A time when the worlds never split, and where parents raised their children on love, teaching us to navigate the perils of life as safely as we could, kissing the cuts and bruises on our real bodies when they came about.

Longing rushed through me, like the waves outside this cavern.

It didn't have to be this way. It was only because families like mine had made it so, and acted as though they were saving everyone from hardship and pain, when really what they cared about most was power and control. My father and grandfather before him took advantage of people's appetite for the virtual and the division it caused. Instead of helping heal the discord and teaching people to navigate between the virtual and the real, they exploited it and pretended like they'd done something noble for the world.

I snatched my hand away and stood over my father.

What would happen if we took people like Jonathan Holt and Jude Cruz and Emory Specter *out* of power? Would people truly want a life without their bodies?

Would people truly not ever want to swim in the real ocean and walk on the real beach again? Could Apps ever replace the stuff of this world in a way that was satisfying enough to let go of this world altogether?

So many of us were never given a choice, not a real one.

And now, without bodies to come back to, the remaining plugged-in generation wouldn't even get the chance to think about a real life or a real future at all.

I opened the latch on the glass box and the top sighed open.

Then I slid the tablet that controlled the plugs in this room from my pocket and began to tap in the code I knew by heart.

And I waited. And watched.

Suddenly the pinkie finger on my father's left hand twitched slightly.

Skylar wanted to do an emergency broadcast to warn people what was happening in this world, to give them a choice of staying plugged in or reclaiming their bodies.

Well, my father was the king of the emergency broadcast.

I tapped in the next set of numbers.

I watched, now, as Jonathan Holt's foot shifted ever so slightly.

I kept tapping, one code after the other, noticing how his knee jerked a little, then his elbow. Being plugged in made a person so vulnerable, even someone like my father.

It was time to take him out of power, at least for a little while.

My fingers *tap, tap, tapped.*

He owed me that much. And he owed Skylar, too.

Suddenly, finally, Jonathan Holt heaved a great gasp.

His lungs rose and fell in ragged breaths.

I checked the time. By tomorrow morning he would adjust enough to be lucid.

Color flooded into his cheeks.

My father didn't know it yet, but he was about to help us do the most important emergency broadcast of everyone's lifetime, more important even than the one where he announced the borders had closed. What's more, I was ensuring that he didn't disrupt our plans once they were in progress.

I watched as his eyes fluttered open, waited until he seemed to focus, knowledge coming into his gaze— knowledge and recognition.

My father saw me. Finally.

That's when I spoke.

"Hi, Dad, it's been a while hasn't it?" I said.

And then I smiled.

37

Skylar

gestures

AS THE AFTERNOON waned, I watched the beginnings of my plan leap into motion. Adam and Zeera met with the seventeens to explain how the Shifting App would work. They would all be posing as buyers at the market, scattered throughout the real Body Tourists. After I made the emergency broadcast and bodies began to shift back to the Real World and awaken, everyone's job was to take advantage of the ensuing chaos and begin ushering people to safety. Messaging on the tablets was on a need-to basis only. And absolutely no gaming.

"We can't have you distracted," Adam kept emphasizing. "People could die if you're not paying attention. Skylar could die."

Everyone turned and looked at me.

As much as I wanted to, I didn't turn away. Tomorrow I would be at their mercy, as would so many other bodies. I needed them to see me, to remember the stakes. I was sitting there off to the side, listening to Adam and Zeera go over everything a second time, when Rain came into the room and beckoned me to follow. He led me to the other side of the mansion, where no one lived.

I eyed Rain with suspicion. "What's this about?"

"Just trust me," he said. "Please?"

I didn't respond. But when he opened the door I went inside after him, surprised to see my own Keeper standing there.

"Hi, Skylar," she said. Her eyebrows arched. "You seem . . . tired."

I hugged her fiercely. Her arms were a relief around me.

"I sent word to the Keeper that we'd need her help," Rain explained.

I looked from one to the other. "Help with what?"

The Keeper gestured toward the bedroom. "See for yourself."

Rain hovered close behind me as the two of us entered the room together, the light soft in the surrounding darkness. I nearly backed away the moment I saw who was there. A man lay in the narrow bed, far older than our years. His skin seemed to sag with the effort of existing.

I turned to Rain in shock. "Your father decided to unplug?"

Rain shook his head. "No. I decided for him."

"But why?"

Rain arranged two chairs next to the bed. "I worried if we surprised him, that he'd interfere with our plans. My father doesn't like to be left out of things." Rain sat down and I did the same. "But I also thought he could help us."

I looked at the man in the bed once again. I was used to seeing Jonathan Holt plugged in, his face always at peace, his body relaxed, as though his position as Prime Minister was his most natural repose. Here, his muscles seemed tense, his face exhausted. I wondered if he was having terrible dreams, still hovering in that surreal state between unplugging and waking up to this world. He seemed so vulnerable, his body on the verge of collapse. "How can he help us by being here?"

Rain's hands rested in his lap, but then he reached out, his fingers curling around the sheet near the place where his father's arm lay exposed. "By staying out of your way." Rain turned to me now. "Remember how when you shifted, you found many doors, not just one of them?" I nodded. "That gave me an idea. Forget about going to Trader's house. Tomorrow, when you shift, you should look for the door that leads directly to Jonathan Holt's office, the one in his house. Conjure it, Skylar. From there, we'll have all we need for the emergency broadcast."

My brow furrowed. "We?"

Rain seemed uncertain. "I'm planning on plugging in here at Briarwood and meeting you in the App World to help. I've watched my father do emergency broadcasts my entire life and know how to access his special downloads." His eyes sought the floor. "Also, I didn't want you to have to do this alone."

I was quiet a moment, taking this in. "Rain," I said eventually. "Thank you."

The trace of a smile appeared on Rain's lips. "I'm glad I could do something right."

I stared into Rain's sea-green eyes, waiting for my heart to run to him. When it didn't, I knew it was safe to say and do what I did next. I took his hand. "You do a lot of things right," I said, and then I smiled.

But when he smiled back I knew my gesture was a mistake.

There was hope in his expression.

I felt my heart falter a little inside my chest. I waited a beat, until it could right itself, and then I got up and walked out.

Tonight, like always before something big was about to happen, there was a party at Briarwood. This time, instead of a skating pond, there was a softly lit room that flickered with candles; the mood hushed, with occasional laughter breaking in through the quiet. It was already crowded when I arrived.

Adam stood at the door with a basket, collecting everyone's tablets.

People seemed reluctant to let them go. Some of the devices seemed stuck to their fingers and palms like glue.

"Zeera needs to upload them with the Shifting App," Adam explained to those who were so reluctant they resisted handing them in. "You'll get them back. Promise."

I walked up to him. "Isn't Zeera coming?"

He leaned in and whispered. "Yes, but I figured the party wouldn't be as fun if everyone was off in a corner on their own, tapping away." He nodded toward a table piled with food. "Parvda's over there if you want to say hello."

"I want," I said and headed her way.

She looked up from her plate. It was piled high with food. "You look pretty."

I laughed. "I can't decide if that was a compliment or an insult. You sound so surprised."

Parvda rolled her eyes. "Skylar, you're always beautiful, but tonight you look different."

"Different?"

"Yes," she said, drawing out the word. "Like you took care deciding on your outfit." She took the hem of my long top into her hands and inspected the fabric. "Since when do you wear shimmery blue silk?"

My cheeks grew hot. "Since tonight I guess," I mumbled. I dug through the bag over my shoulder for the thick gray winter sweater I'd stuffed inside for later. When I pulled it out Parvda stopped me.

"Don't put that on! Not yet." She took the sweater and put it back in the bag.

"I'm suddenly cold," I said.

She smirked. "You are not."

I scanned the room for Kit. I worried he wouldn't be able to tear his eyes from the monitor that showed his sister. I wouldn't blame him. I sighed when I didn't see him anywhere.

Parvda offered me her plate. "Are you nervous?"

I didn't take anything. The thought of food right now turned my stomach. "About tomorrow? Definitely."

She laughed. "I wasn't talking about tomorrow."

I followed her gaze toward the door and noticed Kit hovering just inside. When his eyes landed on me they brightened. "Parvda! Stop making me blush."

"I don't think it's me making you blush, Skylar." She nudged me. "Go talk to him." She got on her toes to whisper in my ear. "Tell him how you feel. You don't know what's coming tomorrow. Don't waste this chance."

I looked at her like she was crazy.

"Go, Skylar," she said, and gave me a gentle push.

I walked away from Parvda, her advice still ringing in my ears. When I reached Kit, I opened my mouth to ask him a question, but he put a finger to my lips before I could get any words out.

He shook his head. "No more talk of plans and sisters and rescue tonight. Okay?" He took his finger away.

I could still feel it there, pressed lightly to my mouth. "Okay," I whispered.

Kit shifted from one foot to the other. "I know it's early, but do you want to get out of here?"

Don't waste this chance, Parvda had said. I felt shy as I answered, "Yes."

"I'll go get the bike and meet you at the front door?" Kit asked.

I nodded. "See you in a few minutes."

Without another word, he slipped away.

I was on my way out, lost in the wonder of where this night might lead, when Lacy stepped out of nowhere and blocked my exit. She wore a slinky green dress that showed off her long freckled legs. I did my best not to compare my own outfit with hers. She always managed to seem glamorous, even in the Real World.

"Where are you off to?" she wanted to know. "This party's barely started."

"Lacy," I said tightly, stepping aside to move around her. "Why do you even care?"

She played with her shoulder strap. It was as thin as the sharp edge of a blade. "I just think you're being hasty. You're missing out on all the secrets this place is keeping."

I stopped midstride. "Secrets?"

Lacy smiled that wicked smile of hers. "Oh yes. Follow me."

I knew I shouldn't succumb, but I couldn't help myself. Lacy had me curious. At first I wondered if she'd take me to the room where Jonathan Holt slept, thinking I didn't already know he was awake, but I followed her to a part of Briarwood that I'd never visited before, that no one visited as far as I knew. We wound our way through a long dark hallway, and just as we arrived at the end of it, Rain stepped into our path.

"What are you doing?" The question seemed like it was aimed at both of us, but he only looked at Lacy.

The right strap of her dress slid down Lacy's shoulder and she smiled. "The party is boring. Skylar and I were just trying to spice up the evening a bit."

Rain's face flushed. "You should get back to it. We all should. I'll walk with you."

Lacy didn't budge. She glanced at me, then back at Rain. "Isn't there anything you want to tell Skylar before we go?" she hummed. "Or show her?"

Rain whispered angrily in her ear. I couldn't catch the words, just the tone of them. "No" was all I caught, his voice cold and hard.

My eyes shifted to Lacy, waiting to see how she responded. Disappointed when her only reply was a glare for Rain, I pulled the sweater from my bag, followed by my coat, and began to put them on. "Well, if there's nothing else, then I should be off." I took a deep breath. "Have fun at the party, and I'll see you at the meeting spot in New Port City, bright and early."

Surprise stormed Rain's eyes. "You're off where?"

I shrugged. "Don't worry. I promise I'll be there before dawn. I just need a little space to collect myself tonight."

"I wasn't worried about timing," Rain huffed.

Lacy stepped between us. "Then what were you worried about, darling? Skylar can take care of herself."

I shrugged the coat over my shoulders and started to walk away. "For once, I agree with you, Lacy. See you tomorrow in the App World, Rain," I called over my shoulder. Then I disappeared down another hallway before either one could say anything back.

38

Skylar

falling

KIT WAS WAITING for me outside, the motor on his bike cutting into the night and the distant roar of the waves. "I thought you might have changed your mind."

I shook my head. "Never."

He looked at me, a wry smile spreading across his face. It nearly made me forget all that was to come tomorrow. He slid backward a bit and tapped a hand on the seat in front of him. "Do you remember how to get there?"

My lips parted in surprise. Kit was offering to let me drive what I thought might be his most prized possession. "I do remember," I admitted. "But another time, another night," I said, passing on his offer. I longed to feel the smooth cold of his leather jacket against my cheek and

I was looking forward to the ride, to not having to be the one in charge. I was in charge of plenty tomorrow.

He nodded and slid forward again.

I got on and we took off.

As we drove away from Briarwood, away from Rain and Lacy, from the friends I'd made and the other seventeens from whom I still felt distance, my heart grew lighter, as though it could no longer be pinned down by gravity.

I clung tightly to Kit as we flew along the cliff because I wanted to be closer, to erase all of the space between us, and because I could never be close enough. I let my hands wander underneath his jacket until my fists closed around the soft fabric of his shirt. I buried my face in the back of his neck and let myself breathe him in. There was something about the dark and the cold and the tiny snowflakes gently falling around us that made it seem like we were the only two people left in this world. I felt wild and other, like a different Skylar had come to take my place, or maybe a dimension of myself that I'd just never met until now. But there she was and she was merging into me, and I welcomed her like a strange and unfamiliar App downloading into my body.

Kit wound the bike along the curves of the road and I leaned forward, watching his face in the mirror. He was smiling broadly now, and making no effort to hide it.

I nearly didn't feel the cold.

The cottage appeared ahead of us, a lonely and stark shadow against the night, its only companion the waves of the sea as they rushed in to the shore. Kit slowed as we approached the yard, and when we came to a stop, my heart was still flying. He put his feet on the ground to hold the bike steady and I swung my leg across the seat and slid to the ground. He parked next to the lone craggy tree, the branches gnarled and curling above him. The two of us hadn't said much since the afternoon, not in words, at least, but it felt as though a million things were passing back and forth between us nearly constantly. The sheer fact of our presence with each other right now was communication enough; the fact that I'd said *yes* to Kit's request, that I'd come back with him alone, because I wanted to and he knew this, said more than any words ever could.

There was a moment, a single fleeting instant, when I thought about Rain, when I remembered that evening on the beach when we almost kissed, just before I found out about the lies and the half truths and before everything else that happened between that almost-romance and today. As these thoughts flew through me and faded away, I realized I was glad that Rain's kiss never came.

I was happy my first real kiss was still ahead.

The wind whistled around the edges of the house.

Like always, Kit threw wood into the iron stove.

While he stoked the fire, I retrieved one of the bottles from under his bed and two short glasses from the cabinet. Soon we were sipping from them, but unlike before, we were standing, not sitting, each of us resting one hand on the kitchen counter, like we needed help holding our bodies upright. We talked about nothing and everything. We avoided tomorrow and spoke only of before and of days that lay far into the future, of worlds that used to exist and might never exist again. We talked until the hour grew late and the night tipped into morning.

Finally, there was a pause.

I ran my hand up his arm and stopped at his tattoos. I lifted his sleeve an inch, until I could see the beginnings of the night sky inked onto his skin. "Why stars?" I asked him. "Why birds?"

He pulled off his shirt and turned so I could better see the scene on his arm in the waning glow of the fire from the stove, the only light inside the cottage. He stared down at them with me. "I love the magic of the sky and everything in it. I love that it's magical but it's real. I don't need the virtual to find magic in the world." He looked up and caught my eye. "If you got a tattoo, Skylar, what would it be?"

I didn't have to think long before answering. I'd thought about this very thing ever since I'd first seen his. "A ringlet of waves around my upper arm. Or maybe around both of them. I love the water. I love to swim."

"Maybe you'll get one someday."

I was glad for the dark, that it hid my face, as I stood there, heart jumping and leaping, in front of this boy I'd known only a little over a week, yet it seemed like years had passed since the day we met. "Maybe I will," I agreed. "Maybe when I do, you'll come with me."

"I'd like that." He hesitated a beat, then spoke again. "My sister could do it. She was, *is* quite the artist. She's the one who did mine."

I held my breath at the mention of his twin, at this delicate revelation. "Tell me more."

"Even better, I'll show you." Kit took my hand and pulled me into his bedroom. He switched on a lamp and retrieved a box from underneath the bed. He sat down, prompting me to sit next to him. We were close, our legs pressed together. He lifted the cover from the box, revealing a series of thin bound books. He took one out and rested it between us. Opened it to the first page.

I gasped. The artistry was extraordinary, detailed and beautiful. But what surprised me most of all was the familiar people the book portrayed. I pointed to one of the panels. "That's Rain."

Kit nodded, staring down at the page. "My sister drew all sorts of chronicles about the famous people in the App World, Rain most of all. She spent her whole life dreaming of living there. Of plugging in. Of meeting someone like him."

I nearly laughed. "When I was a Single there, every girl I knew and plenty of the boys, too, dreamed the very same thing." I flipped ahead, took in the carefully sketched drawings, the imagined stories of the people I'd spent years watching on Reel Time with the rest of their voyeurs. "We'll get her back. And then we can introduce her to the real Rain Holt. Maybe it will make her want to stay in the Real World."

Kit looked up from the book. "I'm not sure I want her to stay if he's the reason."

I felt the warmth of his gaze and I raised my eyes to meet his. "Is that because of who Rain is or because of who he's been to me in the past?"

"The past? Is he, really?" Kit sounded surprised.

"Yes," I said.

There was a long stretch of quiet as I leafed through the book. Eventually I set it aside. "Your shoulder's healing." I peered at the thick red seam along his skin. It cut across the birds inked there.

He nodded. "I'll have a scar."

"I'm sorry," I said, and I was.

"I'm not," he said.

He looked at me with those bottomless eyes, dark lashes fanning out to frame them. I wanted to fall into them, to fall into him. My hand had its own plans, and it was reaching out, reaching up to brush the hair from his brow. He caught my fingers and wove them through with his own. Quickly, he brushed a kiss along my shoulder, his lips like feathers. My heart zipped and dipped through the air on filmy bee's wings. I wished I could catch it, hold it in my palm, soothe its restlessness, but it had taken flight outside my body. When our eyes met again, our mouths were close. I could feel Kit's breath, short, sweet bursts, that made me want to taste him.

Kissing in the App World was always a transaction of sorts.

You'd view the choices of partner, of kiss type and location, the length of time for the experience, the sort of mood you were going for. Boy and girl icons both vied for your attention, they flirted and played coy, until you settled on the one you fancied for the moment. Capital was exchanged, and the kissing session began. With an App you got exactly what you wanted, always the way you wanted it, and with enough capital you could download a parade of kisses, one partner after the other, trying out for the role of romantic ideal, until you settled on the one you liked best. Once Inara and I were old enough, like all thirteens we went through a kissing-obsessed phase, where our lips were nearly constantly purple and bruised, our minds in a fog of post-kissing delirium. But no amount of downloaded kisses could have ever prepared me for what it would be like to kiss someone for real.

To kiss Kit for real.

To feel the first soft press of his mouth against mine,

for the way our lips would part and our breaths would mingle; for the way I would feel his fingertip running down my arm as though he was touching all of my skin at once; for what it was like to kiss someone until I was no longer in control and I no longer cared; or for how not knowing what would happen next could be thrilling. Kit kissed me until my mind no longer mattered, until I was all body, all skin and bone and flesh and beating heart. He kissed me until I was sure that I was real, that I'd always been real, that I'd never been more real, that I was meant to be real and not virtual ever again. And when he pressed me back into the soft blankets on the bed, I found that it was exactly what I wanted. As he kissed a trail down my throat and across the soft skin of my neck and I lost the power of speech, I found other ways to communicate, marveling at the entirely new language of sighs and moans and touches and laughter that my body seemed to know instinctively.

Love was a miracle we could not catch. It lived in the ether like the sweet smell of pollen, it dwelled in the highest eaves we could never reach, and it swam in the deepest crevices of the ocean.

But sometimes, when we were lucky, love settled like gold dust onto the skin of the body and made us shine like not even the latest, most glorious App ever could. It nestled inside of us like a lazy, sleeping kitten, like it might never rise or find any other place so comfortable as us. Sometimes love made our bodies its home, maybe not forever, but at least for a while, and through the meeting of seeking fingers and the touching of lips and hands that wandered here and there we could breathe love in like it was air, let it melt onto our tongues like it was sweet, sweet ice cream, let it wash over our bodies like a warm summer's rain. At least for a time. At least as long as it lasted.

For this, we were alive.

For this, one day we would die.

For this, fear and fragility and impermanence existed.

For this, bodies were worth keeping, despite everything.

These were the thoughts that bloomed in every part of me when, in the very early hours of the morning, Kit and I finally, after all this time, drifted off to sleep.

39

Kit

trade

WHEN I WOKE up, she was gone.

Skylar was gone.

My heart lurched. We didn't even say good-bye.

I dragged myself out of bed and got dressed. For a long time, I stood in my kitchen, trying to warm myself, unable to stop shivering. Guilt bloomed like a gunshot wound throughout my chest.

Was I really going to do this?

I went to my room and opened the drawer where I kept my shirts, digging around underneath them until I came up with what I wanted. My sister stared up at me from the photo. I slipped it into the pocket of my jeans. When

I went to retrieve my winter jacket, I noticed a tiny note gently balanced on top of the doorknob. I picked it up.

I love you, Kit. Skylar

I stared and stared at those words. I stared until a strip of light the color of rust streaked the horizon and my heart started beating again in my chest. I should've left thirty minutes ago. I eased the note into the same pocket as the picture. Then I walked out the door into the freezing cold and started up my motorcycle. Riding wasn't the same without Skylar, I thought to myself, as I took off along the sea.

I knew exactly where to go.

I'd known all along.

I parked my bike in an alley, walked right up to the front door, and knocked.

Jag answered immediately. He stood there, nearly as big as the doorway, staring at me with cold eyes. "What do you want?"

"I've come to free my sister," I said, unflinching.

He laughed, but not kindly. He pretended to look behind me. "I don't see the merchandise. No merchandise, no trade."

Was I really going to do this? I asked myself again. *After last night?*

I took a deep breath, and let it out. Then I spoke the words I'd never be able to take back. "I have information to barter with," I told Jag. "Information about a rebellion Skylar is leading."

Jag laughed again, this time in disbelief. His thick body shook with it. "What makes you so special she would tell you her plans?"

I dug in my pocket and produced the note.

Jag read it.

He stopped laughing and stepped aside.

I didn't need any more of an invitation. Without another word, I walked through the doorway and into the darkness behind him.

40

Skylar

false starts

WE MET BEFORE dawn in an abandoned building just outside the Body Market. The nearby hotel was a looming shadow against the dark sky, the glass windows reflecting the lingering moon. My group consisted of Adam and Parvda, two seventeens, both girls I'd only met once before, and Trader.

He eyed me as I propped my bicycle against the wall. "Nice wheels."

"I like them," I said, slipping the hood from my head.

Trader gave me a knowing look. "There's something different about you this morning."

Red crept up my neck to my face. I did my best to cover it up. "Risking one's life will change a girl."

Trader put an arm around me and pulled me close, with an affection that surprised me. "I'm not going to let anything happen to you today."

I looked up into his black eyes. For once, they were sincere. "I actually believe you."

"Good, because it's true," he said quietly.

Everyone gathered together, and I learned that the other seventeens' names were Shereese and Niki. They'd just come back from scouting the best way into the market.

Niki checked her tablet. Her long braids brushed her shoulders. "The market opens in fifteen minutes for viewing, but the bidding and buying don't start until ten a.m. That gives us three hours."

Shereese was the tallest person here. She towered over everyone, all lean muscles and sleek limbs. "We think the best way in is through the side entrance. It won't be as busy as the front one, but it will have enough activity that we can blend in. Then we'll head to the spot we picked out underground for you."

"They seem to have a storage space of sorts," Niki said, picking up where Shereese left off. "There are a few spare plugs, I guess you could say, which makes our job easier since we don't need to kick anybody else out."

I nodded, but the idea of "spare plugs" worried me. "Are they spare plugs or are they empty ones, because the bodies were already sold?"

Shereese shrugged. "Could be, but we don't have time to worry about that." She glanced at her tablet. "We've got to get moving."

Trader grabbed a black bag off the ground and said something to Parvda. Everyone began to file out of the building into the cold dark streets, but Adam hung back.

"You okay?" he asked.

I shrugged on the hood of my coat, pulling it around my face. "I'm fine. I just wonder what this morning will bring."

"Well, let's go see," he said.

The two of us slipped into the darkness with the others.

The Body Market was just as I remembered it.

Lush red carpet. Gleaming glass. Guards everywhere, eyes vacant, though I was certain they were watching. Even this early in the morning there was an air of excitement, Body Tourists from all over the world streaming inside, speaking so many different languages, eager to start the buying that brought them here, dressed and ready for the market to reopen.

My stomach churned, taking it all in.

We moved through the aisles with the rest of the crowd, winding our way down below. I followed Shereese and Niki, and Adam, Parvda, and Trader hung back. The sheer number of bodies around us was enormous. There must be tens of thousands. Shereese and Niki led me to a door in the far corner of one of the lower floors, nearly hidden in darkness. We looked around to make sure no one was watching us and went inside.

There were glass coffins with nothing in them, save the cradle for plugging in.

"You ready, Skylar?" Niki asked, all business.

I took a deep breath and nodded. Shereese popped open the latch and I climbed inside, setting my arms and legs gently into the rests. Maybe Rain was doing the very same thing right now out at Briarwood. It was a relief to think he would meet me once I got to the App World, that I wouldn't be all alone today. I was just laying my head back when Trader and everyone else came through the door. But the second my head hit the cradle, a wave of exhaustion flowed through me, followed by shards of fear and doubt.

Should I have gone straight to bed last night? Or was it simply the upcoming task of shifting that sapped my body of its energy?

Trader stared down at me, tablet in hand. "It's time, Skylar."

"I know," I replied, my voice hoarse. Then I took a deep breath. "I want this over with."

Trader nodded and attached a sensor to the underside of the headrest, the one that tracked my brain waves and would amplify the power of the App. Without waiting for him to tell me we were ready or that I could go, I closed my eyes.

My last thought was of Kit, his face, his eyes, his mouth so close to mine.

And then I fell under.

I stood on a cliff.

Snow was falling. Lightly. Gently.

I put out my hand and waited for the cold specks to melt against my skin. The cool and ice in my palm made me smile. When I looked up again, the snow fell harder, so hard it was like a blizzard, a harsh wind searing through my thin clothing, sleet pelting my face.

I searched and searched through the driving snow.

Wanting him to appear.

The faint outline of a boy took shape, not far away.

I pushed against the wind and the ice, trying to get to him.

The moment I got close, he disappeared.

My heart hurt so much it left a hole in my chest.

I put my hands to my face.

My cheeks were wet, soaked, I thought from the snow.

But then I realized they were streaked with tears.

I opened my eyes.

I tried to sit up.

I couldn't.

My wrists and ankles were tied down.

I was lying flat, on a soft red carpet. I could feel the cushion of it along my spine, at the back of my legs and underneath my shoulders. I yanked hard with my hands but it was no use. I couldn't break free.

That's when I heard the whispering. At first, I couldn't hear what was being said or who was saying it. Then I began to hear bits and pieces.

Bid . . . pricey but . . . how much? . . . sister . . . so many uses for a body like that.

My head throbbed, my limbs cried out. Everything hurt from the strain of listening, from the strain of fighting against the bonds that held me tight to the ground. I was able to budge only enough so I could shift my face toward all those whispering voices.

An enormous crowd looked back at me.

Hundreds. Maybe thousands.

They hushed as they met my gaze.

The blood rushed through me, loud in my ears.

The Body Market. I am being sold on the Body Market.

I'd failed. *Failed.* My sister won and this was my punishment.

Then someone in the crowd began to call my name. Again and again.

"Skylar! Skylar!"

They yelled, they chanted.

My name, again and again, and I was powerless to do anything.

Trapped.

About to be sold.

I started to scream.

Air, I couldn't get any air.

Then a burst of it filled my lungs and I gasped it out like it was water trying to drown me. My throat was raw, everything was raw. My skin and my muscles felt battered. My eyes flickered open.

"Sis?" Trader looked down at me. His eyes were worried.

"Is it over?" I croaked. Pain shocked my brain. I saw stars, my vision streaked with colorful lightning, followed by the hot burning pink of sunset. Trader didn't speak. Instead he placed his tablet before me so I could see the time. Only ten minutes had passed. There was an urgent message on the screen from Zeera. I lifted my head. Shereese and Niki were whispering to each other in the corner. "What happened?"

"I don't know. Your body, your brain . . . maybe this is too much for it to handle. This is the third time you've tried to shift in just a couple of days. I've never even done that."

Adam appeared at my feet. "Maybe we should message

everyone that there's been a change of plans."

"It would have to be that our plans are over," Trader said.

"No," I protested. "No way. Let me try again. Maybe it was just a false start."

Adam was shaking his head. "Skylar, you could get hurt. I knew this was a bad idea. You could be damaging your brain."

I laid my head back against the rest, blinking up at the ceiling. "I don't care. Tell Zeera everything is fine." I squeezed my eyes shut. By now I knew how this worked, so before anyone could tell me not to, once again, I fell under.

I stumbled along the shore, kept stumbling, tripping over rocks and slipping on kelp, the world spinning.

Why couldn't I stop spinning?

The sky was a strange shade of yellow, so bright it hurt my eyes. There was a terrible smell in the air. I sniffed at it. Rotting fish. I kept pushing forward along the cluttered beach, but it seemed I was going in circles. I was lost.

And this was an island.

My entire body was exhausted. I wanted to lie down on the beach and go to sleep.

But wait . . . I'd been here before.

I looked at the tall trees at the center of everything, and as I did, it started to rain. There was something I needed to remember, something pushing at the edges of my brain, wanting my attention.

Inara, went a whisper, somewhere deep inside of me.

I went plowing through the brush, shaking away the water soaking my hair, my face, until I made it to the clearing. There, underneath the biggest tree, sat Inara, just as I remembered from Odyssey.

"What are you doing here?" I asked. "Am I dreaming?"

She looked up. "Skylar, I need you." She blinked her big eyes. "Come and find me beyond the room with the doors."

The room with the doors, repeated my mind.

My brain suddenly lit up, and so did the sky.

The rain stopped, the sun came out, and the landscape began to change.

I was walking through a dream and I needed to take control of it. And when I did, I'd find my way into the App World.

The App World. I'm going to the App World.

That's what I needed to remember.

Cool relief showered my tired mind, my tired limbs.

Just before the landscape could shift away, I looked at Inara. "Don't worry. I'll be there soon," I told her.

This time, when I walked forward, I did so without stumbling, I did so with full awareness of why I was here. I walked and walked, watched the sky as it changed colors and the ground as the sand gave way to a narrow street, which eventually became a floor that looked like it was made of wood. Soon, tall walls rose up around me.

I'd found the room with the doors.

Once more, there was a different number. I was prepared for this, but what I wasn't prepared for was how different in number they'd be.

There were too many to count. Hundreds. Maybe thousands.

Door upon door upon door.

A fun house of doors that wasn't fun at all.

Was my mind playing tricks? How in both worlds would I find the door to Jonathan Holt's office? My heart sped, panic clawing at my insides, and the doors seemed to multiply as I stood there watching. I ran from one to the other and the next, doors of all colors and sizes, doors made of concrete, of wood, of soft thatched grass, of glass, and even one of storm clouds. I turned this way, then that, dizzy and lost.

All over again, I was losing my grip on the dream.

I halted, midfrenzy, closed my eyes, and took a deep breath. Focused on the one door I needed, Jonathan Holt's office door.

You can do this, Skylar.

When I opened them again, the endless doors were still everywhere around me, but they were blurry and out of focus. All except for one.

Straight ahead, I saw a door that was remarkably

familiar. It was metal, maybe steel, and looked as thick as the door that led to a vault. As thick as the door that led to the weapons room at Briarwood. In fact, it looked exactly like the weapons room door. I shook my head. I bet Marcus Holt had designed both. He'd built a weapons room for himself in the Real World and then duplicated its design in his new and improved virtual one. People were predictable. They might cede an entire life and their bodies with it for the promise of a virtual existence, yet then spend so much of that virtual existence trying to get back what they once had in the Real World they'd left.

I went to it now and placed my hand against the cold smooth metal. Closed my eyes, concentrating, then pushed hard.

The heavy door swung open.

A rush of cold air like winter met me on the other side. I stood in the threshold a moment between worlds, between the dreamy land where the shift took place and the virtual reality that lay on its other side. I extended my arm across the border, marveling at the way I immediately changed once I reached the App World. The part of me that remained in the room with the doors still had the same golden-brown skin I'd grown used to on my real body. That part of me was flush with color and life. Whereas the arm I'd extended into the App World lost its color altogether. It was faded and pale, the basic virtual self always awaiting the magic of an App.

As I stood there, my head began to throb.

Maybe the body, regardless of its makeup, didn't like being suspended between worlds. I took one last look at the part of me still vibrant with color and then shut the door to Jonathan Holt's office behind me.

I was in.

I looked around.

Where was Rain?

The Prime Minister's office was enormous but uncluttered. A large imposing desk was placed at one end of it, a long table with chairs in the middle, but otherwise, it was empty. Sleek but lonely. The room seemed designed to have the qualities of a basic virtual self, so it could show off the presence of the latest in Apps. One entire wall was made up of floor-to-ceiling windows, and I went to them, stalling, hoping Rain would appear soon. The Water Tower stood directly outside, blue and moving, so like the real one, but now I could see differences that gave this one away as just a copy, the way the edges of the building curled ever so slightly, the color of it exceedingly bright, every detail exaggerated just enough that someone with a careful eye would know that what they were seeing wasn't reality.

Maybe this was one of the dangers of the Real World.

If you spent too much time there, you'd begin to see the cracks in this one.

Voices floated up from the ground below.

I strained to see where they came from.

A parade of people walked alongside the park.

Protests? In this tony part of town?

Time to focus, I reminded myself.

Rain had yet to arrive, but I couldn't wait any longer. I turned away from the windows and went to the place in the wall he'd told me about, where Jonathan Holt's personal App Store was hidden. It looked like nothing was there. Just gray, cold concrete.

But I did as Rain instructed and got closer.

And there it was.

It almost looked like a glitch in the atmosphere, a round blurry hole just big enough for a finger. I touched it, then stepped back to wait.

Slowly, an icon appeared far behind the wall, like a fish swimming up to the surface of the ocean, rippling the water as it rose, getting bigger as it got closer. Closer and closer it came, until finally it burst into the room and hovered in front of me.

It didn't look like much.

A small red cube. It could be anything.

It emitted a soft hum. The hum got louder the longer it floated in front of me. At first, it was tolerable, but eventually the hum got so loud I thought my head might burst from the noise, so loud it was screeching, so loud that there was nothing else I could do but download it in the hopes that the noise would stop.

So that's what I did.

The moment I reached for it the horrible hum disappeared and the Emergency Broadcast App flowed into me. There was the familiar icy feeling seeping through my code, but this download was unlike any other I'd experienced. My mind seemed to expand suddenly, my entire being did, really, but in the end, my eyes were the most affected.

The App made it so that I saw differently.

I could see . . . everything.

The entire world, the City as a whole.

Each blink had me in a new place, a new living room, a new breakfast table, a new room in a building or spot in Main Park. At first it was dizzying and I couldn't control it. I blinked and blinked and flew from one place to the other, confused and lost, the startled faces of citizens blinking back at me, then disappearing, replaced by others. At one point I opened my eyes and found myself face-to-face with Sateen, a Single I thought I'd never see again. She only managed a single syllable, "Skye—," her voice thick with shock, before I'd moved on, my virtual self still there in her presence, but my eyes elsewhere.

I was everywhere and nowhere at once.

I had to slow down. Catch my breath. I was sick, I would break apart with it, my virtual self wasn't coded to contain so much, to see so much at the same time. I closed my eyes, pressing my lids tightly to my cheeks, trying to block out the many images, the way they flew by, one after the other. I concentrated on breathing, one slow breath after the other. In. Out.

In. Out.

Then, suddenly, I felt a hand gripping mine, steadying me.

Grounding me, like an anchor.

At first I thought I was imagining it, but then I looked down and there it was. I focused on it, focused hard, like my whole life depended on hanging on to this particular vision. When I felt ready, when the world stopped spinning so quickly, I let my eyes travel up the arm and then to the shoulder and the familiar face attached to the hand woven through mine.

I gasped. Rain had joined me in the broadcast. "You made it," I whispered, my voice hushed.

His big blue eyes were sincere. "Sorry I'm late. And don't worry, they can't hear us yet."

I swallowed. My code stopped racing, slowing enough that I gained control of my vision, and the dizzy feeling of my mind expanding to encompass an entire world began to dissipate, the vertigo of it fading, and I could breathe normally again. "I'm glad you're with me," I added, because this was true. I *was* relieved, I *was* grateful, I was something else, too, something I refused to name, now, at least.

"Are you ready?" he asked.

I nodded.

"I'll start," he said. He pressed his fingers against his throat as though turning on his voice, then stood tall, like the son of the Prime Minister everyone knew him to be, the prince of this world finally returned. He looked out over the living rooms and the people of the City alongside me. "Citizens of the App World," Rain began. "As most of you know, my name is Rain Holt, and I was left on the other side of the border while doing my Service. I will return there, once this broadcast is over, but my father has authorized me to speak to you now, and to cede this message to someone with important information affecting the fate of everyone in this City. Please give her your undivided attention," he finished.

Then Rain looked at me.

It was my turn to speak.

So I took a deep breath, and I started to talk.

"Good morning," I began. "My name is Skylar Cruz. None of you have reason to know me. When I lived in this world I was a Single. But I ask for your ear, because I have important news, maybe the most important news of your virtual existence. Very soon, in the next hour, you are going to be asked to make a choice, a choice that could change everything about your future."

I paused and focused a minute on a living room where a family of four was in the middle of breakfast. They sat there, all of them holding hands, the two mothers blinking up at me with worry in their eyes. Then I switched scenes until I came upon a girl not much younger than me, alone in the corner of a broken-down house in what might be Loner Town. I switched again until I was in the common room of Singles Hall, a crowd of Singles staring up at me, so many of their faces familiar. A pang of regret, of loss, of missing the life I once led here sparked through my code. I let it run through me and then I continued on, my eyes going from one Single to the next as I spoke.

"Your bodies are in danger. You've all been told that the Race for the Cure has been won, that your bodies are being disposed of so you can live here in virtual eternity. But what you've been told about your bodies is a lie. A political group of former Keepers that call themselves the New Capitalists will not be disposing of your bodies, they'll be *selling* them, some for parts, some so that new minds and personalities can be downloaded into them, some for uses we can't even know just yet."

I let my attention shift again, this time in a way that was directed, until I was looking into the eyes of Mr. and Mrs. Sachs, hovering over their familiar dining room table just as Jonathan Holt had so many months ago. I faltered a bit as I saw their tired, frightened faces, the trace of anger in Mr. Sachs's eyes. To him, I'd betrayed their family. I wanted to reassure them about Inara, that I would get her to safety. Instead, I readied myself to finish the broadcast, Rain's closeness a comfort, helping me forward.

"Many of you may not care whether your bodies are sold or disposed of. But many of you may want to protect your body. If this is the case, listen carefully. The choice you are going to have to make is to stay here, plugged in, or to unplug and come back to the Real World. In the next few minutes an App is going to appear to each and every citizen of this City. You are free to ignore it, but if you care about the future of your body, you must download it. It's called a Shifting App. Once you touch it, it will allow you to transition out of this world and back into your bodies. You'll fall into what feels like a dream, and in the dream you will cross through one door that leads you out of the App World. On the other side of it you'll immediately see another, and this one will take you into the Real World. We have people waiting to help you to safety once you wake up." I took a deep breath. *Almost there.* "It's your choice. I wish you luck with this decision. I wish there was more time for you to make it." I glanced back at Rain, who nodded. "Thank you for listening," I finished.

Then the Emergency Broadcast App drained away.

I blinked.

The first thing I saw now was the view out the windows, the Water Tower stretching high into the atmosphere, a shimmery blue against the pink and orange of the morning. I was back in Jonathan Holt's office and a relief like static crackled around me. I looked around for Rain, but he wasn't there. *Where could he have gone?* I sat down in one of the chairs at the long table at the center of the room, to wait things out until it was time to shift back into the Body Market and, hopefully, find my own way to safety.

Then I heard a noise behind me.

"Rain?" I called out.

No answer.

A chill walked itself up my virtual spine and, slowly, I turned around.

There was Jude, standing in the doorway, staring at me.

A virtual Jude.

And next to her was Emory Specter.

41

Rain

like daughter, like mother

WHEN I CAME to in the Real World, a pair of familiar blue eyes blinked down at me, and for a moment, my heart surged.

Then I remembered. "Mariela," I said. "You pulled me out too soon."

Skylar's mother helped me up from the cradle where I'd plugged in at Briarwood. I curled my fingers around the edge of the glass box, the same one where my father had lain only the day before.

"How is she?" Mariela asked, concern darkening her expression.

I tried to get up, but the world started to spin. I gripped the glass harder, trying to hang on to something solid and get my bearings again. Eventually, my vision steadied. "She's fine at the moment. You would have been proud to hear her speak."

The trace of a smile ghosted Mariela's lips. "I'm sure."

I was about to say something else when I noticed the tablet, *my* tablet, sticking up from the pocket of Mariela's sweater. "How long was I out?" I asked her carefully.

Her eyes slid away from mine. "A while. A couple of hours."

I reached out and took the tablet back. Mariela tried to grab it from me but I held it away. I brought up the messages, but there were none. They'd been erased. "What have you done?" I asked her.

"Nothing," she said.

I studied her. "I don't believe you."

"You can believe whatever you want."

"Tell me," I pleaded. "Who have you been talking to?"

"It doesn't matter. All that matters is that my daughter will be safe."

"Mariela—"

"You love her, don't you?" she asked.

I gaped at her.

Her eyes narrowed. "You do, don't you?" she pressed.

"Yes," I admitted. "But—"

"—then stop worrying and let me plug you back in." When I hesitated, Mariela's eyebrows arched. "I'll answer your questions after this is over. Right now you need to focus on Skylar. Think of how happy she'll be when you reveal that you've found me."

I took this in. "You're willing to see Skylar now?"

"Yes," she said.

Suspicion flared. "What changed?"

She looked away. "Can't a mother simply want to see her daughter?"

"Nothing is simple in your family. Or mine, for that matter."

Mariela turned back, her eyes shiny with tears. "Please, Rain."

"All right. Questions later. But I won't forget them," I added. And then I slid back into the cradle and closed my eyes.

42

Skylar

truce

I STARED AT Jude and Emory in shock.

He was the same as I'd always remembered, not too tall, eyes cold and calculating, body tense, like it was ready to spring. A smug smile played at his lips. He wore a suit, every inch the Defense Minister. The only difference now was that I knew he was my father. But the virtual Jude was strange to take in. She was Jude, but she wasn't. Gone was the golden color of her skin, replaced by the pale basic hue of Caucasian 4.0, her dark hair reduced to a faded brown, limp and straight around her face. Her eyes, though, were the same eyes as ever, a shade lighter blue than mine, big and familiar, but without a trace of the warmth I'd grown used to as a small child, before everything about our worlds and lives changed.

Warning signals shot through my code.

I stood quickly, knocking over the chair I'd been sitting in.

The crash of it on the floor made me jump.

Jude and Emory looked at each other and chuckled.

They're enjoying this.

Rage replaced the fear, and I looked at my hands, saw the red tinge that flowed over them, satisfied by it. The virtual Jude couldn't hurt me, not in any lasting way. And it was the same for Emory Specter. I had nothing to fear, not really. But then, faraway voices began whispering through my mind.

Hurry. This way.

I'm frightened!

Are we really going to do this?

There, there! There it is.

The App. The App was already downloading throughout the bodies in the market and through every single virtual person.

My body is my body . . .

Why should we trust a lowly Single?

What if this kills us in both worlds?

I tried to shake away the voices, but they pressed into my brain like the footprints of tiny mice, slight but urgent. I conjured a door in my mind and walled them off, but I could tell that it wouldn't last long. It shook even now.

Emory was looking between Jude and me with something like pride. "It heartens me to know I have such ambitious children, even if those ambitions are sometimes at odds."

I hated him and I gaped at him now. How could our genes be shared? "Sometimes?"

He stood there appraising me. "Well, we all certainly share a desire for power, even if only two of us openly acknowledge this." His gaze shifted to Jude as he said this.

"I'll never call you Father," I said.

He narrowed his eyes. "Good. I don't like acknowledging Singles trash in the family, so I'd prefer it if you didn't, at least not in public. But privately?" That smug smile returned to his face. "Honestly, I can see so much of myself in you."

I turned away from him in disgust.

Jude walked up to a chair at the table and sat down, all business. "I've come to make you a deal."

My lips parted. "What?"

"I'd like to negotiate a truce."

I crossed my arms. Jude's words didn't match her tone, which sounded bitter. "Are you sure that's what you want?"

"No," she said. "But I'm tired of warring with you and all the others. I'd like to salvage what I can." Jude sighed deeply. "That App of yours is already wreaking havoc."

My lips parted in surprise. "How did you know about

that? How did you know I'd be here, for that matter?"

Emory eyed me. "It turns out that not everyone on your 'side' is actually on your side."

I stared at him straight on, like this didn't matter, and busied myself righting the chair I'd knocked over so I could sit while my brain raced at the thought that someone in the Real World could have betrayed us to Jude. "Tell me your terms for this truce," was all I replied.

"I'll leave you two sisters alone to negotiate," Emory said. He turned on his heel and walked out.

Just like that, like I didn't matter at all, like he couldn't care less that his daughter was sitting right in front of him, for the first time aware of their relationship.

"He's right, you know," Jude said. Her voice was soft. Sad even.

I studied her in surprise. "About what?"

"You're ambitious, Skylar, and you've become powerful, even if you don't like to think about yourself that way. We're more alike than not."

I huffed. "If I am powerful, it's only because you put me in this position."

She shook her head. "Maybe that's how it was at first, but it isn't that way anymore." She placed her hands on the table. Flipped them over and stared at her smooth pale palms. "I love it in the App World." She chuckled. "Maybe I'll retire here and someone in the Real World can profit from my old, withered body."

I stared at her, mouth hanging open. One minute Jude was regal, untouchable, and the next she was someone who seemed vulnerable and human, showing me a glimpse of the sister I'd longed for all those years as a Single. "Jude, what's going on?"

"Ever since the night of the fire, I've been plugging in." She wouldn't look at me. "Here, I'm whole again. Here, my face is perfect."

Now it was my turn to avert my eyes. "I'm sorry," I whispered. "I really am. It wasn't my intention . . . to . . . to . . ."

"To disfigure me?" Jude asked, finishing the thought for me. "Well, you did."

I forced myself to look into my sister's virtual face and then I spoke the thought out loud that had crossed my mind on more than one occasion since that terrible night. I did my best not to sound accusing. "Why don't you avail yourself of your own market? Take advantage of all those 'natural resources,' as you put it, to help yourself?"

Jude cocked her head, studying me. "What, an eye for an eye, Skylar? Is that what you're suggesting?"

"I'm not suggesting it, I'm just—"

"I did consider it," she cut in. "Believe me. But in the end, I couldn't do it."

I looked at her in surprise. "Why not?"

"I know you think I'm a horrible person, but while I'll certainly take advantage of the selfishness and foolishness of citizens of the App World for the benefit of New Port City, like I said before, I don't want to be at war with you." Jude spread her pale hands on the table, pressing down. "It feels wrong. And while I'm not accepting total defeat, I know when I need to meet the other side at least halfway."

I searched my sister's face, and all I saw in it was sincerity. Regret. Sorrow. I reached out and placed my hand next to hers, our fingers nearly touching. "I don't think you're horrible. Sometimes I can see so clearly that you're not. Or at least, that you don't want to be."

A single tear sparkled brightly on her pale cheek, and the atmosphere between us grew heavy with mist. "So you believe me?"

I hesitated. Did I? "I don't know," I admitted. "The Body Market is wrong, no matter how you try and spin it, and nothing changes the fact that you're behind its existence."

Jude snatched her hand away and the mist evaporated. "You're so naïve. Somebody in charge needed to get practical, Skylar, and selling bodies is the most practical option we have."

My eyes held steady on my sister. Jude's other side came creeping back, reminding me we were still at odds. "The body isn't a thing to be sold. These people who say they don't care what happens don't even know their own bodies anymore, or remember what it's like to be real." I leaned across the table. "If they did, they wouldn't give them over so easily. You're taking advantage of this."

A flicker of sorrow passed across Jude's eyes like a bird in flight, followed by a knowing look, like she held information that I didn't. "What, Jude?"

She looked at me hard, her virtual skin like stone. "Everyone is capable of betrayal, Skylar. In the end, we all betray each other somehow, even the ones we love."

"I don't believe that," I said.

Jude straightened, chin up, shoulders thrown back, every bit a woman capable of ruling, which meant she was also capable of cruelty. "You can't hear an apology when someone is offering one," she stated.

My brow furrowed. "You were apologizing just now?"

"In a way, but you're too deaf to hear it."

I looked at my sister, saw how her iciness caused a layer of frost to crawl down the walls of the room. "I guess you're too proud to say sorry directly."

Jude rose from her chair, smoothly, so steady a stack of books on her head would easily stay in place. "It doesn't matter what I am, Skylar," she said. "Or even if we apologized. Someday, down the road, we'd just betray each other again. And when love is involved, the betrayal is always worse." She walked around the table and faced me. "Someone you care about deeply was willing to use you, Skylar, to get something he wanted even more," she started, but then her eyes shifted behind me.

I heard someone else enter the room and turned to find Rain standing there. It was like Jude conjured him. Was that who she meant? Had Rain betrayed me yet again?

"Skylar, what is Jude doing here?" he asked.

Jude was shaking her head at me, as though she knew my thoughts. "Skylar, I wasn't referring to *him*."

"What is she talking about?" Rain asked.

I ignored his question, gripping the edge of the table as something unpleasant, a fear or an ache, lapped at my edges. "Who, then?"

Jude dug into the pocket of her jacket and produced a tiny slip of paper. "I made a virtual copy just in case I needed to prove it to you." She held it out so I could see.

But I didn't need to. I already knew exactly what it was.

"Does the name Kit ring a bell?" she went on. "Your bounty hunter friend showed up at my head of security's door this morning with this note as proof of his access to you. We let his sister go in exchange for the very valuable information he passed to us, and here we are! You were foolish to get involved with a bounty hunter, Skylar. How else do you think we knew what you were up to today?"

My virtual self seemed to turn to stone, just as I'd seen Jude's do, my skin taking on the gray sheen of steel. *Kit betrayed me. Kit betrayed me.*

Kit. Kit. Kit.

As my outsides roughened, my heart shattered inside of me.

I felt an arm slide around my waist, keeping me steady. I looked up into Rain's eyes, grateful that I was no longer alone.

"As a gesture of goodwill, I let him go, Skylar," Jude said. "Both he and his sister are free. Aren't you relieved to hear such news?"

"Thank you," I said, but my voice was black with regret.

Jude's eyes were steady on me. "It's punishment enough to see him again and know that he betrayed you right at the moment you loved him most. Isn't it, Skylar?"

Pain spread through me, a pain so severe I was sure it wasn't only my virtual self experiencing it, but my body, too, the real and the virtual at war with my vulnerable heart. Jude was right and I knew it. I couldn't breathe. I tried to gather myself, leaning into Rain for support. "You said you were here to make a truce. Get on with it."

She nodded. "You've gotten your way, Skylar, and given everyone a choice. I want you to stand by your words and allow us to sell all the bodies forfeited by their owners. *With no further interference from you and your friends.*"

"And in exchange?"

"I'll let everyone who unplugs go, even you," Jude said.

My mind spun. I turned to Rain for help. "What do we do?"

Rain seemed so calm, much calmer than I felt. "It's not

a perfect deal, but it's better than the alternative, which risks everyone, including you."

I took a deep breath, my stomach churning. "All right," I croaked.

Jude smiled. "Part of being a leader means making hard choices, Skylar. Maybe now you'll understand me a little bit better. And our father, too." Her eyebrows went up. "Maybe you'll even forgive our mother someday, too," she added cryptically.

Then she turned and left the room.

I walked away from Rain and collapsed into a nearby chair, trying to process all her words and what I'd just done. My head went to my hands, my virtual self turned to water, my hair and skin wet with tears. They fell from the ceiling like a storm.

Come on. This way!

Mommy, please—

The voices were pushing through the wall again.

My head screamed in agony. For a second, everything went black. Then a hand clasped my shoulder, and my sight returned.

"Skylar." Rain's voice was gentle. "It's getting late. We need to go."

I looked at him, my eyes swimming, brain throbbing. I let him pull me from the chair to the door that led out of his father's office.

Suddenly, we were spilling into the room connecting

the two worlds, the room full of doors from every part of the App World, and I understood the voices I'd been hearing. People streamed by us, some of them at a run, some of them with fear on their faces, others with a mixture of confusion and regret, calling out as they went. As they passed through you could literally see their Apps draining away, wings disappearing to nothing, models' legs growing shorter and plumper, magical attire evaporating to be replaced by the plain basic clothing of the virtual self, skin the color of green and blue or covered in glitter fading back to Caucasian 4.0. For a while the rush was like a stampede of strange animals, mythical creatures running from an unseen foe.

But eventually the exodus steadied to a trickle.

Where was Inara?

I hadn't yet seen her.

I took a step, stumbled, again my mind, my sight, flickering out. I was on my knees, hands pressed against the floor. A man nearly tripped over me on his way out of the App World, but my eyes were too blurry to make him out clearly.

"Skylar," Rain was saying. I could hear his voice somewhere above me. "You're scaring me. This is too much for you to handle."

"You go," I told him, getting to my feet, everything so unsteady. "Unplug now if you need to. I'll be okay."

"I'm not leaving you behind," he said.

My vision cleared and I focused on him. "I have to wait as long as I can, remember? I haven't seen Inara. And I have to be the last one out."

"Skylar, come on," Rain urged.

A girl, maybe a nine, went by us, leaving behind a trail of delicate swan feathers, the ballet shoes on her feet transforming to regular slippers with each step.

"People are still coming through," I said, hoping Inara would suddenly appear. "I can't go yet. If I do, the people left behind will be sold by Jude."

The floor shook underneath us. A crack appeared in the ceiling above, from one side of the room to the other, and searing pain pierced my head like lightning.

Rain's eyes were panicked. "Your mind can't hold this much longer."

At first I nearly couldn't respond, but then the pain faded to a throbbing, dull ache. "Please. I'll join you soon. I promise." A man who must have downloaded a James Bond App raced by us, leaving behind a sleek pistol. It clattered to the floor. The lady on his arm faded to nothing and when he walked through the door he was nearly six inches shorter, his hair a dull blond again after that sleek and shiny black. Just then, the red-lacquered door to my right crumbled to nothing.

"Skylar," Rain was yelling.

Bits of ceiling began to pour down around us.

Rain grabbed my hand and pulled me toward the blue

door. It was moving and swaying, like the surface of the Water Tower, but this time it wasn't just an effect. The portal I'd created to the Real World was breaking apart.

A woman holding a child was picking her way through the debris.

"You're almost there," I yelled over the din.

She looked at me, eyes wide as she came toward us. Rain was nearly on the other side of the threshold. Just a little farther and he would be gone. I held fast to the edge of the frame, even as it fell apart in my hands. The woman had nearly reached us. My head throbbed so hard I almost couldn't open my eyes, and my heart raced so fast I was dizzy.

Then, right as the mother and child made their way through, I saw her.

Inara.

The ceiling was falling down around us, but she was almost here.

"Skylar," Rain was pleading.

"Just," I began, each word an effort like I'd never felt in my life. "Let. Go."

The roar of the collapsing landscape was so loud I wasn't sure Rain could hear me.

In the end, it didn't matter.

Inara was so close. "Skylar!" she shrieked.

But the top of the door slid downward, like a shade being pulled shut. It knocked Rain away, his hand leaving mine. It was all I could do to keep the door open high enough for Inara to slip underneath what was left of it.

The pain was so strong I was nearly blind with it.

I felt Inara move past me. "Thank you," she whispered.

Then she was gone.

But it was too late. *I* was too late.

The door slid farther toward the ground and I was on the wrong side of it.

My virtual self, my body, whatever I became when I was in this shifting state, seemed to be breaking apart with the room itself, with everything around me. There came a great rumble, a roar that seemed to come from the belly of the world and rise up through the floor and press down from above.

The last thing I remembered was seeing a great beam coming toward me.

And then, then . . .

Nothing.

THREE DAYS LATER

43

Skylar

the new world

I PUT MY hand to my mouth and laughed.

I was so happy I didn't know what else to do.

Kit circled my wrist with his fingers, then he leaned in to kiss me, slow and gentle. His eyes were bright as he pulled away from me, enough to speak.

"I love you," he said.

The cool remnants of an ocean wave tickled across our feet.

"I love you, too," I told him.

We clasped hands and began to walk, our bodies bumping into each other, the length of our arms touching. We floated over the sand. Occasionally we stopped to kiss. I longed to go back to the cottage, to slip under the covers of Kit's bed and spend the rest of the afternoon there with him, but the anticipation of this was sweet enough to allow me some patience.

My whole body was impatient for Kit.

I'd never felt anything like it in my life.

To think, as a virtual girl, I would never have felt this at all.

As Kit and I walked hand in hand, our bodies electric, lit up with love bright as the sun, I thought about all that we lost when we plugged in, chose the virtual over the real. I understood why some of us did this, too. The virtual self is stunning on so many levels, all that it can do, survive, repair, the millions of possible experiences it offers us and with complete and absolute safety. We can skydive and fight lions and leap from cliffs with total confidence that all will be well. We can feel the thrill of falling from great heights or swooping up toward the clouds on feathered wings. We can change our code to make ourselves more beautiful, or ugly, try on new personalities, and all the other strange and wonderful and frightening things that the people who code the Apps can imagine. The imagination in the App World was extraordinary; it allowed us to live things that the real body can never know because it is too fragile, because it is limited, finite, mortal, because though it is capable of great imagination as well, that imagination often stretches us far beyond what can ever be real. But then, the real body is made for other things that the virtual self can never hope to know.

I wanted to know all of those things with Kit.

I wanted to find them out with him. I never wanted to stop.

"I love you," I told Kit, a second time.

He smiled and leaned in for a kiss.

The sun shone down on us, warming our skin, heating us up.

Wait, whispered a voice, darkly, inside of me.

Wait.

Something is off.

Something was off. Something was off.

A heavy gray cloud passed overhead, blocking out the sun. I shivered, suddenly cold. No, suddenly freezing. I pulled myself away from Kit, a gesture that physically hurt, that pained my heart.

"What's wrong?" I started to ask, but then I saw his face, no, his eyes, how they'd grown blank, expressionless. Indifferent. As though he couldn't even see I was there, or worse, that we'd somehow scrolled back in time to that very first day when all I was to Kit was a thing to be bartered. As I stood there, trying to get him to look at me like I was the girl he'd just told that he loved, a gust of wintry air rushed over everything and his features seemed to dissipate, as if Kit was merely a projection and one whose source was weakening.

My teeth were chattering hard. "Kit?"

I could see through him now.

"Don't go," I cried. "Come back! Come back! Please!"

But my pleading didn't matter.

He was gone.

"Skylar?" said a voice. Male. Familiar.

"Skylar?" said another. Female. Also familiar.

"Skylar, can you hear us?" said yet another.

My eyelids were so heavy, heavy like someone was pressing them down into my cheekbones, but eventually I managed to push them open. For a while my vision was blurred and all I saw were dark shapes moving in front of me.

"She's waking up," said one of the women's voices.

I blinked and blinked, kept on blinking until the film cleared from my eyes and I saw who was standing around me. The first face I recognized was Rain's, and he smiled broadly now, his eyes alive with relief.

"Welcome back to the Real World," he said.

The Keeper reached out and took my hand, squeezing it. "You had us worried."

I tried to sit up but my head throbbed. Everything about me ached and groaned with the slightest movement. I was back in my room at the Keeper's apartment in the mansion, the same room where I'd woken up the first time I'd unplugged. "Is everything okay? Did people make it out of the market?" My voice was hoarse. "What happened? Where's Inara?"

"You need to rest," the Keeper replied.

"Tell me," I pleaded.

Rain nodded. "Inara is okay. She'll see you when you're feeling better."

I took in a long breath, feeling relieved.

"And let's just say the Body Market is severely diminished," Rain went on. "The plan worked enough to not only allow the people to wake up on their own, but to scare away the vast majority of the Body Tourists."

The Keeper chuckled. "Apparently, they didn't like the idea of buying a body that might suddenly come to life."

I searched their faces, my mind stuck on one of Rain's words. "It worked . . . enough?"

Rain sat down on the bed. He glanced at my hand, and I wondered if he might take it. He didn't. "Well, while many citizens of the App World don't want their bodies sold, they don't want a life unplugged either. We're in the process of plugging them back in at facilities where their bodies will be protected, starting with Briarwood."

"But at least they have the choice," I said.

"At least they have the choice, yes," the Keeper echoed.

I sensed there was more. "And . . . ?"

Rain's eyes darkened. "There were also plenty of citizens who gave their bodies over to the New Capitalists' cause, as Jude hoped."

I swallowed, my throat dry, taking this in. "Well, at least they made their choice," I repeated, though the words sounded hollow. It was difficult for me to imagine people just donating their bodies to be sold, but then, we had to respect their decision. Not everyone wanted a real life. For some, obviously for plenty, the virtual life was the only life that mattered.

Rain glanced at the door. "Skylar, there's plenty of time to fill you in when you're feeling better. But right now, there's someone else here who really wants to see you."

Kit?

His name swept through me like a storm. I couldn't stop it.

My heart soared and then plummeted as everything that Jude had told me, the shock and the pain of it, came rushing back. I tried to sit up a little higher, my gaze caught on the jar of sea glass sitting on the bedside table where I'd left it. I didn't know whether I wanted to pick it up and hug it to my chest or send it flying across the room to smash into a million pieces against the wall.

"Who is it?" I finally managed.

Rain nodded at the Keeper.

I nearly couldn't take a breath as I waited to see who would walk through the door.

"I searched everywhere, Skylar," Rain was saying. He sounded excited. "I thought maybe if I was able to find her, somehow you'd come back to us, and here you are."

Her?

Right then she walked through the door—no, she rushed—rushed to my bedside.

"Mom?"

"My brave girl," she said, and threw her arms around me. "We have so much to catch up on, so much to talk about."

I let her lift me up off the pillows, reveled in the shock and comfort of having my mother, this woman I'd longed for all my life in the App World, with whom I'd still only had a precious few minutes many, many months ago, right here with me.

We were safe, we were together.

Finally.

When she pulled back to look at me, I glanced up at Rain, who was still standing there, taking in this reunion he'd orchestrated. Gratitude flooded every part of me, and as it pulsed across my skin, I did something I never thought I'd find myself wanting to do again. Even as my eyes caught the glare of the colorful blue glass on the table next to me, a glare that reached straight inside to the very center of my heart, slicing through it, I reached out and wove my fingers through Rain's, and then I smiled.

Keep reading for a glimpse at

THE MIND VIRUS,

the conclusion to the

UNPLUGGED

series.

Let us pass, then, to the attributes of the soul. . . . If it be true that I have no body, it is true likewise that I am capable neither of walking nor of being nourished. Perception is another attribute of the soul; but perception too is impossible without the body . . . I am—I exist: this is certain; but how often? As often as I think; for perhaps it would even happen, if I should wholly cease to think, that I should at the same time altogether cease to be. . . . I am, however, a real thing, and really existent; but what thing? The answer was, a thinking thing.

—René Descartes,
"Of the Nature of the Human Mind; and That It Is
More Easily Known Than the Body,"
Meditations on First Philosophy (1641)

1

Ree

virtual mortality

"A LIFE ON the Apps is the only life for me."

That's what Char kept saying, over and over. Ever since that chick Skylar gave her emergency broadcast. Char was lying on her back in the grass of Main Park, staring up at the Night Sky 3.0. This one featured the Southern Cross, and it sparkled above us like a shining sword. Honestly, I preferred Night Sky 5.0, because Orion was more my thing.

It was a beautiful evening, regardless, like all evenings here.

Same as usual, in other words.

The only difference was that this evening was the day after half the City had unplugged at once. Half the people we knew in this world were, *poof!* Gone.

"Like, who cares about a clunky chunk of flesh when I have the entire virtual world at my fingertips?" Char went on, laughing, her voice alternately a shriek and a cackle, sounding like she'd downloaded one of those Wicked Witchy Apps when on the outside she was all Betty Boop and Pinup Girl, her plump, red heart-shaped lips all pouty and pursed. "Can you believe that Harry left? I mean, how dare he! I was totally going to Kiss App him at some point."

I closed my eyes, brain-blocking her. I didn't want her to know my thoughts at the moment, which weren't pretty. I let them flow freely now, in the newly locked safety of my virtual head.

Yeah, that's easy to say when your daddy got rich on Pharmaceutical Apps and you have an endless source of capital.

Why am I friends with you again?

Has anyone ever told you how annoying you are sometimes?

I opened my eyes again and let Char back in. If I kept her from poking around in my head much longer, she'd guess I was having nasty thoughts about her.

Char swiped a finger across the atmosphere and her App Store gathered around her like a cozy bowl of candy. Char's icons always came in bright shades of pink and yellow and green and purple and blue. They squeaked and giggled and played with her hair and tickled her ears. One of them even settled happily into her cleavage, and she smiled down at it like a dear friend.

She turned to me, head lolling to the side, her shiny black locks sultry and smooth. "What next, Ree? How shall I celebrate my continued virtual existence? Hmmm?" She put out a hand and a crowd of Apps settled into her palm like pastel-colored insects, looking at her adoringly, hoping to be chosen. "Ree? Ree! Are you listening to me!"

I crossed my legs, the grass tickling my thighs. They were bland and pale next to Char's rosy, flushed virtual skin. "I'm listening," I droned. "Why don't you try something new for a change?"

Char's pout grew even more pronounced. "What do you mean, *for a change*?"

I sighed. "I mean, why don't you pick Personality over Appearance?"

She glared. "I care about more than Appearance Apps."

"All right. So prove it," I dared.

Her long-lashed, dark-lined eyes narrowed. "You could use a Personality App today."

"You first," I said, crossing my arms to match my legs. "Then me."

Char turned her attention back to her Apps, trying to choose. She sat there pondering, lying back on her elbows, legs crossed, one red-heeled foot bouncing in the atmosphere in a classic pinup pose, like she had all the time in the world, when suddenly an App I'd never seen before rose up out of the swarm. "Oooh! What's that?" she cooed.

The two of us stared at it in awe.

Even I was captivated.

It took the shape of a present and glittered with every color in existence. It didn't flirt or cajole, it just hovered in the air like a Queen Bee who knew all she needed to do was stand there and wait to be adored by admirers.

"I've never seen anything like it," I admitted.

"I don't care what it is, Ree, Personality or Appearance or whatever else it could possibly be, I'm picking it."

"I thought we had a deal," I said, but only halfheartedly. In truth, I wanted Char to download this App. I wanted to see what would happen when she did.

She didn't even bother to reply.

Char just reached out a long, red-lacquered nail and touched it.

The second her fingertip met the icon, she gasped. Her Pinup features immediately began to transform, fading away. Char's wide dark eyes lolled back into her head with pleasure.

Or, at least, that's what I thought at first.

Quickly, far more so than was normal, Char changed back into her basic virtual self. I waited, impatient to see what new and exciting features would replace the basic ones. Her arms and legs began to twitch, just a little. But then they began to jerk. Char's elbows slipped out from under her and her head crashed to the ground.

I scurried over and lifted it, cradling it in my hands. "Are you okay?"

"Let me go," she growled.

I lay her head back on the grass and moved away, watching as Char's virtual skin now turned from Caucasian 4.0 to a dark shade of gray. Something was wrong. Her mouth opened and closed, opened and closed. "Wait a minute," she choked out.

It sounded like someone was strangling her. "Char?"

"Ree," she coughed.

Her skin was an ugly purple now, all of it like a bluish bruise covering her virtual self. Then, right before my eyes, her skin began to slip from her body like one of those Real World animals I downloaded once that shed their skin every so often, emerging renewed. But Char wasn't looking renewed. She was looking like . . . she was looking like . . .

Death.

But that was impossible.

Death was impossible. Death had been overcome.

Her eyes kept going in and out, like someone suffering a brain stall.

I leaned over her. "Char, what do I do?"

A scream lodged in Char's throat. She gasped, working

her lips, trying to form words, her breathing hoarse and hiccupping. Finally, she managed a single word.

"Poison," she wheezed.

"Poison?" I said, reaching for her, but afraid to touch her, too. "The App was poisoned?"

By now a crowd had gathered around us. People stopped to watch the scene Char was making as she twitched and jerked and choked in the grass. Parents out with their children for a nighttime stroll, Lullaby Apps tinkling softly above their carriages. Businessmen on their way home through the park. A crowd of young women heading to the bars for the evening, decked out in pricey Model Apps. A gang of fifteens, covered in tattoos and chains, trying to look badass but tittering and giggling underneath all those downloads, stood off to the left. As they watched, their laughter disappeared, their hands going to their mouths in horror.

I looked from one group to the other, waiting for them to do something.

No one stepped forward.

In fact, most of them began stepping away.

"Can't anybody help us?" I cried out.

Not a single person answered. Everyone seemed frozen.

As I sat there next to my friend, I watched the virtual Char I'd known my entire life slip away entirely, until all that was left was a giant string of tiny numbers, tightly wound, weaving in and out of themselves again and again.

There was nothing left of Char but code.

The numbers began to break apart. Disintegrate like ash.

And then, suddenly, they disappeared altogether.

Char was gone.

Vanished from the atmosphere, as though she was never there at all.

At first, everyone around me was silent. A collective shock fell across the park, across those of us who'd witnessed Char's quick and ugly demise.

I scrambled to my feet, unsure what to do. Who to call. What came next.

Then, one of the models, a tall, bone-thin girl in a too-short dress, teetering on spiky heels made out of lightning bolts that flashed as she moved, began screaming.

"Virus! Virus!"

That was when everyone turned and ran.

READ THEM ALL!

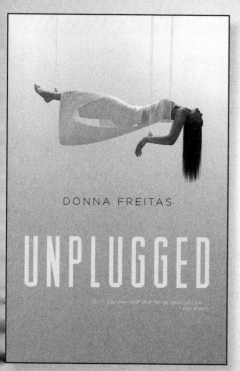

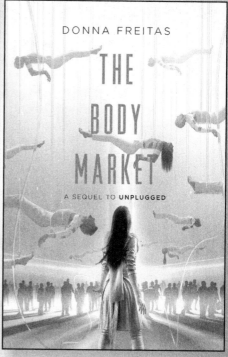

JOIN THE Epic Reads COMMUNITY

THE ULTIMATE YA DESTINATION

◄ **DISCOVER** ►

your next favorite read

◄ **MEET** ►

new authors to love

◄ **WIN** ►

free books

◄ **SHARE** ►

infographics, playlists, quizzes, and more

◄ **WATCH** ►

the latest videos

www.epicreads.com